"*Cool Beans* is like a long s ... and delightful! Erynn's bo ... of laughter, romance, and ... generous dollop of fun!"

— BETSY ST. AMANT, author of *Return to Love* and *A Valentine's Wish*

"With witty and energetic prose, Erynn Mangum taps into the mind of a twentysomething searching for her place in life. Her latest book holds magnetic appeal for all ages and guarantees you will laugh, cry, and sigh with heartfelt delight. Blending brilliant characterization with an infusion of spiritual truth and a shot of romance, *Cool Beans* is an experience to savor and will leave you with a little caffeine buzz all of its own!"

— REL MOLLET, Relz Reviewz

"Erynn Mangum has the amazing ability to create characters so vivacious and fun that you just wish they could be as real as they seem. I honestly believe that you could get a caffeine buzz just by reading this."

— LORI FOX, reviewer, TitleTrakk.com

"What happens when you take one highly caffeinated heroine and knock her faith into the half-caf zone? *Cool Beans*, another fun read from the pen of Erynn Mangum."

— TAMARA LEIGH, author of *Leaving Carolina* and
ACFW Book of the Year winner *Splitting Harriet*

a maya davis novel

COOL BEANS

erynn mangum

NAVPRESS
Discipleship Inside Out™

NavPress is the publishing ministry of The Navigators, an international Christian organization and leader in personal spiritual development. NavPress is committed to helping people grow spiritually and enjoy lives of meaning and hope through personal and group resources that are biblically rooted, culturally relevant, and highly practical.

**For a free catalog go to www.NavPress.com
or call 1.800.366.7788 in the United States or 1.800.839.4769 in Canada.**

ISBN-13: 978-1-60006-711-2

Cover design by Alexis Goodman at The Visual Republic
Cover image by Getty Images

This novel is a work of fiction. Names, characters, places, and incidents are either the product of the author's imagination or are used fictitiously. Any resemblance to actual events, locales, organizations, or persons, living or dead, is entirely coincidental and beyond the intent of either the author or publisher.

Unless otherwise identified, all Scripture quotations in this publication are taken from the New American Standard Bible® (NASB), Copyright © 1960, 1962, 1963, 1968, 1971, 1972, 1973, 1975, 1977, 1995 by The Lockman Foundation. Used by permission; All rights reserved. Also used is the *Holy Bible, New International Version®* (NIV®), Copyright © 1973, 1978, 1984 by International Bible Society, used by permission of Zondervan, all rights reserved.

Library of Congress Cataloging-in-Publication Data
Mangum, Erynn, 1985-
  Cool beans : a Maya Davis novel / Erynn Mangum.
    p. cm.
  ISBN 978-1-60006-711-2
  1. Coffee shops--Fiction. 2. Dating (Social customs)--Fiction. I.
Title.
  PS3613.A5373C66 2010
  813'.6--dc22
                              2009037827

Printed in the United States of America

2 3 4 5 6 7 8 / 14 13 12 11 10

For Jon O'Brien, Doug Mangum, Bryant Mangum, Caleb Mangum, Greg O'Brien, Allen O'Brien, and Thomas O'Brien. Thank you for showing me what a real man of God looks like. I'm so blessed to be surrounded by such incredible men!

ACKNOWLEDGMENTS

Lord, this book is all for You. I pray that those who read it will be drawn closer to the One who created them. You always answer me when I call to You. Help me to be quiet and listen.

Thanks also to:

Jon, my favorite husband, for kissing me every morning and saying "I love you" every night. Every day with you is a gift from God. I'm so proud to be known as your wife. I love you!

Mom and Dad, for sharing your wisdom about marriage and always welcoming us over for dinner, movies, and visiting. You are amazing!

Bryant, Caleb, and Cayce, for being the best siblings and best friends I have. You guys are always able to make me laugh. You are awesome!

Nama, for calling and e-mailing and being the most amazing grandmother ever. You are my hero!

Connie and Greg, for welcoming me into your fun and amazing family. I'm so blessed to have such incredible in-laws!

Allen, Vicky, Tommy, and Ashlee, for being the best brothers-in-law and sisters-in-law I could ever have imagined!

Jon's and my extended families, for all of your support, prayers, and laughter. You are precious to me.

Shannon Kay, Barb and Walt Kelly, Jen and Greg Fulkerson, Eitan and Kaitlin Bar, and Elisa Wingerd—I'm blessed to call you friends.

Eliya Kirby, for giving me a behind-the-scenes pass to Borders Café—Thanks for letting me stalk you and for being willing to answer my questions about life as a barista!

Shannon Harden, Jon-Erik Golob, Kelly Rowe, Leslie Poulin, and Amy Lee—for working at an amazing tearoom with me, giving me a glimpse of the restaurant business, and making it tons of fun!

Steve Laube, my incredibly talented agent and friend, thanks for answering my zillion questions and for encouraging me when I feel like I've got nothing left!

Rebekah Guzman, Kris Wallen, Amy Parker, Tia Stauffer, and the rest of the NavPress team—you are fabulous!

The Christian Writers Guild, for continuing to celebrate contracts, answer questions, and be wonderful friends. Thanks for everything you do!

CHAPTER ONE

The October day is perfect. The sun is shining. The air is crisp. The birds are chirping. The faintest mist is just fading in the earliest rays of light.

It's morning.

"Miss?" There's a man in a rather dorky-looking outfit staring at me. "Miss?"

"Oh, it's Maya," I correct him.

"Maya. Did you want something?" He's frowning at me now.

"What?"

"Did . . . you . . . want . . . something?" he says, slower, waving his hand around in a circle. "From the concession stand?"

I suddenly realize there are rows and rows of candy behind the dorky man. "Oh!" I say. "Sorry. Yes, I would like a Milky Way."

Dorky Man's frown deepens. "A what?"

"Milky Way. A Milky Way. Milk chocolate, caramel, that squishy stuff that I can never remember what it's called?"

"I've never heard of a Milky Way."

"Are you kidding?" I am aghast.

And barefoot. Suddenly, there is a damp sensation on my toes. I look down and see my pink toenails gradually disappearing into a large puddle forming near the concession stand.

"Apparently there's a leak," I say, pointing.

Dorky Man isn't finished. "And chocolate. What is chocolate?"

SPLASH! I slip and fall flat into the puddle. I'm gasping for breath. "Chocolate! Chocolate!"

He apparently doesn't notice my fall. "Don't know what that is. Go somewhere else. Next!"

A dog starts a mournful howl somewhere in the distance that echoes the cry in my heart. He doesn't know what chocolate is! *The dog gets louder.* What if my whole life was a wonderful dream, and this is reality? *And louder. Now it's a mournful, yipping bark.* What if I am stuck in this puddle forever? What if—

"SHUT UP!!!"

I gasp, jumping, falling off the bed and landing with a resounding *crack!* on the floor.

Calvin, my beagle, is still barking his head off. I close my eyes and rest my cheek on the cool wood floor.

It's 2:24 a.m., Thursday. I don't have to look at the clock to know this.

"Ohhh . . ." Now my mournful moaning is in competition with Calvin's. With my ear mashed against the floor, I can hear the stomping getting closer. I feel like an Indian in one of those old movies who can tell when the posse is coming.

"Maya Elise Davis!"

Jen is not happy on this Thursday early-*early* morning.

"Mmm?"

"Your dumb dog has been going at it every Wednesday night for the last six months, and I'm sick of it!"

I scoot around on the floor a bit so I can see my wild-haired, pajama-clad roommate and, I guess, former best friend, standing in my doorway, dimly lit by the hall light.

Poor Calvin is now lying prostrate in front of Jen, head between his paws, making little *rooo . . . rooo . . . rooo* noises.

"You scared me," I mumble. "I fell out of bed."

"How can you sleep through that?" she huffs. "Whatever. Now that he's done, I'm going back to bed." She leaves, flicking the hall light off.

"Roo . . . rooo . . ."

"She's gone, Calvin."

The dog sighs and then doggy crawls to where my left leg is and rests his head on my ankle.

I close my eyes again.

Mmm . . . Chocolate . . .

I sigh. Hot chocolate. No, no! Even better! Mocha.

"Ohhh . . ." I lick my lips.

Opening my eyes, I'm immediately confused. Usually, my first view of the morning is the clouds, rainbows, and little bluebirds I painted all over my ceiling. Today, I'm staring underneath my armoire.

Yuck. I need to remember to vacuum under here.

Apparently, I am on the floor lying on my stomach. My head is on my hands, and my left leg is completely asleep.

I look down and see why. "Calvin."

I swear the dog shakes his head.

"Move, Calvin."

He grunts but pulls his long-eared head away from my ankle.

I push myself to a standing position and immediately groan. Sleeping on floor: bad idea.

I shuffle to the kitchen, eyes half closed, one hand holding my lower back, the other grabbing the high counter.

Jen, looking smart in a blazer, pants, and heels, shakes her coifed head at me. "Wow. Welcome to life."

"I dreamed—I had such a nightmare." I collapse onto one of the bar stools. "There wasn't any more chocolate, and a man in a dorky outfit didn't even know what it was." I hold my head in my hands. "It was terrible."

Jen doesn't say anything for a minute. "Your cheek has your class ring imprinted into it." She pokes my face. "*Cal-Hudson. 2006.*"

"Swell."

"Calvin was at it again last night. I hate that dog. Every Wednesday night, Maya! And why were you sleeping on the floor?"

"Hey, Calvin can't help it." I look over to where the little beagle is emerging from my bedroom, eyes all sleepy. "He just hears something every week. You scared me when you yelled, and I fell off the bed." I point to my imprinted cheek. "This is *your* fault."

"No, it's Calvin the Blunder Dog's fault." She finishes her cup of blackberry-orange tea and rinses it out in the sink. "What time are you working today?"

"Ten to close." I yawn. "I might go in early for a mocha."

Ooh. Mocha. Just saying the word makes my whole body crave it.

Jen watches me, finally smiling. "You are ridiculous. I wish you could see your expression right now, all wistful and sappy looking. And just over the mention of coffee."

"Not just coffee, Jen. *Mochas.*"

"Whatever." She rolls her eyes but grins wider. And my best friend is officially back. Jen's not a nice person until after she gets her tea fix. She's weird that way.

"Well, have a good day. I'm off. I'll be back around six-ish." She grabs her briefcase and flicks me in the forehead.

"Ow."

"Laters." The door clicks after her. I look over at Calvin, who sits in the middle of the hallway, staring lazily at me.

"You do not get to eat breakfast in there. If I have to make it to the kitchen, you do too," I tell him.

Calvin huffs.

"Tough."

Letting out another huge breath, he trips into the kitchen and falls in front of his bowl.

My dog and I are way too alike in the mornings.

It's seven thirty, and it's a gorgeous October day.

"Eat up. We're going for a jog."

Calvin's ears perk up at this, and he gobbles up the food I pour in the silver bowl while I go back to my bedroom to pull on some workout clothes.

The apartment I share with Jen is just perfect for us. It has two bedrooms, two bathrooms, a big living room, and a kitchen that is more pretty than functional but fills our microwaving needs.

Aside from an occasional cookie fiasco, neither Jen nor I is a big cook. Jen claims she's too tired after legally assisting her lawyer boss all day. I tell the truth and just say I don't like cooking.

My plan is to marry Emeril Live.

And, yeah, I know that's not his last name. It doesn't really matter because I have a pretty good feeling that's not God's plan for me. So, *bam!* I'm just going to have to be content with TV dinners.

Which I am. Sometimes the little chicken nuggets are shaped like flowers, and this makes me happy.

I flip on the light in my room and flop down on my unmade bed. I slide my Bible and a pad of sticky notes over.

God has been attempting to teach me to (a) be more thankful and (b) keep my mouth shut more often.

This is hard because (a) while I am a positive person, I don't always remember to be thankful; and (b) my second favorite thing to do is talk.

So, we're working on this, me and God. Obviously, because today's Bible reading is Philippians 4:6: "Be anxious for nothing, but in everything by prayer and supplication with thanksgiving let your requests be made known to God."

I reach for a sticky note.

Today I Am Thankful For:
1. Cushioning wood floors as opposed to cement. No broken bones.
2. Proudly wearing my college and graduating year on my face.
3. Mochas. Milky Ways. Cocoa Puffs. Hot chocolate.
Cold chocolate. . . .
4. Chopping my hair off last week. It will not take
forty minutes to dry it today.

Calvin is back in my room, fed, awake, and, as the Dixie Chicks would say, "Ready, ready, ready, ready, ready to ruuun!"

"One sec, Cal."

Most people assume I named my dog after my school. This is not the case, however. He is named after Calvin Klein and my first pair of $80 jeans — marked down to a gorgeous $23.50. I bargain shop.

I have on a pair of gray jogging shorts and a bright pink

T-shirt. Calvin starts to go ballistic when he sees me pulling on my jogging shoes.

"Let's go, bud." I hook his leash on, and we half-stretch, half-walk toward the door.

Twenty-four minutes later, we both drag ourselves back into the apartment. I'm sticky from the humidity and coated with a thin layer of dirt, compliments of a Nissan pickup. Little Calvin is wheezing harmonically. He ate a cricket, so I can understand why.

"Shower. Must shower."

Calvin is right on my heels.

"Yeah, right." I nudge him out of the bathroom. I turn the faucet on full blast and start shampooing. Yet another reason I'm grateful for cutting my hair. It now bounces right above my shoulders in a curly, layered style. I won't use half the shampoo I used to when my hair was halfway down my back.

I yank open the tinted glass door and stop, inhaling through my nose, arching my back, and achieving what my Pilates instructor would call "core stability."

French roast.

I close my eyes now. This is apparently our dark roast for the day. I sniff harder, focusing on the scents. Maybe Italian? I can't distinguish the medium roast, which disappoints me greatly. But the decaf is definitely my own creation: half decaf French, two sprinkles of cinnamon, and the rest is a light Breakfast Blend.

Ahhh . . .

You know how in those sappy romances, the people are

always like, "I knew he was the one because I felt like I was coming home when I was around him"?

Cool Beans evokes that feeling for me.

See why I love my job so much?

"Hey, Nut-job! Close the door."

I open my eyes and squint at the tall, skinny, dark-haired guy behind the counter. Jack Dominguez is grinning, wiping his fingers on a towel, and causing a little group of twentysomething women sitting at the table closest to the counter to start twittering.

"Totally ruining the moment, Man versus Wild." I frown at him a minute longer and then close my eyes again, breathing deeply.

That's it. . . . Feel your navel pressing against your spine. . . .

I've always wanted to ask the perky Pilates lady if she's ever really felt the inside of her belly button pressing against her spine. I mean, she's skinny enough that she might have, but really, wouldn't that sensation kind of creep you out? Like, oh my gosh! Where are my intestines?

I don't know. Just a thought.

I let my breath out finally and close the door. Cool Beans is not crowded this time of the morning. Aside from the women, there's a bald guy with a laptop and two guys in suits discussing something about stock presentations.

Here's how Cool Beans is set up:

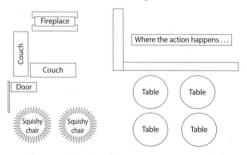

There is always a blend of fifties and big-band music playing quietly over the speakers. Everything is decorated in retro colors: cerulean blues, cherry reds, lots of white leather and silver. There are five art-deco bar stools by the counter, near the fireplace.

Jack throws a towel at me as I walk through the little swinging door next to the counter. "Morning, *Sciurus*," he says, smirking.

I catch the towel and pop it at his leg. "Hey, how's the zookeeping?"

Jack is still in the process of majoring in biology with an emphasis in animal behaviors. A degree like this will open doors.

Zoo doors, at least.

Just so you know, *Sciurus* is the Latin name for *squirrel*. I do not appreciate him calling me this, especially since he does so because he's convinced my brain activity is a lot like a squirrel's. Quick, pointless, and scattered.

Which is also the reason he calls me multiple related nicknames: Nut-job, Nutkin (from Beatrix Potter), and Pattertwig (compliments of C. S. Lewis and *Prince Caspian*).

"Just fine; thanks for asking."

He takes a red-headed girl's order and starts making an espresso while I tie on my cherry red apron. He grins over the machine at me. "I think I might get that internship at the Hudson Zoo for next semester." The automatic espresso machine is humming quietly.

I can't help the smile. "Awesome! That's really good, Jack."

"A friend who works at the zoo said that if they don't like your application, you find out in a week. It's been nine days." He smiles into the espresso. "It'll look really great on a résumé for the San Diego Zoo."

I've known Jack since the second grade. We were both assigned to the same lunch table — which was fortunate because his mom always packed him tamales for lunch, and my mom always packed me tuna fish. I hate tuna fish. Jack doesn't like tamales. So, we became lunch-swap buddies.

We lost track of each other through high school, but both ended up in the same fitness elective junior year at Cal-Hudson. And we both started working at Cool Beans that same year.

So, we've been friends for a while.

Jack has wanted to work at the San Diego Zoo since he visited there as a third grader. Hudson is about an hour northeast of San Diego.

Once my apron is on, I start grinding a fresh batch of the Italian medium roast.

"So guess what?" Jack asks over the buzz of the grinder.

"You decided against a career in shoveling manure?"

"Funny, Pattertwig. No, I'm parrot-sitting this weekend."

"Won't that hurt the bird?" I ask, tilting my head.

"What?"

"If you sit on it."

He sighs.

I grin.

"I thought you were working on the sarcastic comments," he says, joining me by the coffee grinder.

"I have been. I thought that was a smooth delivery."

"Nutkin."

"Sorry." I smile toothily at him. "Don't expect miracles overnight."

Sometimes, my sarcasm can be more . . . um . . . hurtful than funny. I'm attempting to work on this because I don't mean to hurt people. And as a Christian, it's probably not the best witness to go around insulting people all day.

So Jack decided to be Jiminy Cricket and help me keep my mouth shut.

"At least it wasn't mean," he concedes.

"You might want to let the parrot owner know that you don't think it's mean to sit on the poor bird."

"Maya!"

"Sorry!" I tuck the coffee filter filled with grounds into the basket, slide that into the coffeemaker, and snap the switch to On. It immediately starts gurgling like Free Willy out of water.

Jack's laughing.

"So, what's the parrot's name?" I ask.

"Polly."

"Please tell me you're joking."

"I'm joking."

I nod. "Good. How unoriginal can we get?"

"The bird's name *is* Polly, though."

"You said you were joking!"

"You asked me to say that," Jack says.

I cover my face. Talking with Jack hurts my head. I start making myself a mocha. Cool Beans lets us have as many drinks as we want while we're on duty. It just makes us huge enough caffeine addicts that we're constantly coming back for more, even on our days off.

I pour milk into a metal pitcher and start the steam wand in it. Bubbles float to the top as the espresso lightly trickles into a mug for me.

"So, Polly. Does she talk?" I ask.

He makes a face. "More than you, even. It will be a loud weekend."

"It's good for you." I smack his shoulder. "Makes you tougher."

"And deafer. The bird screams. And sings. And whistles."

I laugh. "When are you becoming the proud guardian?"

"This afternoon when I get off work." He glances at the clock. "Five hours, forty-five minutes, and counting."

"Hey, this is good experience for becoming an overseer of wild beings."

"No, it's not. This parrot is an *Amazona aestiva*. Blue-fronted Amazon. Those are commonly kept as pets. If parrots could be domesticated, this one would be." He hands the girl her espresso. "This one is not wild."

I roll my eyes and pull the wand out of the pitcher. I start pouring the milk into my espresso and chocolate syrup, holding most of the foam back. "Well, maybe next time someone with a hyena will go out of town, and you can hyena-sit."

He immediately brightens. "Do you know someone with one?"

"No."

"Oh."

"You have problems." I stir my mocha and inhale, sighing.

He smiles. "Probably."

My lunch break is at one thirty, but by one o'clock, I'm starving. My stomach is trying to eat itself, and I keep patting it, attempting to reassure it that I'll feed it before I die of missing organs.

Note to self: Regardless of the label, Snickers bars do not satisfy your hunger all morning, thereby making them bad breakfast food.

"Whoa, Maya. Miss breakfast?" Jack asks, after my stomach rumbles in protest of a late lunch. He just got back from his lunch break and is retying his apron over his black collared shirt and straight-cut dark jeans.

"I had a Snickers bar," I say.

"Healthy."

"It has peanuts. That's protein."

"And milk chocolate. That's calcium."

I grin. "Exactly." I turn to a short older woman who has gray hair, blue eyes, and a white smile. She's wearing what I assume is trendy old-lady clothes: khakis, a silky floral blouse, and, in not-so-old-lady fashion, a bright pink cardigan.

She clears her throat. "I would like an extra-large iced mocha with two extra shots and whipped cream, please."

I stare at her. "Okay."

"And one of those coffee cakes. Those aren't reduced fat, are they?"

"Uh . . . no."

"Excellent." She pulls her credit card out of a blue leather purse.

I ring up her total. "Is this for you?" I ask hesitantly.

"Of course, dear. Who else?"

I'm in awe. "I want to be you when I grow up," I tell her.

Jack starts laughing as he steams the milk. The lady—Autumn Reeve, according to her credit card—grins at me.

"Oh? Why is that?"

"You're drinking a mocha on steroids and eating coffee cake."

She slides her card back into her wallet. "And most old fogies don't do that, do they?"

"Not even that. Most women in general."

She smiles again. "Well, thank you for the compliment, dear."

Jack hands her the drink. "Take care, ma'am."

"Here's your cake," I say.

Autumn takes both, waves, and then sits on the sofa near the unlit fireplace. She pulls a copy of *Good Housekeeping* out of her purse and sets a pair of bifocals on her nose.

Jack pokes me in the back. "Stop staring."

"Ouch. Invasion of personal space."

"Nutkin, you have no personal space."

My stomach growls again, and I sigh longingly at the glass case of doughnuts along the back wall. Jack rinses the pitcher he used to steam the milk while I wipe off the steam wand and then squirt another blast of steam out to clear it.

"Why didn't you eat breakfast?"

"I went for a run instead."

"You can't do both?"

"At the same time?" I make a face. "I can't eat and run. I get cramps."

"Nutkin."

I rub my cheek. Actually, the reason I only got a Snickers was because we're all out of cereal, and Jen and I are too lazy to go buy more that early in the morning. And I typically forget after work.

"We're all out of breakfast foods, and I never remember that unless it's breakfast."

Jack digs around in the catch-all drawer under the cash register. He pulls out a pad of paper and a bright green pen. He scrawls something.

A guy in his late teens comes up to the counter then, and I stop watching Jack. "Can I help you?"

"Cappuccino, please."

"Okay. What size?"

"Uh . . ." He makes a weird face at something behind me, and I turn to look right as Jack smacks a piece of paper on my forehead.

"Ow!" I yelp, more out of surprise than pain. The paper is stuck there with tape, and I yank it off.

To Whomever Is Reading This: Please remind me to buy cereal. Thank you.

I glare at Jack, who is smirking by the espresso machine. The kid in front of the counter is gaping at us.

"Uh. You should . . . buy cereal," he says, staccato-voiced.

"Thanks."

"Yeah." He stares at me for a few more moments. "Uh. Large cappuccino, please."

I ring it up on the cash register and tell him the total. Jack finishes making the cappuccino and slides it over the counter.

After he leaves, I turn to Jack. "Good grief."

"You're telling me. It's one thirty. Go eat."

My stomach is dancing happily at this news. I grin and pull my apron off. "See ya."

"Eat more than a Snickers bar this time, Pattertwig," he calls after me. I dig my purse out of a cabinet and run for the door, waving.

My cell phone is vibrating as I shuffle through my purse for my keys. The screen reads, "1 New Voice Mail."

I check it as I unlock my ancient blue Jeep Wrangler.

"Maya! Call me as soon as you get this!" *Click.*

It's Jen. I'm trying to decide what could be so enthralling at her law office. Maybe her boss closed his tie in one of his legal dictionaries again.

For as cool and collected as they make lawyers look on TV, Jen's boss is one of the biggest klutzes I've ever met in my whole life.

I push speed dial number four. Here's what my speed dial looks like:

> #1 – Voice Mail.
> #2 – My mom, who lives an hour away in San Diego.
> #3 – My dad. Even though I drive to San Diego every Sunday for dinner, my dad still likes me to call every once in a while and let him know how the Jeep is.
> #4 – Jen.
> #5 – Jack, who likes to send me random text messages on my days off.

I listen to it ring as I back out and start driving toward the nearest Panda Express. Cheap Chinese food — is there a better lunch?

"This is Jennifer Mitchell, legal assistant to Wayne Davids. Please leave me a detailed message including your name, number, and best time to reach you, and I'll return your call promptly. Thank you."

So businesslike.

"Jen, it's me. I'm on lunch break until two. Call me."

I hang up, make two right turns, and park in a front parking spot. One thirty is too late for lunch but a great time to eat if you're trying to avoid crowds. No one is even in line.

"The two-entrée plate, please. Orange chicken, beef and broccoli, and fried rice." I can feel my salivary glands working overtime, and I focus on not drooling on the nice man in a hairnet helping me.

"Anything to drink?" he asks, giving me a weird look as I use my sleeve to dab the moisture from my mouth.

"Dr Pepper."

My phone rings right then. I hand the man a ten and answer it. "Hi, Jen."

"Guess what!"

I yelp, yanking the phone away from my ear and earning another weird look. Seriously, I should be the one giving him odd expressions. He's wearing a hairnet over a buzz cut, for goodness' sake!

I take my change, Styrofoamed meal, and empty paper cup to the beverage island, turning the volume down on my phone as I do that.

"What?" I ask Jen.

"No, no, you have to *guess*."

"Wayne's giving you a raise."

"Nope!" She is giddy.

Weird. Jen is rarely giddy. It's what makes her a good legal assistant. She laughs and has a fairly good sense of humor, but she's rarely hysterical.

"Uh . . ." I stick the cup under the Dr Pepper. "You got your own case."

"No! Try again!"

I pop the lid on and sit at the nearest table. "You met Orlando Bloom?"

"In Hudson? Heh. Right. No, Maya! I . . ."—her voice drops fourteen volume levels to a whisper—"I got asked out." She immediately starts giggling.

"Oh yeah?" I'm not seeing the big deal here. Jen gets asked out an average of five times a week by Wayne's clients. It's not that unusual. Especially if you've got long, sandy blond hair, big green eyes, and lashes to kill for.

Certainly not unusual enough to elicit giddiness.

"Yeah," she sighs. "Oh, Maya, he's so cute. And a Christian

and my age! I can't even remember the last time that happened."

I grin. Okay, so it's true that she's usually getting offers from men twice her age and just out of divorce court. Part of the price of working for a family lawyer.

I stare at my fork and suddenly frown. "It's not Adam, is it?"

"What? No, it's not."

"Good. Adam was a jerk."

I hear her sigh. "He wasn't a jerk, Maya. Be nice." She's giggling again. "This guy is so sweet! I met him on lunch break."

I breathe a sigh of relief. As long as it's not Adam. "Cool, Jen!" I say. "That's so exciting! When are you going out?"

"Tonight."

"Wow. Quick. He doesn't waste time."

"And isn't that a great quality?"

"Uh. Sure."

"Maya, I'm so excited! Promise you'll be home when I get back from the date so you can meet him, okay?"

"As long as it's after ten, I should be there." I take a bite of fried rice. "I'm closing tonight, remember?"

"Oh. Be careful, Maya. I don't like the idea of you being there all alone."

"Jack usually stays and studies after he gets off."

"Good. Okay, well, I just wanted to tell you." She's back to giggling. "I have to go. Love you; see you tonight!"

"Have fun, Jen!"

I hang up and concentrate on my orange chicken. How do they make orange chicken, anyway?

I grin, thinking about Jen. She's really excited. Jen doesn't make personal calls during business hours. Not because Wayne doesn't let her but because she thinks it's unethical.

Silly Jen.

This guy must be really something. Just as long as he's not like Adam, the last guy she dated. Adam was a jerk.

He made Jen cry. That is not okay in my book. Or Jack's. He was ready to kill Adam.

I glance at the clock on my phone, gasp, and inhale the rest of my food. I jump up from the table, toss the Styrofoam, and refill the Dr Pepper.

I get back to work at 2:03. The school crowd will be in the building in exactly twenty-two minutes.

"Late, late." Jack is tsking at me. He is making another pot of coffee in anticipation of the crowd.

"Jen called. She's got a date tonight," I say, tying on my apron.

"Better not be with Adam."

There's a subtle threat to his words, and I smile. Jack is like my and Jen's big brother. He watches out for us.

"It's not. Actually, I don't know this guy's name. But it's not Adam."

"Good." He grins at me. "So, you're closing tonight, right?"

"Yeah."

"Okay. I'm going to go get Polly the Parrot settled in my apartment, and then I'm coming back here to study."

"I don't understand why you can't study at home."

"It's too quiet."

"Won't Polly take care of that?"

He gives me a look. "A whistling bird is not going to help my studying."

I shrug. "Okay, suit yourself." Honestly, I like it when he studies here. And he has ever since a group of rough-looking guys came in about a year ago right around closing time and gave me a lot of trouble when I tried to get them to leave.

Yet another way he plays the big-brother role.

The school crowd rushes through the doors and keeps us on our toes until it finally slows way down right as Jack is taking his apron off at four.

He waves. "I'll be back in a little bit."

"No rush. Say hey to Polly for me."

He rolls his eyes as he leaves.

Nine forty-five. And Cool Beans is officially the most boring place in the whole town of Hudson, California. It's a school night, so I knew it wouldn't be like a Friday- or Saturday-night close, but this is ridiculous.

I lean over the counter, resting my elbows on it and cradling my cup of French roast with two shakes of cinnamon, one of nutmeg, and a smidge of cream and sugar.

Jack is busy reading a book about how to keep parrots happy and healthy. Apparently, the bird said nothing. Just sat on her perch and stared at Jack and his mutt, Canis.

Just so you know, *Canis* is the Latin name for *dog*.

Nerd alert. I know.

Jack is occasionally calling out parrot facts. "Did you know that parrots can live up to a hundred years?"

"I did not," I say, sipping my coffee. "I hope no one leaves me a parrot when they die."

"Wouldn't that be awful? Apparently, they bond extremely well with their family and have bouts of depression when they're gone." He looks up from the book. "Great. I'm going to have a depressed bird this weekend."

I laugh at him.

There's one other person in here. A woman, about thirty, is

sitting in one of the squishy chairs reading a romance novel titled *To Ache Is Life*. Without the racy cover, I would have assumed it was a book about ibuprofen or workout addicts. Every once in a while, she suddenly sniffles and grabs for a Kleenex. She's drinking a triple-shot mocha and is only halfway through the book, so I'm assuming she's planning on staying up tonight and reading.

The door opens, letting in a rush of cool night air. I quickly move my cup to the shelf under the counter. Drinking in front of customers is a definite no.

It's Jen, and she's by herself. I would take this as a bad sign except for the huge grin on her face.

"Where's the gent?" Jack calls from his chair.

"Hey, Jack. Oh!" she sighs and clasps her hands at her heart. The woman reading the romance novel sets it down to watch Jen. "Oh, Maya, he's so *dreeeamy*! He's so sweet and nice and funny and charming and—"

"Not here?" Jack says again. I grin.

"He's parking the car, you big dolt." She comes over to the counter and pulls off her soft brown jacket. "Maya, he's adorable. You'll love him."

"Oh yeah?" I pull my cup back out from under the counter. "I take it dinner was good."

"It was wonderful. We went to Gina's."

I nod appreciatively. "Nice, very nice." I lean back down and grin at her conspiratorially. "You obviously like him."

"First impression . . ." She glances to make sure he isn't inside yet and then looks back at me, voice lowered. "He's great."

"Good! Yay!"

"Hush, here he comes." She immediately straightens, perfect posture back in place.

The door opens, and I gasp.

It's Travis Clayton.

CHAPTER TWO

So not *funny, God!*

Jack and Jen are giving me weird looks, but I try to cover the gasp, acting like I just cracked my finger on the counter. "Ouch," I say suddenly. "That stings."

I look up at the guy who just walked in again. Yeah, no doubt about it. He's definitely who I thought.

Travis Clayton. Six feet, two inches of muscle and athletic talent. Blond, blue eyes, the whole California surfer package. Slight drawl he inherited from his midwestern mom. He's got a bad habit of playing with his class ring when he's nervous, sings in the car to oldies music, and broke his wrist as a sophomore in high school when he crashed into his surfboard.

And he's the guy I dated the last three years of high school and freshman year at Cal-Hudson. We broke up right before Jen and I moved in together and right after my hopes of marrying Travis Clayton were dashed like his scaphoid bone against his board.

Jen has eyes only for him, but I can feel Jack's stare.

"Hey." I clear my throat, waiting for him to recognize me. It's been five years. My hair is short and its natural color, not long and blond like before. I've lost about fifteen pounds, and

I've embraced the natural makeup look as opposed to the china-doll appearance.

Travis looks exactly the same.

My heart is pounding. The adrenaline rush is making my hands tremble, so I hide them behind the counter. He looks good. He always did, but he looks especially good with the matured face, the slight stubble.

He smiles politely at me. "Hi."

He doesn't recognize me! Thank You, God! I'm still upset at You though. We will discuss this later.

Travis interrupts my prayer of thanksgiving. "Well, by your name tag, I take it you're Maya, Jen's best friend and roommate." He holds his right hand out over the counter. "I've heard a lot about you."

Apparently, not enough that he's heard my last name. "Yeah. Same here." I shake his hand lightly, disappointed in my weak grip.

Act natural. Act natural. Think natural thoughts. *Coffee. Ice cream. Sundaes. Maraschino cherries. The cute little baby jars of maraschino cherries.* I try to regulate my breathing, focusing on the Pilates core muscles.

Jack stands and comes over to meet him. "Hey, I'm Jack Dominguez. I'm a good friend of Jen's and Maya's."

He's sizing the guy up, and this makes me want to laugh. Jack is tall, yes, but big, no. Kind of on the skinnier side. Travis is not skinny. He's still got his football-player–sized shoulders and wide back.

"Nice to meet you." Jack nods.

"Thanks for introducing us, Jen," Travis says sarcastically, wrapping one arm around her. I blink at the casual way he does it. This is their first date, right?

Jen rolls her eyes at Travis. "I'm sorry, okay?" Then she looks at Jack's book and back up to Jack. "Why are you reading about parrots?" She frowns.

Jack sighs.

I force a light laugh. "It's a long story, Jenny. So, do you guys want anything to drink? On the house."

Jen stares at the menu for a second. "Can I have the English Dusk tea?"

Yuck. It's basically just a plain loose-leaf black tea with a hint of mint and some sort of flower in it. And zero caffeine. Of course, the only time I ever drink tea is when I'm sick, and I'm a firm believer that taste buds change when you're not feeling good. So maybe the tea is decent.

It'll never beat coffee though.

I know exactly what Travis will want. Small dark roast. Black as the refrigerator with the door closed.

"I'll take a small dark roast, please. Black."

I nod, fiddling with my hands, memories swimming in my head like ducks. "Okay." I put a spoonful of English Dusk tea in a little strainer sack, attach it to the cup, and pour hot water on top of it. Then I pour Travis's drink.

"Here you go."

"Thanks, Maya." Jen winks at me. "You're closing tonight, right?"

I look at the clock and nod. "Yep. Just now."

The woman with the aching book takes her cue and leaves, tossing her Kleenex and empty cup in the trash.

"Well, we'll leave too, so you can clean up," Travis says. He takes Jen's arm. "Nice meeting you, Maya. Jack."

"Yeah, you too," Jack says.

"Mm-hmm." I nod as I start running the cleaning cycle

on the espresso machine.

They leave. Jack immediately comes behind the counter and stands there staring at me, leaning against the sink.

"So?" he says after a minute.

"So what?"

"You know that guy, don't you?"

"Yeah. He's Jen's date. If you're going to be behind the counter, you can help clean." I toss him a wet towel, and he catches it, frowning at me.

"Nutkin."

"Jack."

"Come on, it's me. Talk to me."

I hiss the steam out of the wand, run a clean towel over the wand and trays below it, and then turn the espresso machine off. I rub my hands on the towel and just look at Jack.

He's still leaning against the sink—and still frowning.

Well, it's not like it won't come out eventually. Travis will probably have one of those aha moments they have in cheesy made-for-the-Hallmark-Channel Christmas movies tonight and come clean tomorrow.

I wince, thinking about the emotional repercussions of that one. Jen will be heartbroken but too loyal to me to keep dating him, even though I'll tell her to "just keep dating the guy even though it weirds me out."

Yucky.

"Okay. I dated that guy before," I admit in a quiet voice.

"And . . . he didn't recognize you? What was he, blind before?"

"Well, it was in high school. And freshman year at Cal."

Jack nods. "You haven't changed *that* much, Pattertwig." He starts wiping the counter with the towel. I toss the few pastries that are left in the display case into a bag for him to take home. Either Jack takes them home or we throw them away.

"You didn't know me in the blond years." Aka, age fifteen to nineteen. The day after Travis and I broke up, I marched to the salon and had them rinse my hair to its natural dark-chocolate brown color.

Mostly because it was Travis who kept me dying my hair for that long. He liked blonds. Still does, apparently.

"So it was like . . . what? Five or so years ago? Because when we became friends again, you didn't have a boyfriend."

I nod. "Yeah. Five years."

"Huh." Jack finishes with the counter and tosses the towel in the dirty hamper under the sink. "Wow. Well, that's awkward."

"Um, *yeah*." I say this like *duh*.

He rolls his eyes at me. "Please, Maya. Dating drama is so high school. He'll figure out who you are eventually, and it will be fine. After all, it was five years ago."

"Yeah . . ."

"And you're both adults. And Jen's a great girl, and she'll be understanding about it. And you'll be fine because you're an optimist, and you've got one heck of a best friend, who is also your co-worker, so why wouldn't you be fine?" He grins.

I smile back. "You know what? You're right. I mean, seriously, how awkward can it get?"

Reasons It Is Okay for Jen to Date Travis:
1. As Pumbaa would say, "You got to put your behind in your past."
Hakuna matata.
2. People change, and we both certainly have. Blond to brunette,
for example.
3. Jen's happy. Yay! It's been too long since she met a nice guy.

4. Travis isn't Adam. Yay! I don't have to punch someone's lights out tonight.

I stare at my scribbled sticky note under the dome light in my Jeep. I'm parked outside my apartment building.

Well, *technically,* I'm parked outside my apartment complex. In a guest parking spot. Someone in a bright red Nissan pickup took my allotted parking space right below my apartment. I'm guessing his name begins with a *T* and ends with an *S*.

We will need to discuss this issue. I'm not the guest here; he is. So he can park a block down and across the lot.

I shove the sticky note into the pocket of my jeans and climb out of the car, grabbing for my purse—which is really just a big messenger-style bag. I loop the strap over my neck and shoulder, crossing it over my chest, and start the trek home, frowning at the pickup.

Empty car equals man in apartment. This is going blatantly against The Apartment Code Jen and I wrote three years ago. No first dates allowed inside the apartment. Keeps temptation at bay and roommate out of awkward pajama scene when she's just trying to get a glass of water before bed.

And yes, this happened to me. With Adam actually. He brought Jen home late, and I was standing in the kitchen in a spaghetti-strap top, no bra, shorts, and slippers. The next morning, we wrote the code.

I get to the base of the apartment and hear voices above me over the iron-railed staircase. Just like Jen. Following the letter of the law, not the intent. Apparently, they are standing outside the front door, talking.

I climb the stairs and give a polite smile to both of them.

They are leaning on the rail gabbing. "Hi, guys. Good to see you again, Travis. Night, Jen."

"Good night, Maya."

"Nice to meet you too," Travis says. An odd look crosses his face right before I shut the door.

No drama tonight. I'm tired.

Calvin skips over to meet me, wriggling happily. I pick up the little dog and kiss his silky ears. "Hi, baby. Did you have a good day?"

"Roo! Roo!"

"Yeah? That's good." I tuck him under my arm, and he kisses my chin. "How about a bedtime snack, lovey? I'm thinking a sundae. Lots of chocolate for me."

This appeals to Calvin. I usually let him have his own bowl.

I set him down, lay my purse on the counter, scoop the vanilla ice cream, and spoon a generous helping of hot-fudge sauce on top of mine. Calvin trots behind me to my room. I set my bowl on the nightstand, his on the floor, and change into my bright pink pajama bottoms and a plain white T-shirt. I leave my bra on. Better safe than sorry, as my mom always says.

I have this theory about bright pink pajama bottoms and chocolate: The two combined can cure anything. Even the confusion I'm feeling right now.

Finishing off his bowl, Calvin jumps up on the bed next to me, and I flick on my little TV. "So, do I tell her?" I ask him.

He sighs and buries his nose in his paws, watching Stacy and Clinton on *What Not to Wear* lecture some poor girl with straggly red hair and a makeup-free face about wearing PJs in public.

I lick my spoon and squish back against the pillows on my bed, sitting right smack in the middle of the queen-size mattress, both feet stretched out in front of me.

Calvin makes a little noise, eyes still on the show.

"I know. I don't like that outfit either."

Calvin is a very fashion-astute dog. He carries his name well.

I'm scraping the bowl a few minutes later. Nick, the scissors-happy hairstylist, is attacking the redhead's hair and leaving her with a shorn 'do about fifteen inches shorter than she started out with.

I flick the TV off before the makeup artist starts and slide under the covers, turning out the light, snuggling into my pillow, and shutting my eyes.

Well, Lord, today was an interesting day. Please help me not to be all dramatic about Travis and Jen. They might make a good couple.

I listen to Calvin's breathing for a few minutes and sigh.

Travis is back. I can't help the weird little clench in my chest even at the mention of his name. Five years is a long time, but apparently not long enough.

And God, please just help it not to get awkward. I hate awkwardness.

CHAPTER THREE

I'm at Cool Beans by ten thirty Friday morning. I didn't even see Jen this morning because I decided to skip the morning run and sleep in until nine thirty. Which is why my hair is still wet from my shower and pulled up in a short little ponytail.

Jack is yawning behind the counter, wiping down the espresso machine as one of our regulars, Lana, leaves with her daily mocha.

I wave to Lana, drop my bag in the cabinet, tie on my apron, and look at Jack, who is yawning again.

"Late night?" I ask.

"The bird. Is nocturnal."

It's never good when Jack uses two sentences when he could've used just one. I wince.

"Nocturnal, like she's loud at night?"

"Nocturnal, like she kept me up all night." He sets the towel down and grabs his head. "Screeching and hollering. And I now know her owner's favorite movie. Polly quoted *The Mask of Zorro* the whole night."

"Hey, that's a good movie!"

Jack glowers at me under his hands. "Not anymore, Nut-job. All night! 'He probably wears the mask to hide his bald head and unsightly features.'" He sighs. "Go ahead and laugh."

I do. "I'm sorry, Jack, but I have to admit: This is hilarious!"

"No, it's not. I do not want to fall asleep hearing, 'The pointy end goes into the other man.' I like *silence*. Complete silence. Polly does not understand this. She even whistles that song Zorro and Elena dance to."

I'm impressed. "Wow. Can I meet her?"

"Yeah, but you'll have to come after sunset to hear her talk. She's nocturnal, I swear. Not a word, not a peep all day and then she morphs into Ebert and Roeper overnight."

I giggle and start foaming milk for an extra-large triple-shot cappuccino for poor Jack, who is leaning weakly against the counter, staring at a group of men doing a Bible study.

"Here." I hand him the drink.

"Thanks, Nutkin."

"Welcome."

He sips the cappuccino and smiles weakly. "Very good." He shakes his head and tries to straighten off the counter, then gives up and leans back against it. "So, any more awkwardness last night?" he asks me.

"Well, they were talking on the porch when I got home. I still don't think he recognized me, but I don't know. I went inside. My motto last night was 'No Drama.'"

"Probably best."

"Yeah."

Our boss, Alisha Kane, walks in right then, tucking her sunglasses into her dark hair.

Alisha is a good boss. She's flexible with schedules, gives raises regularly, and always has a funny story to share with us. In all, Cool Beans has five baristas, but Jack and I are usually paired together.

She comes in once a week just to make sure things are running well. There's a little café across Hudson that she owns, too. Alisha spends most of her time there.

"Hi, guys," she says, coming over in front of the counter and setting her briefcase down on it. She digs through the pockets and pulls out a bunch of white envelopes.

"Hey, Alisha, how's it going?" I ask. I start making an americano for her. Alisha loves americanos.

"Good." She gives Jack a look. "Jack, you look a little down."

"He's bird-watching this week," I say.

"You're what?"

Jack smiles tiredly at Alisha. "I'm babysitting a parrot who likes night best for talking."

She laughs. "Ah. Sorry, Jack."

"Not your fault. It's mine."

"Is it a school project?" she asks.

I hand her the americano and answer for him. "No, it's just Jack not being able to say no."

"It sounded like a good idea at the time." He rubs his face. "Extra money, good experience with birds, not a lot of work. . . . Yeah. Regretting this one."

Alisha sips her coffee. "Well, kids, I only have a few minutes, but I wanted to drop by and see how it was going. Here are your paychecks, by the way."

"Yay!" I say for the both of us, since Jack is now sleepily staring into his coffee mug.

We talk income for a few minutes, and she gathers everyone's time cards for the last week.

"Have a good day, guys. Call if you need anything," she says, as is her custom, and slides her shades back on as she leaves.

Three o'clock, and I'm officially done for the day. I untie my apron, hang it on my hook inside the kitchen, and grab my bag.

Jack's leaving too. Our replacements, Carmen and Lisa, are already here and in place behind the counter, giggling over something Lisa did yesterday.

"Bye!" I wave at them as I leave, holding the door for poor, exhausted Jack.

"Bye, Pattertwig." He yawns. "See you tomorrow."

"Sleep well, Jackie."

He gives me a hug before I get in my car.

Calvin is yipping excitedly as I walk in the door. "Hi, boy!" I pick him up and rub his big ears. "How are you?"

It's a gorgeous day, and I decide Calvin and I are going on a walk. I change into my jogging pants and a T-shirt. I have one arm in the armhole and the other is trying to find the opening for my head and other arm.

Right then, of course, the phone rings.

"Calvin, can you get that?"

I yank the shirt on and answer my cell, my left eye involuntarily winking because some fuzz from my shirt is in my eye.

"Yeah?"

"Well, hi; hello to you too."

"Hi, Mom. Sorry, I couldn't see." Still can't. I rush for the bathroom, wondering if people can go blind by T-shirt fuzz. I don't think this shirt is 100 percent cotton. That's bad, right? According to the Style Network, that's very bad.

I think it's because people are into the all-natural stuff now. You know, green is the new black and all that. If you want my opinion, I think "going green" sounds like someone's either very jealous or on the verge of being awfully seasick.

Mom asks, "What are you up to?"

"Is polyester bad for your eyes?"

"Probably," my mother says, all cheerfully, apparently not having that whole mother's intuition thing to know that her daughter is going blind.

"Oh." I start splashing water in my eye. I'm still holding the phone with my right hand and my aim is bad to begin with, but I find out it's a lot worse with my left hand.

Water drenches the front of my pants.

Swell.

"What is going on there?" Mom asks.

"I had fuzz in my eye, so I was trying to get it out before I got polyester poisoning of the retina or something, but now I have water all over my front like I couldn't hold it long enough."

"Pleasant, Maya."

"You asked!" I blink, and the fuzz leaves my eye. So easy now that I'm soaking wet, of course.

"Well, I was actually calling for a reason."

"Beyond just concern for your favorite daughter?"

"With a daughter like you, I've learned just to live with concern."

I grab a towel for my pants, sit on the toilet-seat cover, and start dabbing. "Gee, thanks."

"You're welcome. Now. About Sunday."

Calvin and I drive two hours roundtrip every Sunday to eat dinner with my parents in San Diego. With gas prices what they are, I believe I deserve the Daughter of the Year award. Calvin doesn't get anything. He's just a dog, and he likes the wind in his face. It's a treat for him.

"Zach and Kate are coming to town."

My brother, Zach, is four years older than me and married to Kate. They don't have children, and they're like the worst communicators on the planet.

Obviously.

I can barely contain my joy. Right. "They're in town?"

"Well, they will be tomorrow. So, they'll be here on Sunday, and Dad thinks we should go out to dinner. I was calling to see if you'll meet us at The Cheesecake Factory in Fashion Valley Mall."

Well, if Zach's here, then yeah. Bring out the fatted calf.

I squint my eyes shut and pause with the towel. *Sorry, Lord. That wasn't a good thought at all.*

Here's the thing about my brother, Zachary Robert Davis: He's pretty much brilliant. He made straight As from kindergarten to graduating from med school. He's a doctor in Phoenix. For sick little children in the largest children's hospital in Arizona.

I'm a barista in Hudson. The difference, needless to say, is glaring.

"Sure. What time?" I say. Short answers are best here.

I can almost hear Mom looking at the clock and thinking. "Maybe around five? That will give you enough time after church, right?"

"Uh-huh."

"Wonderful. See you in a couple days, sweetheart!"

Mom hangs up, and I set the phone on the counter. I keep working on the wet spot.

Don't get me wrong; I love my brother. I really do. He's usually a good brother, especially now that puberty is long past for both of us.

I just have self-esteem problems after a family dinner involving him. He's always talking about some child he cured of a deadly disease, and what am I supposed to say? "Oh yeah? Well, without me, some poor lady would have had a horrible caffeine headache all day long!"

Kind of loses something.

It's hard being the sister to a genius. It was hard in grade school when we had the same teachers and they'd all say the same thing at the beginning of the year: "Oh, wonderful! Another Davis child!" You know, expecting another straight-A student. By the end of the year, they were like, "Oh. We thought you were related to Zachary Davis."

It never gets easier.

I abandon the towel and head to my room. Calvin follows me, curious about when exactly this walk will happen. "Just a second, kiddo."

I grab a sticky note from my bedside table.

Reasons It's Okay to Be Me:
1. This is exactly how God wanted me to be.
2. We don't all have to be doctors!
3. If everyone were a genius, we would have no normal people, and then geniusness would be normality. Without me,
Zach is not a genius.
4. Even though it is for Zach, I still get Cheesecake Factory too! Yay!

Between Zach and Travis, the walk turns into a jog, the jog into a run, and the run into crashing on the sofa, sweaty, worn out, and holding a package of Oreos and a jar of marshmallow creme.

Calvin falls with a huff on the floor beside the couch, tucking his head between his paws.

"Sorry, bud. Guess I pushed us kind of hard today."

He sighs his agreement.

I think one of the best, albeit most disgusting-sounding, desserts ever is Oreos dipped in marshmallow creme. It's amazing. I always feel sorry for people who don't know of this remarkable combination.

I flick the TV on and rise off the couch for a brief second to pop in *While You Were Sleeping*, probably my most favorite Sandra Bullock movie of all time.

It's Calvin's, too. I know this because usually he sleeps through movies, but anytime I watch this one, he perks up and stays awake through the whole thing.

Jen walks in right when Lucy and Jack have their first kiss under the mistletoe. "Oh!" she sighs, drops her purse and coat on the floor, kicks off her heels, and falls to the couch. "I love this movie."

"Hi, Jen."

"Hey." She reaches for the Oreos, bypassing the marshmallow creme. "So, is this the grand plan for tonight?"

"What?"

"Oreos. Squished-down marshmallows in a jar. Bill Pullman."

I lick the crumbs from my thumb. "I'm putting in *Elf* next."

"Maya, it's October."

"Jen, it's funny."

She giggles and pulls her hose-shrouded legs up underneath her on the cushions. "You're right. Can I watch it with you?"

"Yep." I watch her tie her hair up in a sloppy bun on top of her head. "What should we have for dinner?"

"Wayne gave me a gift card to Macaroni Grill today. We could have pasta."

"I don't feel like showering."

She nods. "I don't feel like putting those heels back on. Honestly, Maya. You should be thankful your career actually encourages good podiatric support."

"Speaking of podiatric and doctors and stuff, Zach's back in town." I pop another marshmallow-covered Oreo in my mouth and watch the screen in crunching silence.

Jen looks at me. "Thus the cookies and the comedies."

Jen knows all about my sibling rivalry with Zach.

"Well . . ."

She reaches over and rubs my arm. "I'm sorry. It'll be fine, you know."

"Yeah. Let's make tortellini for dinner."

"I thought you just said you didn't want pasta."

My mouth is watering. "I said I didn't want to shower." And by *make* tortellini, I really mean dump one of those frozen bags of pasta into a boiling pot of water.

"Oh."

I look over at her. "Hey, why did you get a gift card anyway?"

She blushes lightly. "Well, Travis is a big client, and he sent flowers to the office today. Wayne was proud of me, so he gave me a gift card."

I'm frowning. "Wayne was proud you got flowers, so he gave you dinner for you and you alone?"

She shakes her head. "I never claimed he was brilliant, Maya."

"This is true."

We watch the movie for a few minutes. Jack and Lucy are dancing around the "I like you" issue, and it's pretty adorable. This is how Jen and I watch movies: We talk until we get to a scene we love; then we shut up and watch it.

Travis sent Jen flowers.

I chomp another Oreo and glance over at her profile. She's concentrating on the movie, mindlessly nibbling on a cookie.

I know exactly what flowers he gave her: tulips. It's Travis's favorite flower, and he gave me tulips the whole time we were dating. Even though I specifically mentioned on multiple occasions that I love daisies.

Especially the happy little white ones.

This will work out nicely for Jen, though.

"He even brought me my favorite flowers," she says quietly after the scene ends.

"Really?"

"Mm-hmm. A huge bouquet of tulips." She sighs. This is the second time, and she's only been home for fifteen minutes. "I really like him, Maya."

I have to laugh at her dismal tone, even though my stomach suddenly starts cramping. "So why the depression?"

"I don't want to get my heart involved so fast. You know?" She rubs her face. "Things were good. It was me and God, and I didn't need anyone else."

"And now?"

She finally meets my eyes. "Now . . ." Her voice trails off, and she looks back at the TV.

Bill Pullman is paying his toll with a ring. I know what Jen's thinking.

"It'd be nice, huh?" I say.

"Yeah."

I nod and stand as the happy couple kisses. I walk into our tiny, nonfunctional kitchen. "Okay. No tortellini. We're going the extra mile tonight."

Especially since we're both dealing with issues involving the same guy.

Awkward. *Awkward!*

"What are we having?" Jen calls from the couch, looking at me over the high counter that's directly over the sink.

I open the cabinet that serves as a pantry. "Pie."

"Pie? Like pot pie?"

Ah, Jen. Ever the nutritional optimist.

"Like apple pie. Or cherry." I have canned fillings for both. Never as good as my grandmother's homemade apple pie, of course, but desperate times call for desperate measures.

And I can't cook to save my tush.

"Maya." She comes into the kitchen, her white collared shirt and skirt looking rumpled after lounging on the couch. "We can't have pie for dinner."

"Why not? We're young. We exercise. And besides, this is the highest our metabolism will ever be. We should be taking advantage of this." I'm waving the cans at her as I talk.

Jen works with a lawyer all day. She recognizes logical thinking when she sees it. "Okay, you win. But I'm fixing a salad."

"Spoilsport."

"Sugar nut."

"Don't say that in front of Jack; it'll give him another nickname."

She grins as she pulls a packaged salad from the fridge.

CHAPTER FOUR

Ten o'clock Sunday morning. I'm slouched in one of the very uncomfortable folding chairs in a freezing-cold classroom inside Grace Bible Church. I'm cradling my coffee with both hands, slumped over, and my left eye is half open like the Hunchback of Notre Dame.

Jen's sitting next to me, but unlike me, she's sitting straight-backed, smiling, eyes wide open, her long, shiny blond hair in perfect place. She's wearing a skirt and a subtle pink top and looks like Miss Teen California all grown up.

Ugh.

Definitely not a good idea to start the A&E *Pride and Prejudice* at ten thirty last night. It's downright impossible to stop that movie in the middle!

So, there I was at two thirty at night, cuddled up with Calvin on my bed, sighing over Mr. Darcy's faltering speech and dripping wet hair. "Beg your pardon, your family is in good health?"

How come nobody talks like that anymore? If I could time travel anywhere, I'd jump to England in that exact year. Bring a basket of deodorant, a pair of blue jeans, and Bath & Body Works soap, and I'd be a happy camper.

By the time I turned the TV off and fell asleep, it was

after three thirty in the morning.

Our singles pastor, Andrew Townsend, stops in front of me and pokes me in the forehead.

"Mmpgh."

Andrew is way too much of a morning person. "Harken! She speaks!"

This is what I say: "Leave me alone."

This is how it comes out: "Leefmaown."

Andrew just laughs and moves on, greeting the people sitting in a half circle around the classroom. There are about twenty or so people here; most of them come to our Wednesday-night Bible study as well.

Andrew Townsend is twenty-nine, single, used to play hockey but still has all his teeth. I find this a big perk for an ex-hockey star. I heard he could've gone pro, but he decided not to because he wanted to be a pastor.

Anyway, he's this big broad-shouldered guy with tons of thick, beautiful, sandy blond hair that he keeps on the longish side. It makes him look like a modern-day Viking. I've told him this before, and he said, "*Arg!*"

Which is actually more pirate-sounding than Viking, but what the heck.

Jack drops into the seat on my right. "You okay?"

"Mmm."

Jen leans around me. "She watched *Pride and Prejudice* last night."

Jack frowns. "So she's depressed?"

"When did you finish it, Maya?" Jen asks.

"'Bout three or so."

"Last *night?*" Jack is grinning. "They invented a Stop button, you know."

"But good things came from this," I say around a mouthful of coffee.

"Like what? Poorer posture? You can win in the Hudson County Fair Slumped Shoulders Contest?"

I blink at Jack. "They have that?"

"No, Nutkin."

"Oh. No, I discovered I do not under any circumstances want to be a newspaper delivery guy. I heard him at three thirty this morning, and I think that's a form of punishment. What did he ever do to deserve that?" I ask.

"They get paid really well," Jen says. "So, I've heard it's worth it."

"Okay, everyone, chatter needs to cease," Andrew says, pulling a little stool under him and sitting in the middle of the half circle.

It always is a little humorous to see big, stocky Andrew on the little, rickety stool. One day, I swear it will break.

It'll be funny in a morbid kind of way.

He's balancing a huge ceramic coffee mug on one knee that says: *Donate Blood. Play Hockey.* It's filled to the brim with dark, rich coffee, and this is where Andrew and I have a connection. He's a major coffee nut, too. He comes into Cool Beans on a regular basis.

"Today, lads and ladies, I want us to discuss your thoughts on how aggressive Christians should be in today's culture."

"You mean, like, evangelism?" Natalie, one of the girls in the class, asks.

Andrew shrugs. "Sure. In every area of life."

Jack leans back in his chair. This means he's going to speak. "I would say it's enough to stand up for what you believe, not so far as to beat them over the head with it," he offers.

"Explain that," Andrew prompts.

"Well." Jack adjusts his pant legs now. This means he's not sure how to put his thoughts into words. "I'm not sure how to describe it. Like stating what I believe in a way that is loving, I guess." Then he exhales. This means Jack is done talking for the rest of the class.

I smirk into my coffee.

"Very good, Jack." Andrew nods and continues. We spend the next thirty minutes in discussion, and then Andrew tells us we're going to read through the book of James. "This is such a great book on not backing down. So, get ready, strap your helmets on, and aim for the puck because this book is one of my favorites."

Andrew sometimes forgets he's a pastor and not a hockey player, I think.

He prays, and we all stand and start folding up the aforementioned uncomfortable chairs like we do every Sunday. I'm still freezing cold, and now I get to waste three and a half hours before I start the drive to San Diego.

"Jen, want to go to Kohl's?"

This is sort of like asking a demolition crew if they want goggles. The answer is fairly obvious.

"No thanks," she says sweetly.

At least I thought it was. I don't even hear her answer at first; I'm so convinced I know what she'll say. "Okay, we can go before—wait. What?" I sputter.

"Um. Not today." She fidgets and smoothes her skirt.

Jack is grinning. "Got something else to do, Jenny?"

She winces, blushes, and smiles all in about three and a half seconds. "Maybe."

Travis.

I sigh. "Okay. Well, maybe another time." I sling my purse over my shoulder, trying not to be depressed. Especially after such a great lesson. Great lessons by Andrew usually perk me up for the rest of the day, enough that Calvin and I usually discuss it on the way to Mom and Dad's.

Jen looks at her watch and smiles softly. "Well, I have to go, guys. Have a great day!" She waves and is off.

I look at her swooshing hair as she leaves and then at Jack. He's smiling one of those "It's okay" smiles, which are perfected by the medical profession. I know. Zach does it.

"Kohl's?" he asks.

"I don't know." I shrug. "It was mostly an excuse to burn three hours before I leave to go see Mom and Dad and Zach."

"Zach's in town, huh?"

"Mmm."

He gives me the same smile but pairs it with a shoulder squeeze. "Maybe he's more tactful now."

"Maybe."

Andrew comes over as everyone else in the room has left. "Hey. So?"

"Two thumbs up." I show him my thumbs.

"Really? Cool beans!" He shoves his elbow in my ribcage. "Get it? Cool Beans? Like where you work? Get it, Maya?"

I rub my side. "Ow."

"What's the game plan for you today?" Andrew asks.

"I'm going to see the parental units this afternoon," I say. "I think you bruised me."

"Oh yeah, your Sunday tradition. Bruises are good for you; they toughen you up."

"Tonight it's at The Cheesecake Factory, so I've got three hours to kill. And I don't want tough sides."

"Get the key lime cheesecake; it's stinking awesome." He grins at me. "No tough sides? Like beef jerky or something?"

"Dude, I saw this woman at my apartment pool the other day," Jack starts, covering his eyes with his hand. "Her skin looked like my mom's suede couch. It was gross. There is such a thing as too tan."

Andrew laughs. "Total agreement here, man. Hey, what are you guys up to for lunch?"

Both of us shrug, which spurs Andrew to clap his hands and order us to go to lunch with him at Kaiser, a local deli.

We arrive with the rest of the after-church lunch crowd and wait about ten minutes for a table. When we finally get seated, Andrew plops in his chair and grabs the menu. "Man, I'm starving. I can't even remember the last time I ate."

"Breakfast?" I ask sweetly.

"No breakfast. I'm out of Eggos. Ruined my whole morning."

"There's more to life than Eggo waffles, Andrew," I say.

"But not more to breakfast." He slams the menu down, and I jump. "I'm getting the number twelve."

I look down at it. *Ham, turkey, pastrami, salami, bacon, and three fried eggs on a toasted bun with lettuce, tomato, cucumber, guacamole, and cheddar and Muenster cheese. Big enough for two!*

"Looks hefty," I remark.

"Sounds good," Jack says. "Hey, what exactly is pastrami?"

"Beef, kid. Cured beef."

"Basically, it's left out to dry, and they run out and get it right before it spoils, then stick it on a sandwich," I explain.

"Sounds great." Jack says this unenthusiastically.

"Doesn't it, though?" Andrew says, all cheerful. "My mom used to feed us pastrami and bologna on bagels for our after-school snack." He inhales, getting nostalgic. "I never eat it without thinking about her."

"I hope that my future kids remember me for more than nearly spoiled beef," I say.

"You sentimental fool." Jack grins at me.

The server, a cute brunette who can't be more than five foot one, comes to take our order.

"When did Zach get in town?" Jack asks me.

"Uh, yesterday, I think."

"They going to be here long?"

"I don't know, actually. Mom didn't say how long they are here."

"Excuse me?" Andrew waves over the server. "Could I get extra cheese on that number twelve?"

"Extra, sir?" She sounds like he just ordered a pig with an apple in its mouth. "It comes with cheddar and Muenster already."

"That guy who just got served?" Andrew points nondiscreetly at the table next to us. The guy, a nice-looking man in his forties, looks at Andrew and holds up his sandwich like the monkey holds Simba on *The Lion King*. You can almost hear the African safari music starting.

"Yes?" the server asks.

"Is there swiss on there?"

"Yes, sir. Swiss and colby jack."

"Yum. Could I get both on my sandwich, please?"

She nods. "Sure. It'll probably be extra, just so you know."

"Fine."

She leaves, and Andrew turns back to us. "What were we talking about?" he asks.

Now I know why Andrew is the barrel-shaped giant he is. "Glad to see you're taking that Atkins diet to heart," I say.

"I'm not on Atkins. I could never survive without Eggos."

I just smile.

It's three fifteen, and I'm busy grabbing a few things for my weekly trip. Calvin is racing excitedly around my ankles. He loves Sundays.

I'm still debating if I should take him. On the one hand, he'll be ecstatic to ride in the car. On the other hand, he'd have to wait in the car through dinner because we're not going to Mom and Dad's first.

"Roo! Rooooo!"

Take him, I decide.

"Ready, baby?"

"Roo!"

"I'll take that as a yes." I pop a collar around his neck. It's bright cherry red and Calvin's favorite.

Jen isn't here, neither is a note from her. If I had to guess, I'd bet she hasn't been back all day. Her car isn't in her allotted parking spot, so there's no telling where she is.

I pull a Dr Pepper from the fridge and a box of Junior Mints from the pantry. I've got my jacket for later when it gets dark and drops the whole ten degrees that makes us Southern Californians cold. And I changed clothes from jeans and a sweatshirt to my black pants and a cerulean silky long-sleeved top. It makes my eyes look really blue, and with my hair fixed curly, I look fairly decent, if I say so myself.

You might think this is too dressed up for The Cheesecake Factory. I would completely agree with you. But Zach is always dressed in Dockers and usually has a sport coat with him. And Kate, his wife, typically looks like she has stock in Ralph Lauren or something.

Me? I'm all about denim. Give me a quality pair of jeans and I'll wear them until they fall off my body in tatters that would make that "Feed the Birds" lady on *Mary Poppins* proud.

I open the door, and Calvin runs out, down the steps, and over to my car, wriggling excitedly. I grin, lock the door, and then go open the car for him.

We listen to my classic Elvis collection on the drive over. Calvin has his head out the window, tongue flapping, for the entirety of the trip.

I get to The Cheesecake Factory at exactly 4:57, which officially makes me early. I remind myself of a few rules: "Make friendly conversation, keep Travis and Jen out of it, and order the Godiva chocolate cheesecake." Turning the car off, I look over. "Sit tight, don't eat the seats, and stay out of my Junior Mints," I lecture Calvin, who then falls with a huff on the passenger seat.

He curls into a little ball and looks up at me like, "Fine, whatever."

Climbing out, I straighten my shirt and try to see my reflection in the Jeep window. Too dirty. "Cal, how do I look?"

He closes his eyes and conks out.

"Helpful." I grab my purse, press the lock down, and shut the door. There's the tiniest nip of chill in the air, which means San Diego's excuse for winter is on its way. Where's the snow? Where are the happy ski bums? Where's the Dean Martin music?

They're all in Colorado, I guess, because neither San Diego nor Hudson gets squat when it comes to snow. I have at least fifteen adorable scarves that I never get to wear, and if I do wear one, I have to crank up the A/C. I'm moving to the Rocky Mountain state ASAP.

I walk through the doors into the dark, crowded restaurant. People are pressing in all around the hostess station, making the two poor girls tending it duck for cover behind the menus.

"Maya!"

I turn right into my mom's hug. "Hi, baby," Mom says, pulling me tight. "The drive was good?"

"Yeah." I pull away to give Dad a hug as well. "Hi, Dad."

"How's the Jeep running, Maya?"

This is Dad's code for *How are you?*

"Good," I reply. "How are you?"

"Fine. Good to hear that. Bring it by next week, and I'll have a peek under the hood." Dad shifts, looking uncomfortable in his slacks and collared shirt. I give him a sympathetic look.

Zach and Kate stand up from the bench where they were seated, and immediately three little kids plop down on it.

"Hi, Maya." Zach smiles. "You look good. I like your hair."

"Thanks. You look good, too." And he does. He's wearing Dockers (of course) and a white button-down shirt with the top two buttons undone, showing his white undershirt. He's letting his sandy blond hair grow beyond his normal nearly shaved look, and it's slightly gelled to a sticky-up preppy style. Zach looks identical to Mom—blond, green eyes, tall and lean, the whole package.

I look exactly like Dad's mother, Nana. Short, average weight (meaning I have to run to stay lean), blue eyes, and hair as close to black as brown can get.

It's kind of a funny sight when my whole family is together. Mom, Dad, Zach, and now Kate are all above five foot seven, and then there's me.

I like being short though. I even wrote a sticky note why:

Reasons It Is Okay to Be Short:
1. I don't hurt my back getting into the lower cabinets
in the kitchen.
2. I get discounts from people who think I'm younger than I am.
3. I will never hit my head on a fan and cut hair
I don't want cut.

So, it's all good.

"Maya, your hair looks really cute," Kate says, giving me an awkward half-wave. Kate's not big on physical affection. So we wave. Or do the little elbow-squeeze thing.

How very unlike me. The more hugs I get, the happier I am.

"Thanks, it's really good to see you," I return.

Dad's buzzer starts going off for the table. "Davis, party of five," he tells one of the hostesses.

She looks us over to make sure none of us is going to attack her like the impatient mob in the front will and then nods. "Right this way."

We're seated in a booth in the corner of the restaurant, and everyone settles in.

"How's airline mechanics?" Kate asks Dad.

"Good. How's doctoring?" Dad asks Zach.

"Big caseload but fine. How's teaching?" Zach asks Mom.

"Same as before. How's the coffeehouse?" Mom asks me.

"Busy but good. How's the lawyer thing going?" I ask Kate.

"Slow time of the year, so it's going well," she answers.

And then the table falls into complete silence. Out of sheer boredom, I open my menu, even though I already know what I'm going to get.

Sunday evenings when Zach isn't home aren't like this. Usually, I wear my pajama pants over to my parents' house. We play games or talk in front of their huge, gorgeous fireplace. Mom always makes a killer meal, like steaks and mashed potatoes or chicken fried chicken and creamy gravy, and sometimes we roast marshmallows over the fire and make s'mores or pop them in a cup full of hot chocolate. There's nothing like it. Then Calvin and I drive home all warm and full, content to live another week on instant freezer meals.

I haven't figured out if it's Zach or Kate or both who put such a damper on the conversation. But ever since they got married, it's as if talking is too personal.

Dad gives me a pained look over his bifocals and his menu.

"So, um," I start, clearing my throat, "the, uh, funniest thing happened the other day. Um, you remember Travis Clayton?"

Ignoring my second rule, I might as well lay myself on the sacrificial altar for the sake of discussion. I gulp half the glass of iced lemon water our skinny, emo-ish server brings.

Mom immediately perks up. "He was adorable!"

"Who's Travis Clayton?" Kate asks.

"Maya's high school sweetheart." Zach looks across the table at me. "Didn't you two even discuss marriage at one point?"

"Right before we broke up, right before sophomore year." I nod.

"In *high school*?" Kate is incredulous.

"College. I was at Cal-Hudson by then."

"He was a sweet boy." Mom's still gushing. "I never understood why you two broke up. You were the cutest couple ever!"

"He played football," Dad tells Kate. "He got a scholarship to Stanford as a running back."

"Impressive," Kate says.

"He tore his knee last game of freshman year. Never went back." Dad finishes his little tale, and then everyone looks at me.

"Anyway . . ." I finish my story quietly. "Jen met him, and now they're dating, and she doesn't know that we dated because we hadn't met yet when Travis and I were together, and now Travis doesn't recognize me. Has anyone seen the server? I'm starving."

"Didn't he get some high honors senior year at Stanford?" Mom asks. "I seem to remember Gloria saying something about that."

Apparently, Mom is the only one who didn't hear me because Dad, Zach, and Kate are all staring at me like I'm holding a betta fish in my mouth like Giselle on *Enchanted*.

"What?" Zach asks. "How could he not recognize you? He was going to marry you, for Pete's sake."

"Who doesn't recognize you?" Mom asks.

"He's dating Jen? Weird." Dad shakes his head. "Is that weird for you?"

"Who's dating Jen?" Mom asks.

"I think . . . I think you might want to tell her . . . um, soon," Kate stutters.

"You haven't told who what?" Mom asks.

"That's — wow." Zach sits back against the bench and looks at me, eyebrows raised. "I'm sorry, kid. That's got to be awkward — Jen and Travis dating."

"What?" Mom gasps. "Travis is dating your roommate?"

I just sigh.

I am so full that I don't think I'll be able to eat for a good week, maybe two. I puff my cheeks out and look at Calvin, who's happily sticking his head out the window as we drive to Mom and Dad's after dinner.

"No more eating. Ever again," I tell him.

Based on his expression of sheer joy, he doesn't believe me. Either that, or he knows where we're going. Calvin loves Mom and Dad's house. Dad lets him on the couches, while Jen and I have a strict "no dogs on anything resembling furniture" rule. He's a spoiled granddog.

I pull up beside their mailbox and let an ecstatic beagle out of the car. He half-runs, half-hops a dog dance to the front door.

"Hi, Calvin!" Mom says in a high-pitched voice as I open the door.

"Roo! Roo!"

She laughs as he tucks his tail under him and runs to her like she's his longlost best friend. "Wow. Okay. Easy boy."

"Calvin," I call, with warning in my tone, as I pull off my jacket. "No jumping."

He immediately falls to the floor, and Mom starts giving him a deep-tissue back rub. "Is you a good wittle puppy? Yes, you is!" She baby talks to him. He just moans like a cat.

No wonder my dog loves this place so much.

Zach watches the whole thing, arms crossed. "Huh. How come when I run to you, you never give me a back rub?" he asks Kate.

She smiles. "Your ears aren't as cute."

"Well, thanks."

After another hour of sitting straight-backed on the sofa and making awkward small talk, I decide to go home. "Come on, Cal," I call. He gives me a grudging look from Dad's lap, where he's now getting a tummy rub.

"Leaving already, sweetheart?" Mom asks from the recliner.

"I have to open at Cool Beans this week," I explain, finding my coat and purse.

"What time do you open?" Zach asks.

"Seven, but that means I'm there by about six thirty."

He waves his hand. "That's nothing. My early surgeries are all scheduled for six o'clock in the morning. Consider yourself lucky you're not operating on someone when you get to work all tired."

I bite back a sigh. "Right, right." I know he's not trying to point out the vast difference in our careers, but it sure feels like it.

"It was nice seeing you again, Maya," Kate says politely. It looks like she's debating giving me a hug, but then squeezes my elbows instead.

"Yeah, you too."

Zach waves from the sofa. "See you later, Maya."

"Bye, Zach. Bye, Mom. Bye, Dad." I snap my fingers at Calvin and he moves in slow motion off Dad's lap, soaking in every last minute.

"Bye, sweetie," Dad says to me. "Bye, Calvin!"

"Roo." This little yodel is more like a sigh of depression. I shake my head, watching my dog sulk to the front door.

It's going to be a boring ride home. Anytime Calvin feels like I'm making him leave before he's good and ready, he ignores me the whole way home.

I pull into my space in front of our apartment and yawn as I look at the dashboard clock. It's nearly midnight, so already I'm looking at five and a half hours of sleep if I were to get in bed and be immediately asleep this very minute.

Jack is not going to like me very much tomorrow. I'm not a nice person to be around when I'm tired.

I nudge Calvin, who is curled into a little ball on the passenger seat. "Wake up, bud. We're home." He crawls across the seats and snuggles into my lap.

Awww!

I have a cute dog. Granted, he's probably just not wanting to walk upstairs, but he's so cute I can't resist. I pick him up, climb out of the car, and carry him up the stairs.

The light from the TV is flickering in the windows, and I frown. Jen's never up this late.

I open the door.

"You're finally home!" she nearly yells, making Calvin jump. I start a little bit too. "Hi," I say.

She hops off the couch and starts bubbling. "Oh, Maya, it was so wonderful! After church, he took me to this picnic spot that was so beautiful because all of the trees were changing, and he'd packed this whole lunch with sandwiches and cheese and fruit and sparkling cider, and then we just sat and talked for, like, hours, and then when it was time to go, we decided to go get coffee, so we sat and talked for hours there, and then we went and saw a movie at the theater, and then we had dinner, and oh — !" She finally takes a breath. My lungs are hurting just watching her. She falls back on the couch. "It was the perfect day."

No accusing "Hey, you never told me you dated him," so I'm assuming Travis did not recognize me last night. Travis is nothing but honest. If he knew who I was, he'd tell Jen as soon as he could.

I set Calvin down, and he slumps to my room to go to bed. I watch him longingly but recognize the hopeful look on

Jen's face and sit on the couch.

So sorry, Jack.

He's really not going to like me in the morning. But every girl knows that half the fun of going on a date is dishing about it later.

This isn't the first time Jen's told me about a date, but it is the first time she's told me about one without using periods. Normally, it goes something like this: "So, we went to dinner. Then we went to a movie. It was fun." The end.

I try to ignore the tightening in my stomach. Maybe if I just pretend I never dated Travis . . . maybe that could work.

There's a prominent new display of tulips on the coffee table. "He brought a gift, I see." I point to the flowers.

She sighs. "Aren't they beautiful?"

"They're pretty."

"Oh, Maya, he's the sweetest guy I've ever met."

Jen, we dated. All through high school and the first year of college. I thought you should know. And it's late. I'm going to bed.

It sounds good in my head. I open my mouth.

She beats me to it. "And we have *so* much in common!" she exclaims. "We both love movies and hiking and Italian food, and he tells the funniest stories!"

"Jen," I start as soon as she takes a breath.

"Oh! And the dinner! I'll tell you what, Maya, he does not scrimp on taking me out. Flowers, nice restaurants, he always asks if I want dessert. . . ."

She's got this dreamy soft look in her eyes, and the light from the TV is making them sparkle even more.

Oh boy.

"Jen," I try again.

"Oh gosh!" She jumps and looks at the clock. "Work! We

67

both have to work tomorrow! You have to open!" She yanks me to my feet. "Go to bed! I'm sorry for keeping you up for so long." She pulls me into a long hug. "You are the best friend ever for listening to me." She leans back and smiles. "I love you, Maya."

"Love you, too." Which is why I keep my mouth shut and do what the woman says: Go to bed.

CHAPTER FIVE

Monday morning, I get to Cool Beans tired, cranky, and with a headache because Jen and I are out of coffee. (Mental note: Buy more today.) To add insult to injury, I'm opening today. Which means it's 6:25 a.m.

"What's eating you, Pattertwig?" Jack greets me at the door, pulling his keys out of his dark-rinsed, straight-legged jeans. I shrug. He unlocks the front door, and we walk into the cold, dark coffee shop.

I hate Cool Beans when no one is here and no lights are on. You can almost smell the vacancy. It's chilly and dead and clammy.

Jack sighs. "I love being the first one here. It's like this place gets excited to be opened."

Jack is weird.

He pockets his keys and looks over at me. "So, seriously, what's wrong?"

"No coffee at home."

"Sit. I'll make you a cup."

He doesn't have to ask me twice. I flick the switch for the gas fireplace and then plop on one of the couches.

"Don't go to sleep, Maya. You do have to work eventually."

Jack's smiling at me from behind the counter.

I block a yawn and lie down, tucking my feet up underneath me. "I won't." I stare at the fireplace, watching the flames lick around the fake wood. "What's the fake wood in fireplaces made from?"

"I don't know. Ceramic, maybe?" Jack measures the grounds into the ten-gallon basket.

"Do you think there are people whose whole job is making the fake wood for fireplaces?"

"Probably."

"Huh." My cheek is pressing so hard against the couch that I can feel the corduroy fabric indenting into my face.

"Okay, time to get up." Jack comes over and tosses my cherry red apron over my head.

I sit up, rubbing my curly hair, and tie my apron around my waist.

"How's Polly?" I ask Jack.

"She's still nocturnal." Jack closes his eyes.

"You look more rested, though."

He grins at me. "She sleeps on the porch."

"Jack!"

"What? She's the one making all the noise. It's not so cold out that she needs to be inside."

I join him behind the counter and get the decaf started. At exactly seven, about ten regulars will run in on their way to work. And while I've never seen the reason for decaf coffee before noon, apparently other people do.

"How was dinner last night?" Jack asks.

"Not that bad," I concede. Zach was really decent last night. I think it's because he remembers when Travis and I broke up. It was tough, to say the least. "I think the distance is good for me and Zach," I say.

"Good." Jack smiles.

"Seeing each other only once every eight months has been helpful. Any more than that, and we'd kill each other."

He just laughs.

I pour a cup of the freshly made French roast and inhale it. It's 6:56 a.m. By the time I had listened to Jen, brushed my teeth, and cleared my bed of all the outfits that didn't make the cut for dinner, it was well past one in the morning.

Ugh.

I sip my coffee, thinking about Jen. She was still snoozing when I left this morning. On my way out, I passed by the tulips on the kitchen counter, the coffee table . . . and I know she's got a vase of them in her room that she brought home from work.

Honestly, three bouquets of tulips? They've been dating for what? Three days?

"Do you think romance can be overdone?" I ask Jack.

He gives me a weird look and opens his mouth, probably to say something smart-alecky, but right then the door opens and our first regular, Leonard, comes in.

Leonard is a mystery to me. He comes in every Monday morning at 7:01 and orders a french vanilla MixUp (our version of the Frappucino). No coffee, no caffeine, no stimulants at all, save for the couple hundred calories and a bunch of sugar.

Then he sits at the same table, stares out the same window, waits for the shake to melt, and drinks the whole thing in one long gulp. After that, he stands, throws the empty cup away, and leaves.

Every single Monday morning.

Some people would say he's a man of habit. I say he's just strange.

"Morning, Leonard," I say cheerfully.

"Good morning. One french vanilla MixUp."

Jack's already halfway done making it. "Yes, sir," I say over the high-pitched drone of the blender. "Anything else?"

"No." Leonard hands me his MasterCard.

"Scone? Cookie? Cinnamon roll?"

Now Leonard just gives me a weird look. I never probe, so this is out of the ordinary. "No, just the drink."

Boorrring. I swipe the card but frown. I, for one, think Leonard should follow the title of his favorite drink and mix it up a little.

"Add a shot," I whisper to Jack while Leonard sits at his table to wait for his drink.

"What? No, Nutkin, I will not," he hisses back.

"Please? Add some spice to that poor man's life."

There's hoppy fifties music playing, so Leonard can't overhear us. I give Jack my best Bambi expression, but instead of dumping a highly addictive yet very legal substance into Leonard's drink, Jack just raises an eyebrow.

"You look like that cat on *Alice in Wonderland.*"

"Thanks." My Bambi impression must need work.

"Leonard, your drink is ready!" Jack calls.

"To answer your question, yes," Jack says to me at ten thirty when we're in the midst of a brief lull.

"What?"

"Romance being overdone? I definitely would say yes, it can be." He looks up at me from a big bowl of frosting he's mixing for the cinnamon rolls I just pulled from the oven. Cool Beans is renowned for its inventive coffee flavors and homemade cinnamon rolls. Kendra Lee is our chef, and she comes in every night after closing and whips up another batch that rises in the fridge all night, so all I have to do is bake them.

I'm really good at pulling something from the fridge and putting it right in the oven. Pillsbury and me? We're buds.

"Yeah?" I nod and set the hot pan on the counter. "I agree."

"Why were you asking?"

"Three bouquets of tulips. Three days."

"See? That's almost to the point of creepy." Jack frowns. "This guy is trying too hard. You didn't break up with him because he just got out of prison, did you?"

I giggle. "No."

He grins and looks at the frosting again. "Hey, why did you guys break up?" he asks, not looking at me because he knows this is a very personal question. Don't get me wrong—he's one of my best friends, but there are still things we don't talk about.

My chest clenches. "I don't remember," I lie. "A few things."

He's looking at me again. I'm an awful liar, and Jack has always been able to read me like a Little Golden Book.

"It's okay. We don't have to talk about it." He picks up the frosting bowl to pour it on the rolls. "Just wanted to make sure he hadn't knocked off a florist in a horrific high-speed car chase or something."

I grin again. "That's it, Jackie. You're really weird. Have I told you that lately?"

He starts laughing. "Would that be like putting the *petal* to the metal?"

"Oh my gosh," I groan, but I start laughing.

"Like if he—"

"Ugh!" I scream as Jack loses his hold on the frosting bowl and the whole thing dumps right on my shoes.

All eight customers stare at us, and one tentatively claps.

Jack's alternating between snorting and apologizing. "Oh, Maya, I'm so sorry. I—" He half-laughs and mashes his fist against his mouth. "I'm sorry. I didn't mean to . . . uh . . ."

Now he's doubled over, gripping the counter in a full-out wheezing laugh. I stand there, arms crossed over my chest, sugary stickiness saturating my shoes and seeping into my socks.

"Jaaack."

He straightens. "Nutkin." He's still trying hard to hide a grin. His brown-brown-brown eyes are sparkling like crazy and crinkling up on the sides, and his dimple is showing.

I sigh and shake my head. "Nothing." I half-walk, half-slide to the back room to take off my shoes, and I finally start giggling.

"Yuck!" I yell, for Jack's benefit.

He comes in, all apologetic now. "I'm really, really sorry, Maya. I'll pay for new shoes and socks." Then he sees me laughing. "Hey!"

"Do you think this counts as a sugar scrub, Jack?"

He gives me a look. "A what?"

"Sugar scrub. Like an exfoliating thing."

"I'm male," he reminds me, shaking his head and leaving. "Sorry!" he yells over his shoulder.

I get home at two thirty. The perk of working the morning shift is you're finished ridiculously early.

I had rinsed out my socks with the hose out back, and they dried in the afternoon sun. My shoes are toast, though. I'm not too disappointed. They were my ugly work shoes, and Alisha said she'd replace them.

There's yet another bouquet on our porch. I roll my eyes and pick it up as I walk in the apartment. Daisies and cranberry red roses this time. Swell. How come Travis can get daisies now, when it seemed like an impossible feat when *we* were dating?

Calvin is dancing around my feet in a happy doggy four-step. "Hi, baby!" I greet him, still carrying the flowers. "Let me put these in the kitchen, okay?"

The card is popping out of the bouquet, and it catches me off guard when I read my name on the envelope: *Maya Elise Davis.*

They're for me?

I rip open the card, my heart starting to beat a little faster. Hey, I'm a girl. It's allowed.

> *Roses are red,*
> *Violets are blue,*
> *Please accept this*
> *Apology for your shoe.*
> ☺

Jack. I grin and shove my face in the bouquet to inhale their spicy, sweet scent. "Good thing you're going into animal-behavioral biology and not poetry," I mutter, still grinning.

I grab my cell and send him a text:

Mustard is yellow;
Dill pickles are okay.
Thank you for the flowers.
They made my day! :)

Now I turn my attention to Calvin, who decided I hate him and is moping around, tail lackluster.

"Dude, don't be so sensitive," I tell him, rubbing his ears until he perks up again. He gives me a lick on the chin and then trots behind me as I go to my room to change out of my dirty work clothes.

"Work out or veg on couch?" I ask Calvin.

He plops his butt on the ground, and I'd swear he shrugs, but then people would tell me I spend too much time alone and need to get more eccentric friends.

I finger my sweats and my yoga pants.

I did have Cheesecake Factory last night.

Work out.

Tossing my work clothes in the hamper, I pull on my yoga pants and a blue T-shirt that I got in Florida with my family. It says: *Who cares about Prince Charming? My heart belongs to a Mouse.* There's a silhouette of Mickey Mouse behind the words.

I pop a Pilates DVD in the player and push the coffee table out of the way. Calvin stretches out on the floor next to me, where I sit back on my knees and stretch, face against the floor, in what's called "Child's Pose."

He sticks his nose in my ear, and I yelp.

"Ugh! Calvin!"

"Roo! Roo!"

I send him a look and stare at the carpet fibers again. Our carpet really needs to be cleaned.

"Up to Up Dog," the perky little instructor chirps.

Now Calvin's hopping around on all fours. "Roo! Roooo!"

"Not you, Calvin."

"And down to Down Dog."

Calvin immediately falls to the floor, head on his paws.

I disobey the ninety-pound, beyond-humanly-flexible instructor and sit up, staring at my dog. "How come you'll lie down for the lady with the most annoying voice on the planet, but you won't for me?"

"Back to Up Dog . . ." I can tell the instructor is aiming for a soothing voice, but she hits squeaky instead.

Calvin smoothly sits up.

I just stare, open mouthed.

My cell phone rings right then.

"Yes?"

"Honestly, Maya, it's like I never taught you any manners for answering the phone."

"Mom, the weirdest thing is going on! I'm doing Pilates and—"

"Don't tell me. You got fuzz in your eye again."

"No! I—"

"Your mouth? Your nose?"

"Mom, listen to me for a second!"

"Okay, what?"

"Calvin is doing Pilates! He's doing exactly what the lady says to do!"

Long silence.

"Maya . . ."

"Yes, Mom?"

Again, silence.

Finally, I hear her sigh. "It's not worth it. Listen, Maya, I was calling for a reason, actually."

I pause the Pilates. "Go ahead," I tell her.

"Roo!" Calvin protests from the Down Dog position.

"Hush," I hiss at him.

"I'm calling to tell you some of Zach's news, actually," Mom says. "One of the reasons he was here this week was for an interview at the San Diego Children's Hospital. And he just found out he got the job. I guess both he and Kate were ready to come back to California. He starts in two weeks."

I am having trouble wrapping my brain around this fact.

Did I or did I not just tell Jack this morning how great it was that Zach and I were getting along and how I thought it was due to the distance?

Funny, Lord.

Sometimes, I find God's timing to be the most hysterical thing on the face of the earth.

"Two weeks, huh?"

"Yep. He's starting as the head of the Neonatal ICU. Isn't that exciting?" Pride rings in Mom's voice, and I catch a little tiny stab of jealousy in my lower abdominals.

Jealousy or pain. Those scissor crunches will kill you.

"Cool."

"I think this is wonderful. Both of my kids back in California! We can all have dinner together every Sunday night again!"

I feel bad that Mom's so excited and I'm so not.

Now I'll have to feel inconsequential and awkward every single Sunday night.

Whoop-de-do.

"Okay, well, I just wanted to let you in on what is going on. I love you, sweetie. Have a good day!" She hangs up.

I turn off the TV and go to my room. Grabbing my Bible, I flounce on the bed.

Okay, Lord. I'm sorry I feel like this, but I don't know how to stop it.

I flip open the Bible and turn to 1 Thessalonians. "Rejoice always."

I know, God. But good grief! Travis and Zach in one week? Couldn't we space out the men who make me nuts coming back into my life?

"Pray without ceasing; in everything give thanks."

I reach for a sticky note.

Reasons I Can Still Be Thankful:
1. Calvin appears to be wise beyond his breed. Maybe this is a new entrepreneurial enterprise: Canine Pilates.
2. Jack gave me flowers.
3. I have yet to see Travis since our first meeting.
4. Zach got a better position at work. I can be happy for him.
5. God is still in control. God is still in control. God is still in control.

CHAPTER SIX

Every Wednesday night, the college/young singles class has a Bible study that meets at Cool Beans. We close early, which doesn't mean much because we do way more business with the college group than we ever do on a normal weeknight at nine o'clock.

Andrew always shows up a few minutes early and moves the chairs and sofas into a huge circle. Sometimes I help. Sometimes I just watch. Like tonight.

"That looks more ovally than circley." I say this sweetly, a half-dried huge ceramic coffee mug in one hand, a towel in the other. I'm standing behind the counter in my brand-new work shoes that are killing my feet.

"Only people who help get a say in what shape the chairs are in," Andrew retorts, nudging another chair into the circle with his shin. "Can I get my usual, Maya?" He Frisbee-throws me a Visa.

I barely catch it. "Decaf or regular?"

"Regular. It's a long lesson."

"Swell."

"Don't sound so excited, Maya." Andrew grins at me and comes over to watch as I start steaming a bucket-sized mug of what will soon be a cinnamon vanilla latte.

I smile. "Lots of foam or only a little tonight?"

"Happy medium."

"I don't do that."

"Make an exception, Maya. This is the clergy talking."

"Did you join the pastorate just for the handouts?" I accuse.

He thinks about it for a second. "Pretty much, yes."

"So much for me believing you were called to this."

"All illusions dissolve eventually." He accepts his drink with a nod. "Thanks, Maya, this is perfect. I especially like the sunflower mug," Andrew says, rolling his eyes. "Maya, I have to preach on the Bible tonight. Who will take me seriously with this mug?"

"I've wondered that for a very long time."

"Not my *face*, you idiot." He starts laughing.

I grin. "I couldn't resist."

Andrew's still chuckling.

Liz Chapman walks in then. She's twenty-three, a fifth-year senior getting her degree in mathematics, and is not-so-secretly in love with Andrew.

Andrew, on the other hand, claims he's waiting for the human version of post-fins Ariel on *The Little Mermaid*—because she was silent.

I told Andrew he shouldn't have any trouble because he talks too much to let anyone get a word in anyway.

He just rolled his eyes and ignored me.

Anyway, this scene takes place every single Wednesday night, and it hurts my heart. Liz always comes early so she can see Andrew before anyone else gets here.

"Hi, Andrew," Liz says, flirtatiously tossing her long, gorgeous red hair. Liz is extremely attractive. She's tall, and while she's on the thinner side, she definitely has curves that I envy. She has crystal-clear, creamy skin, emerald green eyes, a great sense of style. And she's brilliant. Makes me wonder why she's going after an overgrown, sarcastic Viking like Andrew.

"Hey, Liz, how's it going?" He keeps setting up chairs, and she sways over to help him.

Andrew has to know Liz is nuts about him. It's fairly obvious.

"Good," she answers. "How is your week going?"

"No complaints yet." He responds in a cheerfully yet completely blasé voice.

I sigh silently. I put away the clean mugs I've finished drying and go find Jack in the back room, where he's locking up the cash and making a supply list for Alisha.

"Hey, Pattertwig, how many gallons of milk did we use today?"

I check the fridge in the back, trying to remember how many are still in the small refrigerators under the front counter. "About five, I think."

"Okay." He makes a little note on the clipboard he's holding. Then he looks up at me. Jack looks tired.

"You okay?" I ask him.

"I'm exhausted. I stayed up most of last night studying for a mammal behaviors exam, and it was at seven thirty this morning." He yawns, blocking it with the clipboard. "If I skip Bible study, do you think you can close without me?"

"Yeah, definitely. Go home and sleep. Between Polly and this, you haven't gotten much lately."

He groans. "That's another thing. Polly's owner called, and they'll be gone another week."

"Sorry, Jack."

He gives me a small smile. "Not your fault, Nutkin. Anyone here yet?"

"Andrew and Liz."

He grimaces knowingly. "Got it."

"Andrew knows she likes him, right?"

Jack shrugs. "Maybe. Sometimes Andrew's not the most observant, you know?"

"Maybe his hair gets in the way."

He laughs. "That's a good possibility." Jack sets the clipboard down and slings an arm over my shoulders, yawning again. "I'm tired."

"Go home."

"Okay." He follows me out to the counter. There's a happy chatter coming from the main room. About fifteen people are milling around, settling on couches, staring tiredly at the fire flickering in the fireplace, or squinting at the menu, deciding what they want.

My heart suddenly decides it likes skydiving instead of beating, and I smack my chest to remind my heart of its position in my life.

Jack runs into the back of me, since I stopped with no warning.

"Ow," he mutters. "Pattertwig?"

I bite my lip. Travis Clayton is grinning widely at Jen not more than ten feet away from me.

"Oh." Jack apparently follows my gaze.

I turn around and look up at Jack. "This is weird," I whisper.

He gives me a comforting smile and follows it with a hug. "Try not to worry, Maya. God has the best in mind for you, right?"

"Wight." I nod, my voice muffled in his apron.

He pushes me back a couple of inches, smirking. "Sorry."

I look up at him and smile. "It's okay."

"Maya?" Rachel Townsend is standing at the counter. "Can I get a large mocha?"

"Sure," I reply, cheerful barista voice back in place. "Anything else?"

In all, Jack and I make six mochas, five lattes, seven cups of decaf, three teas, and four MixUps for four very confused people who don't know that you don't order frozen coffee drinks after October 1.

Andrew waits for the guy in line to get his caramel MixUp before starting announcements. "Miniature golf on Friday night, Sunday school on Sunday morning . . . uh, *duh* . . . and we've got a service project at a local food-distribution center on Monday evening for whomever wants to come help sort food for the hungry."

Jack and I are busy cleaning up the back area during this time. We can't do a lot of cleaning, but we can do enough to make the cleanup after Bible study a lot shorter.

Travis is sitting next to Jen, balancing a straight-up black coffee on his leg.

"Let's go sit," Jack whispers in my ear.

"I thought you were leaving," I whisper back.

He shakes his head. "I'm fine."

Something you should know about Jack Dominguez: He's too nice for his own good. I immediately feel bad because I know he's staying just for me.

Maybe someday I'll learn to keep my mouth shut.

I pat his arm and whisper, "Go get some sleep. You don't have to stay for me."

"I'm not. I'm staying for the lesson." He goes around the

counter and falls into an empty chair on the back side of the oval before I can say, *Liar!*

A sweet one though. I smile and pull my Bible from below the counter, going over to sit next to him.

"Continuing our study in Proverbs . . ." Andrew says, plopping his thick leather-bound Bible open. "Proverbs 9, please."

There's the quiet sound of Bibles opening and pages flipping.

"We're going to cover verses 10 through 12, so, um . . ." Andrew looks around, and his eyes land on Nathan, a music major who can pick up any instrument and play it as if he's been playing for years. Impressive? Yes. Irritating to the less musically talented? Yes.

"Nathan? Could you read those verses?"

"Sure thing, Andrew." Nathan clears his throat and starts reading. "'The fear of the LORD is the beginning of wisdom, and the knowledge of the Holy One is understanding. For by me your days will be multiplied, and years of life will be added to you. If you are wise, you are wise for yourself, and if you scoff, you alone will bear it.'"

"Thanks, Nathan."

"No problem, Andrew." Nathan leans back in his chair. It would be a lot easier to be jealous of Nathan if he weren't so darn nice.

"So, this begs the question: Where do we get wisdom?" Andrew looks around the room.

I fidget. Is he asking, or is this a rhetorical question?

"Any thoughts?"

The answers start popping up.

"Bible."

"Parents."

"Pastors."

"Holy Spirit."

"Friends." Jack pauses. "Not the TV show."

Everyone grins.

Andrew is doing the continuous pastoral nod. "Good, good. Sweet answers, everyone. Okay, let's chat for a minute about them."

"Seek out wisdom," he finishes up forty-five minutes later. "Whether that's parents, an older sibling, or a friend, listen with the ears of the Holy Spirit inside you. Let's pray."

He does, and after he says amen, the room erupts into chatter.

Jen comes over, trailed by Travis. "Hi, guys."

"Hi, Jen." Jack smiles tiredly. "Hi, Travis."

"Hey there . . . Jake, right?"

"Jack."

"Got it." Travis looks at me. "Hi again."

"Hey."

He's got to recognize me. I don't understand this at all. It's not like I had multimillion-dollar plastic surgery like those creepy Hollywood stars who are always in their twenties.

Just a haircut and a dye job. Less makeup, fewer inches around the midsection. Not anything drastic. Probably a better sense of style, but it's not like you'd notice that in my jeans and black T-shirt for work.

Travis smiles one of those polite but completely not emotionally engaged smiles at me.

He used to smile that exact same way toward the end of our relationship. If I'd been paying attention—which I wasn't—I would have been able to see it coming.

"I think we're going to head out," Jen says. "See you at home in a little bit?" she asks me.

"Yep." I nod.

Jen gives Jack a hug, and then she and Travis leave.

Jack turns and looks at me. "You've got to tell her, kid."

My stomach hates the thought of that. It feels like I swallowed a paper shredder and it's busy working on my esophagus.

"Yeah."

"Soon." Jack is stern. Then he pulls me into another hug. "Hey, let's finish cleaning so we can get some sleep."

"I got it."

I know he feels like he should stay, but he still looks relieved when I say that. "Really?"

"Go home, Jack. Sleep." I pat his shoulder. "I'll see you Friday." We've both got tomorrow off.

"Okay. Night, Pattertwig." He leaves, yawning.

Everyone slowly trickles out. I finish behind the counter, mopping the tile, disinfecting the countertops, and running the cleaning cycles on the coffeemaker and espresso machine.

Liz and Andrew are the only ones left by the time I'm done. Liz is happily chattering, following Andrew around as he puts all the chairs back where they belong.

"So, anyway, I think Sparky will be okay because he was eating normally again today," she bubbles on about her dachshund.

"That's good to hear," Andrew says mindlessly.

I sigh as I watch them. Poor Liz. Andrew obviously either (a) doesn't care or (b) doesn't have a clue.

I'm voting for choice *b*. Andrew's too nice to let a girl pine after him without addressing the issue.

I reach for a sticky note from under the counter.

Reasons I'm Happy I'm Single:
1. Boys are clueless.
2. No emotional jump rope. Look at how Jen's already flipping out.
3. No dying my hair for a boy. This time, I'm all natural, baby.
4. No watching Braveheart out of compromise. I can watch
27 Dresses as often as I want.

I drag the vacuum over to where we just met. "Sorry, guys, it's loud," I apologize before I turn on the machine. It sounds like the Hulk gargling a couple of prairie dogs.

Liz tries yelling the rest of her story but eventually gives up. Everyone gives up on conversation when we pull the Hulk out. It's a pain for talking, but fun if you want to sing without anyone being able to hear you.

She waves cutely at Andrew, smiles sweetly at me, grabs her purse and Bible, and leaves.

I want to yell after her to stop wasting her time on such a clueless Viking, but I don't.

Andrew is still pulling one of the couches back in front of the fireplace. I push the vacuum over there and suck up every microorganism hiding out in the carpet.

I finally turn off the vacuum.

Andrew rubs his ears. "Dang, that thing is loud."

"Sorry."

"Did you build it or something?"

"What?"

He sticks his pointer finger in my face. "Don't apologize for something that's not in your control, Maya."

"Sorry."

He grins. "Where's the monster go?" He hefts up the vacuum.

"Back room, closet on the right."

He disappears. I turn the fireplace off and yawn.

"So, Maya," he says, coming back into the room.

"So, Andrew."

He's scratching his long blond hair. "I have a question for you. And maybe this is just me being male or clueless or too—what's the word?—egotistical, but—"

"Yes, Liz likes you."

His hand drops. "Really?"

This isn't said with a tone of incredulous joy. Maybe incredulous, but no joy.

I roll my eyes and flop on the couch he just moved back into place, leaning back against the armrest, toeing off my shoes, and pulling my knees to my chest. "Don't take this the wrong way, but I think you got hit in the head with a puck too much. It's ridiculous how obvious she's been."

Andrew joins me on the couch with a sigh. "Swell."

I hold my tongue for all of about ten seconds. "You don't sound so happy."

"Oh, don't get me wrong; Liz is great."

"Well, so are instant pasta dishes. What do you mean?"

A slight smile curls his lips. "You know what I like about you, Maya Davis?"

"What's that?"

"You can always get humor in a conversation." He grins fully now. "That's a talent, and don't you forget it, missy."

"Okeydoke." I hug my knees closer and smile back.

"So, what should I do about Liz?" he sighs. "I'm like a negative three on the scale of understanding girls."

"I don't know how much help I am here." I shake my head. "I would just want the guy to come right out and tell me, 'Look, kid, I don't like you like that.' I'm not sure if that's a commonly held view though." Then I shrug. "I don't know. I've only dated one guy, and that was a while ago." Now I'm kind of embarrassed. "Weird, right?"

Andrew shakes his head. "Not weird. Not weird at all. Actually, I think it's refreshing. Too many girls are constantly on the hunt, going out with whomever asks at the moment. I like that you're not hunting."

I think back to when Travis and I started dating. He was the instigator of everything. Which is good for someone as clueless as I am when it comes to romance. You have to come right out and tell me you like me, or I won't get it in a million years.

I look around. "Well, I'm going home."

Andrew takes his cue and stands.

"Thanks for helping me straighten up," I tell him, standing and stretching, pulling off my apron.

"Of course. Grab your stuff; I'll walk out with you."

"Thanks." I run to the back and hang up my apron, find my purse, and pull on my jacket.

I flip off the back lights and then join Andrew. "So, anyway, be praying for me with regard to Liz," he says.

"I will." We walk outside, and I lock the door behind us. "See you later, Andrew."

"Bye, Maya." He gives me a side hug, and I suddenly feel really, really, really small.

When you're only five foot two to begin with, this isn't the best feeling ever.

He grins, winks, and heads for his truck.

I get home at 11:03 p.m. Jen's car is not in her spot.

Now the dilemma: Do I panic? Do I call her? Do I just

pretend not to notice she didn't come home when she implied she was going to?

I bite my lip and decide I'm overreacting. After all, she could very easily be running to the store because we're completely out of milk. And eggs. And flour, sugar, butter . . . basically anything not a Pop-Tart or a Bertolli frozen dinner.

I walk up the steps and into our dark apartment. Calvin is going nuts around my ankles.

"Hi, baby!"

"Roo! Rooooo!" He starts doing crazy eights around the living room. He's cooped up too much, I think.

"Sheesh. With greetings like these, you'd think I never show you any attention," I tell my spastic dog. He yips and follows me to my room.

I dump my purse and coat on my bed, kick my ache-inducing shoes in the general direction of the closet, and then flounce on the clear spot on the bed. "So," I say to Calvin, who is now in my lap, "call her cell phone, call the cops, or call it a night?"

"Roo! Roo! Roo!"

"No more Pilates tonight, Cal. My gluteus maximus is killing me." I pat his silky head as he huffs his breath out. "You are getting nice abs, if that makes you feel better."

Tail wag, so I take that as a yes.

"You know what? We've been working out very well. Let's get ice cream tonight, okay?"

"Roo!" Calvin jumps off my lap in a happy dog dance. I know some people who argue that dogs can't understand English. I figure their dogs are just a lot dumber than Calvin, because there is a definite understanding of the words *ice cream*.

We decide on cookies 'n' cream, with the added healthy benefits of vitamin C and antioxidants in the form of strawberries and chocolate on mine. I settle on the sofa in front of the TV, trying to be subtle about waiting up for Jen.

Good grief. It's like ten thirty now. And on a weeknight, for goodness' sake!

I flick the TV on and stare mindlessly at the persistent Home Shopping Network saleslady. "And if you buy this *gorgeous* fourteen-carat gold, unbelievably beautiful . . . isn't it *delectable?*" she asks some invisible person off camera. "If you buy the limited-edition bracelet, we'll also send you this pair of matching earrings."

The problem with jewelry on HSN is (a) I can't afford a monthly plan of thirty-four easy payments of $67.99; and (b) it all looks like costume jewelry to me, despite the saliva-inducing adjectives the saleslady is using. Seriously, is she selling a bracelet or a box of Girl Scout Thin Mints?

Calvin harrumphs, which means he want me to change the channel.

I mash the remote. *Gilmore Girls* is on, and we both smile. This show is a favorite.

12:07 p.m.

No Jen.

I squint through the peephole on our door for the twentieth time in five minutes. No Jen outside talking, no Jen inside sleeping, no Jen's car parked in her parking spot.

Worry gave way to panic long ago. I tried calling her cell phone at ten forty-five and got a quick voice-mail pickup, which means it's off. "What is the point of having a cell phone if you won't answer it?" I ask my dog, sounding exactly like my mother used to when Zach was first learning how to drive.

I start pacing in front of the door.

"Travis is a nice guy," I reassure Calvin. He's not showing it, curled up on the couch and all, but he's worried sick. "She's very safe with him." Too safe with him.

Calvin closes his eyes.

I look through the peephole again.

Finally!

Jen's little sedan pulls into her spot. I watch her headlights turn off, and she climbs out of the car, slinging her purse over her shoulder.

I am now faced with yet another dilemma: Do I stand here like I've obviously been waiting? Or hightail it to bed?

I decide to join Calvin on the couch instead and stare back at Lorelai and Rory having a famous *Gilmore Girls* debate. Something about vegetables.

"Hi, Maya," Jen says, tiredly. She pulls her key out of the doorknob and joins me on the couch.

"Hey." I look at her curiously.

"Sorry. We decided to go get coffee. You weren't waiting up for me, were you?" She smiles like she already knows the answer. I shrug and smile back. "That's sweet, Maya, but Travis is the perfect gentleman."

Yeah, I know.

"How was coffee?" I ask, turning off the TV. Jack's voice drifts back to my brain about coming clean with Jen, but I silence it. Just like I've been doing with my conscience.

"Well, I actually got tea."

"No way. You?"

She rolls her eyes at my sarcasm. "And it was very nice."

"You guys have been spending a lot of time together."

"Too much?" she immediately asks, gnawing on her bottom

lip. It's an irritating habit people have. Makes me want to hand them a chew toy or something so they save their lips from tooth scarring. It's a very real deformity, and I know this because I saw an infomercial once on some miracle formula to get rid of the buildup of scar tissue on your lips.

I shrug off her question. "I don't know."

"Huh." She stands and sighs. "Well, I'm exhausted, and my alarm is going off at six o'clock tomorrow morning. We have a staff meeting. Sweet dreams, Maya." She heads to her room.

I look at Calvin, who is completely out, and lean my head back on the couch. I hate how tight my chest gets anytime I'm around Jen now.

The truth will make you free.

I sigh. "Time for bed, Cal." Sometimes I don't like that still small voice at all.

CHAPTER SEVEN

"Look, Mom, it's a spiderweb!" I yell.

"Mm-hmm. That's nice, dear." Mom is not listening.

"The itsy-bitsy SPIIIIDER went up the waterspout. Down came the RAAAAIN and washed the spider out!"

I dump a huge bucket of water on the spiderweb, watching as the spider floats down a little river, hugging its legs into itself.

"AUUUGH!" Zach comes running around the corner. "Maya! NOO! Do you have any idea how long it took for that spider to make that web?"

I stare at him. He's white as a sheet and kind of transparent.

"It took foreverrrrrr. . . ."

"Uh, Zach?"

"Oooooooohhhh." He covers his face. "Why did you dooooooooooo this?"

I jerk awake.

"ROOOOOOOO!"

It's pitch black.

I relax back into the pillow. "Shut up, Cal," I moan.

Thursday, 2:24 a.m.

"Calvin!"

Once again, Jen is not happy.

I hear her door bang open, and in two and a half seconds flat, she's whipped my door open and startled Calvin so much that he yelps and crashes into my dresser.

"Be. Quiet. Calvin."

There's no forgiveness in Jen's tone. She sends my beagle a withering look, glares at me, and then marches out of my room, slamming my door behind her.

Calvin sits up and shakes his head slightly. Huffing, he lies down by the side of my bed and droops back asleep.

I shut my eyes again.

"Maya, you have to do something about that dog," Jen says not so kindly the next morning. She's dressed in a jet-black pencil skirt, a powder blue silky blouse, and three-inch heels. I sleepily eye the heels.

I would definitely kill myself in those heels. It would probably be the first death by footwear ever, so maybe the *Hudson Journal* would run something on it.

WOMAN BREAKS NECK IN HIGH-HEELED HORROR.

"Maya!"

I blink and look back at her. "Sorry, Jen. What were you saying?"

Hey, she's the one who dragged me out of bed this morning so we could "talk." I try never to have a conversation before ten on my days off if I can help it.

So I slouch at the table, wearing pink-hearted pajama pants and a bright pink cami. My hair is scrunched around my head in slept-on frizzies. I have both feet crossed Indian style on the chair, and there's sleep scum half-blocking my vision.

"The dog, Maya. Calvin cannot keep barking every single week like this."

"He probably hears something, Jenny." I rub my cheek. "I mean, wouldn't you rather he barked when he heard strange noises instead of just ignoring them? Maybe we're about to be murdered in our beds every week, and he scares them off."

"That is doubtful," Jen says, legal persona in place.

I sleepily trace a design on the table. The object of the conversation is still asleep in my room.

Dumb dog.

Jen sits at the table with a bowl of some kind of trail-mix cereal. It's turning the milk a light greenish-brown color.

I wrinkle my nose. "What is that?"

"Granola, Maya. It's got oats, wheat germ, sunflower seeds, raisins, cranberries, spelt, and flaxseed."

"The milk's green."

"No, it's not. It's tan."

I point. "That's green."

She sighs.

I shut up.

"You eat what you want to eat, and I'll eat what I want to eat," she says staccato-like.

This means I'll eat Cocoa Puffs like a normal healthy human, and she can keep gnawing on that bowl of something that Tom Hanks would've eaten in *Castaway*, dredged up from the forest floor.

Come to think of it, I've never seen the box for that cereal anywhere.

"Hey, you went shopping!" I accuse, pointing a finger across the table.

She looks at me guiltily.

"Aha!"

"Okay. I did. I'm sorry." She lets her breath out. "I went last night before Bible study."

"I can't believe you went completely against The Code." I put my hand over my heart in reverence for our Sacred Trust of Roommates. "And I quote, Rule #12: 'Should anyone go to the grocery store, she must inform the other party so as to make only one combined trip per week.'"

Miss Legal Assistant penned the wording of The Code, in case you were wondering.

"I'm sorry! Gosh, Maya."

"We happen to be completely out of Bertolli frozen dinners. And Pop-Tarts. And those little microwavable pizzas."

"We eat so healthy," she notes dryly.

"Hey, Pop-Tarts are fortified with vitamins, Jen. Plus, they're like an American tradition. You can't criticize Pop-Tarts. They're right up there next to apple pie and partially hydrogenated corn syrup."

"Don't you ever wonder what natural food tastes like?" She waves her spoon over her bowl.

Uh-oh.

Automatic rewind to six years ago. Travis was standing next to me at my all-time favorite ice-cream place in San Diego.

"I'll have the mocha mint cream in a chocolate-dipped cone, please," I said.

"Don't you ever wonder what natural food tastes like?" Travis said to me.

"No," I tell Jen just like I had told Travis. "If God meant for us to eat only natural food, He would have stopped the creation of Krispy Kreme."

She sighs. "I'm just trying to be healthier."

"And I think that's great. Why?"

"Because, Maya. We're not healthy. We live off instant meals and ice cream. That's really bad for you."

There should be a law about bashing ice cream before eight in the morning.

"Why now?" I rephrase the question.

"I just . . ." she pauses and waves her spoon. "I just think it's time. We're twenty-four; we need to start protecting our metabolisms."

"I run," I tell her. "And you're skinny as a rail."

She sighs and finishes her all-natural sawdust. "I need to go. Wayne gets mad if I'm not early to staff meetings. Have a good day off, Maya."

Jen leaves.

It's one thirty, and I've been standing in this dressing room for the last thirty minutes staring at this exact same shirt. It's blue and fitted and, if I were being completely unbiased, makes me look a lot more, um, curvy than I normally am.

God didn't endow me much, as my mother would say.

"A good thing," my father would retort. Dad wants boys to appreciate me for my character.

I think if he'd known that most guys run the moment they find out about my daily caffeine intake, he wouldn't have worried so much through my high school years.

So, here I stand. Fuller on top and more confused in the head. The problem is, I don't want people to think I'm trying too hard to get a boyfriend. At this point in the day, I don't want a boyfriend Ever. With a capital *E*. Based on my excellent efforts at observation, boyfriends make you give up Cocoa Puffs, and you have to start eating dirt for cereal.

I bet Jen never has ice cream the whole time she dates Travis.

Seriously, is there a good life without Dreyer's Thin Mint ice cream? I think not.

Delight in a bowl.

I sigh at the shirt. "Done."

After I change, I walk over to the cashier and pay a ridiculous amount for a synthetic top.

I climb into my car and sigh at the clock. Days off are boring. Jen's never home because her tightwad boss never lets her have any days off other than the weekend, and I always work all day on Saturday and drive to San Diego on Sunday.

So, that means I have to entertain myself all day.

Time for coffee.

This is what solidifies me in American history as a complete and total dweeb: I go to work on my days off.

It's only to get my fix, but I still feel like a loser anytime I walk through the doors and my name is nowhere near the schedule.

I park and walk in, inhaling. *Yummy.*

Lisa, who works all the shifts I don't have—so I never see her—is behind the counter. "Hi, Maya!" she greets me.

Lisa is adorable. She's twenty-two, about four foot eleven, with platinum-blond chin-length hair, huge gray eyes, and a perky personality. Lisa earns the most tips of anyone at Cool Beans.

"Hey, Lisa, how's it going?"

"Great!"

Tony the Tiger would be proud of her.

"That's good to hear." I grin at her. It's impossible not to smile around Lisa. She's got more energy than Tigger on steroids. And while this could be due to the constant cup of espresso beside her, I think she has a lot of natural perk as well.

"What can I make for you?"

"Can I get an extra-large mocha with cinnamon and caramel?"

"Give me two minutes."

Lisa rings up the total (minus my employee discount), and a couple of minutes later, I'm walking out the door cradling a to-go cup of cinnamony, sugary delight.

Pink tulips meet me at the front door. Make that four bouquets. I pick up the etched-glass vase and walk into the apartment. A little card that matches the flowers is poking out of the bouquet.

For the woman who has made this last week seem like a mere moment.

I'm seriously considering pulling one of the tulips out and using it for a gagging device. Yuck!

I set them on the counter instead.

"Calvin!"

I hear a frenzied yip from the bedroom, and my little beagle comes racing to meet me in the kitchen. "Napping?"

Travis used to send tulips to me all the time, too. Since he went to Stanford, we spent our freshman year of college apart. Once a week, sometimes more, I'd open the door and find flowers with a sappy card attached to them. I used to find it romantic.

Now I think it's kind of gross. A muscle in my cheek starts to jump.

I rub Calvin's ears, frowning.

Walking back into my bedroom, I open the closet door and

pull out a big brown box from the top shelf.

Calvin plops on the bed next to me, and I open the box, finding the little blue shoe box near the top. The first thing inside the shoe box is a white ruled sheet of paper dated my junior year of high school.

My sweet Maya,

I'm going to see you in two hours, but I just wanted to leave a note in your locker letting you know how much I love you! Have a great afternoon!

Love,

Travis

"I know. Sappy, right?" I say to Calvin. He just looks at me. Underneath the piece of paper is a birthday card. A sunflower decorates the front and on the inside is printed, "Happy birthday, sunshine."

Travis's handwriting is underneath.

Maya,

Happy eighteenth birthday! Well, you are finally legal, my love. Welcome to the world of voting and . . . well, voting. ☺ I love you so much, and I'm so proud of you for choosing to do what you love this coming year in school. It will be hard being at Stanford without you, but we'll definitely see each other at breaks. I can't wait until we're together forever—no separations coming!

I love you, birthday girl!

Travis

I close the card, remembering. My birthday was not a happy occasion that year. Both of us knew we weren't going to be living in the same town soon, but we just ignored it. Which was fine with me. But not with him. So he had to go and write it in a birthday card and ruin my whole day.

In all, there are fifty-three notes, letters, cards, and scraps of paper from Travis that I collected over the four years we dated. There are ticket stubs from movies and concerts and a couple of dead tulip remnants. Around three dozen pictures of the two of us are neatly stacked together and rubber-banded. About a year ago I got rid of the stuffed animals he'd bought me when my church was having a drive for our local Christian homeless shelter, but for some reason I couldn't throw away the cards and pictures.

I pull the rubber band off the pictures and rifle through them, frowning. Me as a blond. It wasn't a good look. My hair fell down over my shoulders in blond waves like Jessica Simpson's, but my skin looked ashy from the color difference. My skin is too red-toned for blond hair.

My once-favorite picture of the two of us—I am wearing his high school football letterman jacket, standing in front of him; his arms are wrapped around my shoulders; both of us are full-out laughing—drops from the stack.

Man, Travis hasn't changed at all. Same blond hair, same blue eyes, same tall, athletic build. He led our high school football team to the California state championships our senior year.

He used to tell me he was going to go to Stanford, play four years of college ball, get drafted into the NFL, marry me, and move wherever God led us.

He did go to Stanford, but instead of getting drafted, he tore his ACL in his right knee right before Christmas freshman year. He tried out for the team as soon as the doctor let him the following spring, but he nearly tore it again in practice. He never played again.

And as far as that Christmas went . . .

I put the pictures back in a stack and wrap the rubber band around them, sighing. It felt so *good,* you know? That feeling of belonging to someone . . . almost.

Calvin nudges my free hand, dropping his head on my knee. He looks up at me with his sad brown eyes, as if he's asking, *Aren't I enough?*

"You're not, bud." I rub his ears and reach for my Bible.

There's no biblical evidence that Jesus ever had a girlfriend, but I'm counting on Him being sympathetic to this. Because as much as I hate to admit it, as much fun as I make of Jen being all starry eyed, as much as I get grossed out by Travis's love notes to her . . .

I think I miss it.

I open the Bible and flip to Isaiah 40, but instead, chapter 41 catches my attention. "For I am the LORD your God, who upholds your right hand, who says to you, 'Do not fear, I will help you.'"

Does "upholding" my right hand count as *holding* it?

CHAPTER EIGHT

Friday morning. 6:14 a.m.

Darkness.

Actually, make that fog-ridden darkness. The air is so dense that water droplets are clinging to my car. I squint to see out of my windshield.

I moan and bang my forehead on my steering wheel. "Why am I here?" I say to an empty car.

Foggy, chilly days are best enjoyed in front of my fireplace. Coffee in one hand, remote in the other. Movie in DVD player. Preferably something lighthearted and whimsical. Like *Penelope*. You can't get more whimsical than Reese Witherspoon in that movie. Adorable.

I get out of my car, grumbling to myself, yanking my jacket tighter around my body. I march to the door, unlock it, open it, and stomp into the cold, clammy coffee shop. I throw my purse and jacket in the cabinet and gripe to myself as I turn on all the lights.

"Well, good morning to you, too, Nutcase."

"Mmpgh."

"What's eating you?" Jack pulls on his apron and joins me behind the counter, sorting through the coffee we're making today.

"It's foggy," I growl.

"It's not carnivorous fog, so what's really eating you?" Jack laughs at his own joke.

Zookeepers have a weird sense of humor.

"It's foggy; it's cold; and it's wet; and I'm not at home drinking a caramel macchiato in front of my fireplace with my sweatpants and socks on."

Jack nods. "You can drink a caramel macchiato here instead! We even have a fireplace and a never-ending supply of caramel syrup."

Ever the cheerful optimist. I hate him.

Must find another reason to be mad. I point to my toes. "I am wearing work shoes that hurt my feet."

"Maya, I'm wearing an *apron*. Tell me when the last time was that you saw a straight guy wearing an apron."

"*Emeril Live*," I answer smugly, folding my arms.

"Emeril wears a chef coat," Jack corrects. He flicks me on the side of the head. "If any of us get to complain, it's me."

"Mmpgh."

He raises a coffee mug in victory.

I flip the switch on the coffeemaker holding the dark roast, and it starts gurgling.

"Why are you so grouchy?" he asks.

"I'm not grouchy."

"You are, too. It's like working with that little green guy from *Sesame Street*."

"I'm just tired."

"Liar."

I glare at him. "It's 6:34 in the morning!"

"And come two thirty, you'll be singing praises that you got the morning shift," he calmly replies, putting the grounds in coffeemaker number two.

Have I mentioned I don't like him right now?

"How was your day off?" he asks.

"Fine," I say. After I had looked through and put away all my old Travis stuff, Jen blew in the door, changed from her professional bun hairstyle to a down-curly-and-romantic look; kept the skirt, silky top, and heels; and flew back out of the house in fifteen minutes, yelling, "I'm late to meet him for dinner!"

Meet him for dinner? I thought guys were supposed to pick you up.

"Jack," I say abruptly, "when you take a girl out on a date, do you pick her up or have her meet you?"

He gives me a weird look. "Why?"

"Travis made Jen *meet* him at the restaurant."

"Did he do that to you, too?"

I shake my head. "Not usually. I always drove myself to his football games, but other than that . . ."

"Huh. Well, no. Whenever I go out, I always pick the girl up. Except for once, and that was a blind date."

"That's nice of you to pick her up."

"Nice?" Jack gives me another look. "Picking up a girl is more informational than nice, Nutkin."

I pull a sheet of unbaked cinnamon rolls from the fridge. "What are you talking about?"

"Is she a neat person? Does she still live at home? Have a roommate? Dog?" He shrugs. "You can find all of that out when you pick up a girl." He rubs the back of his neck ruefully, picking up a bright cherry red mug. "I went out with this girl once. She had to dart out of the house like a hamster so her living room wouldn't overflow onto the porch."

I grin, morning fog broken. "Yuck."

He hands me the mug, filled with the macchiato he'd been making. "And good morning, Maya."

I cup my hands around the cup, inhaling. "Mmm. Thanks, Jack."

He grins and starts mixing the frosting while I pop the rolls in the oven.

"You've been on a blind date?" I ask, trying to keep the incredulity from my tone. The idea of Jack dating, especially blind dating, is a little weird to me — not because he's not dating material but because I've never actually witnessed it. I mean, he's attractive in a preppy/outdoorsy sort of way, but I don't remember him ever talking about dates or anything like that.

He sighs. "I didn't tell you that story?"

"Nope."

"Okay, first off, my aunt is one of the sweetest, most innocent ladies on the planet."

"You had a blind date with your aunt? That is a little disturbing."

He shushes me. "Listen to my story. So, my aunt tells me there's this really cute girl at her church and asks if she can set us up on a date. I said, 'Sure, why not?' and we decide to meet at the restaurant."

He suddenly gets this sad beagle look — I know the look because Calvin always looks like that whenever I'm out of ice cream.

"That bad?" I giggle.

He grimaces. "Let's just say my aunt does not have good taste in girls."

I gape at him. "That's mean! What was wrong with her?"

"What *wasn't*?"

"Jack!"

"What? She was three inches taller than me, and unlike Tom Cruise, I'm just not comfortable with that. Especially when I'm six one to begin with. And she talked with her mouth open all through dinner."

"Poor girl."

"She didn't like me either. When Aunt Cathy said I was tall, I think the girl thought she meant I was taller than her."

"Poor girl," I say again. "Yet another perk of being short, I guess."

Jack shakes his head. "Asparagus isn't pretty when it's being gnawed on."

"Gross." I make a wide circle around Jack while he stirs the frosting.

"Oh good night, Pattertwig, I only dumped it on you once."

I point once again to my feet. "I still haven't broken in these shoes."

"Whine, whine, whine."

"Cheese, cheese, cheese."

He starts laughing.

It's one thirty, and I just got back to Cool Beans from my lunch break. The day is still chilly; several college students are gathered around the crackling fireplace; and I'm reading the ad on the back of my Subway cup.

"Hey, did you know that Jared is more recognizable than Ronald McDonald?" I tell Jack, setting my stuff in the back and pulling on my cherry red apron.

He hands a customer an americano and starts working on a mocha. "Who's Jared?"

"Maybe that statistic isn't true," I say.

One of our regulars, Jane, comes up to the counter. She's only a few years older than me and comes in every week to do her Bible study for a class at her church.

"Hi, Jack. Hi, Maya," she says, smiling.

"Hey, Jane." Jack waves over the whir of the espresso machine.

"Hi." I grin. "How's it going?"

"Good." She pulls her wallet out and looks at the menu. "I just love days like this. Can I get an English Breakfast tea?"

"Sure." I ring up her total. "Anything new happening?"

"My brother's moving back to town," she says.

"No way! Mine is too!" I yelp. Jane jumps.

"She's had four mochas and a macchiato," Jack explains to Jane.

I shrug. "They were nonfat."

Jane grins. "That doesn't cancel out the caffeine, Maya."

"But I feel better about myself."

She laughs.

I attach the little strainer sack and scoop the heavily scented tea into it, pouring the hot water on top. "Why's your brother coming back to town?" I ask, handing her the steaming mug.

"Mom finally talked him into it. He's been looking for a job in San Diego and decided to move here to work as a marketing consultant with that computer place on Fir Street," she says, adding honey to her tea. "Why's your brother coming back?"

"He got a job, too. At the hospital. He's a doctor."

"Really? I'll have to bring my brother by to meet you guys."

"Yeah, I'd like to meet him. Have a good Bible study, Jane."

"Thanks!" She goes to her usual seat by the window.

Jack comes over, wiping off his hands on the cleaning rag. "You didn't tell me Zach was moving back." He smiles at me sympathetically. "Yet another reason for Maya the Grouch this morning?"

I hold up my hands apologetically. "I'm sorry. Mom called a few days ago. He was in town for an interview at the hospital. He just failed to mention that."

"So he got the job?"

"Well, of course. He starts in a week and a half." I'm still trying to decide if this is a good thing or a bad thing. On the one hand, he's not a bad brother. On the other hand, he's kind of an intimidating brother.

So maybe it's good *and* bad.

"Well, that's good, right?" Jack asks.

I hate it when he reads my mind.

"Not sure yet," I answer, smiling at the next customer, a nice-looking guy probably in his thirties.

"Hi there," he says. "I'm meeting my new girlfriend here. You haven't seen a short, curly haired, cute brunette around, have you?" He leans on the counter, grinning flirtatiously at me.

Ew.

Jack rolls his eyes and goes in the back. The support he offers me in times like these is just devastating.

How do you answer a question like that? I'm not sure, so I stay quiet.

The man keeps on grinning. "How are you today?"

I'm doing my best to hold back the loud exclamation of *eiegh!* "Uh. Good. You?"

"I'm great. Can I get a small black coffee?"

I'd like to put a note on the counter to future men: *If you are trying to flirt with the barista, please buy more than the least expensive thing on the menu.*

I hand the guy his coffee.

"Thanks, sugar," he says. Then he just looks at me, eyebrows raised. I squirm, feeling under the microscope.

"Did you want something else?" I ask.

"Sugar?" he repeats.

"Oh!" Sigh of relief here. "Over there." I point to the drink-doctoring table.

"Thanks."

He sugars his coffee and leaves with a wink but no tip.

Maybe I should add another sentence to that note: *And always, always, always tip!*

Jack comes back and just shakes his head at me.

"What?" I ask.

"You know, I seriously feel ignored sometimes."

"Oh please, Jack," I say, wiping down the counter. "You get flirted with all the time."

"By lonely old ladies." He winces. "And loud nocturnal birds." Then he grins. "Polly is going home tomorrow."

I watch him for a minute. "Please refrain from dancing behind the counter."

"That was a jig, Nutkin."

Jen's car is in her spot when I get home at three thirty. There's a box of triple-butter movie-theater popcorn and a rental copy of *Runaway Bride* next to me on the passenger seat.

I guess I won't be watching by myself. Good thing I bought the extra-large bags of popcorn.

What's Jen doing home so early?

I climb the stairs and open the door. "Jenny?"

She's splayed out on the living-room floor, dressed in black yoga pants and a powder-blue stretchy top, and a peppy blond Pilates instructor is piping orders to move to the Proud Warrior position.

And where is my beloved beagle?

Yup. Right next to Jen.

"Hi, Maya," Jen pants, mimicking the Pilates lady and spreading her arms over her head.

"What are you doing?" I ask. Calvin's stretching his back legs out, lying flat on the carpet.

"What's it look like?" Jen huffs, moving to a sitting forward bend. "I'm working out." She squints at me. Her face has a healthy flush to it. "Your dog is really odd, by the way."

"He likes Pilates. You took off work to work out?" I set the popcorn on the kitchen counter, speechless.

"Uh-huh," she breathes.

Weird.

Last year, Jen came down with the worst case of the flu I've ever seen in my life. She was throwing up about every eleven minutes and had a 102-degree fever, but she still dragged her snow-white face out of bed for three days, pushed past me blocking the door, and drove to work until her tightfisted boss finally told her to go home early that Friday. She spent the next two and a half days in bed.

That's the last time I can remember her taking off work.

"Did Wayne give you the afternoon off?"

"Nope."

"Then why—?"

"Look, Maya, I'm seriously trying to work out here!" she barks from the Down Dog position.

Sheesh. Touchy.

Calvin's glaring at me too, but that's probably because I bought popcorn instead of ice cream.

And I thought Pilates made you calmer?

I go into my room and toss the movie on my bed.

Uncomfortable work shoes are coming off ASAP. Honestly, you'd think the manufacturers of black ugly shoes would realize that people only buy their product when they absolutely have to. If they made them comfy, maybe they'd be more popular. Comfy ugly shoes. They'd be like the new Crocs or something.

I change into my gray velour pants and a black long-sleeved T-shirt. Today is one of the few days in Hudson when I can wear my favorite wool socks without sweating, so on they go!

I hear someone exhale, and I guess if my life were scarier, I would have jumped. I look up at Jen, who's sucking down a water bottle as if the bad guys in *Batman Begins* actually succeeded in poisoning the water source.

"There's more where that came from," I say.

She looks at me quizzically. "What?"

"Nothing." I let down my now elastic-creased hair from its ponytail and run my fingers through the tangled, curly mess.

"What are you doing tonight?" Jen asks, backhanding her glistening forehead.

"Well, I have a very exciting evening planned. I'm going to watch a man with a really cutely named cat try not to fall in love with a girl who works at a hardware store."

Jen shakes her head, grinning. "You rented *Runaway Bride* again?"

"Maybe."

"Want another option?" she asks.

Oh. Gosh.

Here it comes. I can sense it in the atmosphere, smell it in the air. Like the most predictable couple on the face of this earth, Jen and Travis have just entered the "Why Can't Everyone Be as Happy as Us?" stage.

Crap.

I press my hands to my ears, but Jen's too loud.

"Want to go with me and Travis on a double date?"

I offer up a feeble prayer and an audible excuse. "But it's not called a double date if there's only one extra person. That's called a third wheel."

"Oh, don't worry about that." Jen grins to herself smugly. "Travis has this friend who he says is like the nicest guy on the planet."

Is that the new way of saying "has a great personality"?

"Well, I did rent *Runaway Bride*," I try, pointing to the movie.

"It's a four-day rental. Watch it tomorrow."

"And, of course, I bought popcorn. . . ." Now I sound like Rain Man. Swell.

Jen has yet another answer for my impersonation of Dustin Hoffman. "You bought the most artificial popcorn on the planet. It'll probably be here long after the rapture. Just come with us!"

No, no, no. That's all I have to say to her. *No, Jen. No thanks, Jen. Thanks, but no, Jenny. Find another girl to walk through this phase with you.*

"Sure, why not?" my traitorous mouth mumbles. I try to clasp my hands over my lips, but it's too late. The words suspend in the air like little soap bubbles, floating just out of my reach.

"Great!" Jen's excitement is frustrating. Why can't she be the jealous girlfriend who never shares? They never go through the "Everyone Needs a Mate Like Bambi" phase. They just go through the "Dumping All Their Friends in Order to Spend Time with the Guy" phase.

My stomach is doing slow, nauseating cartwheels.

"We're meeting them at Santiago's at five." Mexican food. That oughta help the stomach.

And what's with all this *meeting*? It's like they're business partners instead of dating.

Jen's glowing though, and I don't think it's the Pilates workout.

"Okay," I manage.

"Since it's Friday night, there was talk about a movie. Have you seen that new Brad Pitt movie yet?" She's now grinning, and combined with that after-workout flush, she looks positively stunning. She'd never believe me though. Jen's a fan of the Kirsten Dunst pale look.

"No," I answer her.

"Oh. Well, I heard it's good. Anyway, I'm going to hop in the shower. Wear something nice because I want to wear a skirt."

She disappears, humming.

As soon as I hear her bathroom door close, I drop my head in my hands. *Oh, Lord, what in the world did I just get myself into?*

Two hours and fourteen outfit changes later, we're both standing in the kitchen. Me, because I'm afraid Jen will hit me over the head with her water bottle if I sit on the couch and wrinkle my clothes. Jen, because she's so busy hydrating that she doesn't notice how uncomfortable her heels are.

I fidget, pulling at the red-and-white skirt I'm wearing. It's knee length, and Jen paired it with a red fitted T-shirt and a dark denim jacket, so I look really cute, but I just don't understand why I couldn't be dressed up in my favorite brown cords and maybe that soft blue-green sweater I have.

Honestly, a skirt to go to the movie theater? Hudson's only theater, Cinema 12, is far from a Hollywood premiere. The odds of some kid in the show before me *not* spilling a Coke on the seat so it's all soaked and sticky are about as likely as me liking my blind date.

"He's super nice," Jen says for the seventeenth time. Jen looks the part of the adorable girlfriend in a white eyelet dress. Her hair is pulled back off her face in a headband.

Each time she says it, I see it as one more strike against this guy's looks. I don't want to be shallow, but please. All of us know that physical attraction is pretty important.

She glances at the clock again. "Okay. We can go."

I nod dutifully and pick up my messenger bag. Inside is my wallet, ChapStick, and cell phone. The only thing I can imagine using tonight is my cell phone—to call Jack to come pull me out of this mess. There won't be any kissing, so I don't need the ChapStick. And I'd better not be paying, so there's no use for the wallet. That's Rule #1 in the dating manual for guys.

We climb in Jen's car, and she heads toward Santiago's, a local Mexican restaurant. The whole time I fret about sitting across from Travis at dinner while he's on a date with my best friend.

Awkward!

We get to the crowded restaurant, park, and squeeze through the doorway littered with people.

"There he is," Jen says, waving.

Travis seems even more good-looking than normal in a navy-and-gray button-down shirt that makes his eyes pop. He grins back at Jen, waving her over to where he is standing near the hostess booth. Note the singular *he*. There is not another guy with him.

"Hi, sweetie," he says, lightly kissing Jen's cheek.

She dimples.

I bite my tongue, stomach folding over painfully.

"Maya, glad you could make it." Travis smiles at me, slightly yelling over the crowd noise.

He *has* to connect the dots eventually, right? Hudson? My name? I'm becoming convinced he has some kind of memory disorder.

"Thanks," I say. I look around pointedly.

"Where's Walker?" Jen asks loudly.

Walker. As in the Texas Ranger? That's my date?

Travis leans his head toward the big sign reading "Baños." "Nerves," he says. He grins at me again. "Walker doesn't get to meet pretty women very often."

"Uh, why not?" I ask, trying not to flinch. Here it comes.

He's allergic to oxygen and lives in a bubble.

He raises cows for a living. Came up to Hudson for good tap water.

He enjoys discussing the chemical makeup of commonly used substances.

"He's a sailor on a crab boat in Alaska," Travis says.

Well, it wasn't my first guess but pretty darn close to the second. "Oh," I say, blinking. Now, I'm imagining a huge, barrel-chested guy with a thick red beard and a stocking cap with one of those little fuzz balls attached to the top of it.

Remind me why I wore a skirt?

"He's back in Hudson for the off-season. His family is out here."

"Oh," I say again.

Travis keeps talking. "I met him two years ago at my church. Neat guy. Cool testimony."

"Oh."

Travis is still grinning. "Here he is." He waves his arm in the air. "Walker!"

Red-bearded barrel man not present. Solidly muscular, shorn dark hair, twinkling chocolate-brown eyes, and tanned man answers to the bad-TV-show name.

"Hi there," he says, looking awkward and unsure of how to greet us. Handshake? Hug? High five?

I spare him the grief and hold out my hand. "Hi, I'm Maya."

He looks relieved. And not just because he just came from the *baño*. "Walker. Nice to meet you."

Jen gives him a handshake, too. "Jen."

"Hi." He's built like a soccer player. Not too many muscles, not too tall, just average, and an all-around good-looking guy.

This guy has trouble meeting women?

Yeah, right. I glance around and find three ladies not-so-subtly staring at him right now.

"Clayton, party of four!" a harried hostess yells.

Travis raises his hand. "Here!" he says, as if she were taking attendance.

"Follow me, please." She leads us through the crowded restaurant and leaves us at a four-person booth with menus and a promise that our server will be right over.

Travis and Jen take one side of the booth. Probably so they can hold hands under the table, which makes my stomach tighten even more than it already is. That leaves me and Mr. Alaska on the other side.

He slides in first, and I follow, sitting a good distance away, right across from Jen.

"Uh, so what's good here?" Walker stutters, picking up his menu.

"The shrimp fajitas are unbelievable," Travis answers him.

"So are the fish tacos," Jen quickly adds.

Now I just stare at both of them. "Didn't you say he works

on a fishing boat?" I ask Travis.

"Yeah," Walker answers. "I'm, um, not sure I want seafood after some of those eighteen-hour shifts." He grimaces. "Plus, uh, outside of Alaska, the freshness deteriorates rapidly."

"I'd go with the chicken burrito," I say to him.

"Uh, okay." He closes his menu and stares silently at his hands, which are clasped on the table.

Travis and Jen are too busy giggling over something on the menu, heads tucked together all close and intimate, to realize that my side of the table has fallen quieter than the Bering Sea at dawn.

"So, Walker," I begin, attempting to at least start a conversation, "did you grow up here?"

"Um, no."

The end.

I frown at him. Suddenly—good-looking or not—I'm realizing why this guy doesn't meet too many girls.

Most girls, myself included, generally like to *talk* to our dates. As shallow as I am, looks don't matter *that* much.

"Me, either," I say. "I grew up in San Diego."

"Oh."

"What do you do when you're not fishing?" Second attempt.

He glances quickly at me and then looks back at his hands. "My friend and I run an online computer-help agency. We freelance for big software companies."

Ah. Add computer geek to the mix.

He goes back to the study of his thumbs, and I brush a curl that is boinging in front of my left eye away from my face. Since when did "he's a super nice guy" become code for "he's beautiful but doesn't talk"? Jen obviously does not know The Code very well.

I would have definitely preferred an unattractive but friendly date.

Note to self: Do not be shallow.

Travis now has his arm around Jen's shoulders. "So, Walker, how was the catch this year?" he asks in his classic easygoing way.

"Good." Walker nods. "Decent at least. Enough to pay for another winter in Hudson."

"That's great." Travis grins.

Travis Clayton always had a great smile.

I catch myself and turn back to Walker, Alaskan Fisher. "You just catch crab, right? Anything else?"

"Occasionally we catch some salmon, but that's not a good sign," Walker says, warming up just a bit.

"Why?" Keep him talking. This has become my evening's motto.

"You can't get even half the revenue for salmon that you can for crab," he explains. "And since most of the guys don't have a winter job, they need to have a good crab season."

Jen shakes her head. "I can't imagine working only one season out of the year."

Walker just nods. "Yep."

Travis and Jen go back to talking about something they had apparently been discussing in a previous conversation.

Our server finally appears. "Sorry about the wait, guys," he says. "What can I get you to drink?"

Waters all around, until he gets to me. "Do you have any coffee?" I ask.

He subtly glances at Walker, who is staring at his hands again, at the space between us, and then at me. Then he grins. "Yeah, we've got a great selection of espressos, lattes, and cappuccinos. Can I interest you in a Mexican latte?"

"Yes, you can," I say, nodding enthusiastically.

"I'll have that right out."

Five minutes of silence later, and he brings out a huge steaming mug of something sweet, cinnamony, and creamy. "Oh," I sigh, like Alvin the Chipmunk when he gets his new harmonica from Mrs. Claus. "Thank you."

The server is so nice that he doesn't even laugh at me — just smirks, looks at my date, and then smirks again. "You're welcome." Apparently, he's been on the receiving end of a "Happiest Couple on Earth" syndrome as well.

"Gosh, Maya, you can drink all that?" Walker asks.

"Walker, I can put down coffee with the best of them."

"It will stunt your growth." He suddenly gasps and looks down at the top of my head, which is a little creepy. "When did you start drinking coffee?"

Way before I started working at Cool Beans. Which was about four years ago. "Around four years ago," I say, aiming for the positive side. "I work at a coffee shop."

"That has to be it," he says, like he just discovered radium.

"Actually, I stopped growing in the eighth grade." And my Mimi was shorter than a fourth grader in heels, but Walker doesn't need to know that.

"Hmm. Calcium deficient?" he wonders aloud, still looking me up and down.

I hate Jen.

I grab our server's apron. "Could I get a refill?"

Eleven forty-five p.m. Jen and I walk into our dark, cold apartment, and I gather Calvin up in my arms.

"Hi, baby," I croon. "It's just you and me forever, okay?"

Calvin is okay with this. He gives my right cheek and ear a good make-out session.

"Maya, you never know until you try, right?" Jen says, excusing my inexcusable date.

"Jen, you are not allowed to set me up on a blind date ever again."

"Oh, good grief," Jen says, kicking off her shoes. "He was cute! And you got a free dinner and a free movie. And movies aren't cheap anymore."

"Well," I concede. I fall on the couch, pulling off my heels.

"What time are you working tomorrow?" Jen asks.

"Noon to close. Why?"

She grins. "Want to have one of our infamous Mitchell and Davis movie extravaganzas?"

"Yay!" I say, bouncing off the couch and running to change. Jen's halfway to her room. You can only have movie extravaganzas in pajama pants. No skirts allowed. And you always have to have some form of chocolate.

I yank off my skirt, shirt, and jacket and pull on a pair of blue flannel pants with clouds all over them and a white long-sleeved T-shirt. I try to pull my hair back into a ponytail, but it's not cooperating with me, so I leave it down and curling in weird corkscrew curls like a more scattered version of Shirley Temple.

Calvin is whirling around my heels the whole time in a happy puppy dance. "Roo! Roo!" he yodels excitedly. Calvin loves movie extravaganzas.

"Hurry up, slowpoke!" Jen yells from the living room. I half-hop, half-trip out of my room, pulling on a pair of fuzzy pink socks.

"I'm sorry. Someone made me dress for my date in multiple

layers," I grumble, falling on the couch. Then I'm happy again. "What are we watching?"

"Want to watch *Runaway Bride* since you rented it for tonight anyway?" Jen's wearing her faded red, silky long-sleeved pajama set. Her hair is piled on her head, and she's posed in front of the TV, holding the rental DVD.

"Yay!"

"I'll take that as a yes," she grins. "Ice cream?"

"Pie?" I say at the same time.

She nods. "Both. We've been working out."

"What about natural dirt foods?" I ask, eyes wide.

She waves a hand while putting the DVD in. "Who cares? It's a girls' movie night, and you cannot have natural foods during one of those."

I like Jen a lot.

Forty minutes later, we're both snuggled under fleece blankets on the couch, watching Julia Roberts try on a backpack for her mountain-climbing honeymoon. I lick the apple pie with melted vanilla ice cream off my spoon. Canned apple pie filling, instant Pillsbury crust—it's like God *wanted* us to have high cholesterol.

"I do not want to climb a mountain for my honeymoon," Jen says, scraping the bowl.

"Me neither."

"I want to go to a spa or a resort or something," she continues.

I frown at the TV. "I want to do something in the snow. Winter is the most romantic time of the whole year!" I throw up my hands in happiness and rain down a sprinkling of apple filling on Calvin at my feet, who yips and then starts licking himself.

"Oops."

"You get vacuum duty."

"I bequeath it to Calvin."

Jen smiles. "I've always liked summer," she says softly and wistfully. "Everything is green, and the flowers have all bloomed."

"The whole 'June bride' type of thing?"

"Yeah."

I shake my head. "Summer's hot."

"That means a strapless dress."

"And a bathing-suit tan," I say.

She starts gnawing on her lip. "Good point."

I toss her one of Calvin's toys, much to his dismay. "Here," I offer. "Have a chew toy; save your lip."

"Funny."

CHAPTER NINE

I pop the lid on a lady's latte and pass it across the counter. "Here you go, ma'am."

"Thanks."

She takes it and settles into one of the squishy chairs, pulling a novel out of her purse. Today is another cloudy, stormy day, and Cool Beans is packed.

Jack is in the back, whistling, while he pulls another batch of our infamous blazzberry scones—that's blueberry and raspberry—from the freezer. Apparently, he left Polly with his apartment-complex office, and the owners were supposed to pick the bird up at two o'clock today. It's nearly four, so Jack has officially been birdless for two hours.

Thus the annoying, nonstop whistling. Earlier, I heard him making up a song about "No more parrots in his 'partment."

It was disturbing.

"Hi there," I say to a nicely aged man in his sixties. "What can I get you?"

He pulls out his wallet. "Just a coffee, missy. And a chocolate-chip cookie, please."

I tell him the amount, while grabbing the cookie and drink for him. "Here you go."

"Thanks," goes the man. *Ping* goes the tip jar.

Yay! goes me.

Jack comes from the back, wiping his hands on his apron, still whistling.

"Wait, is that the victory theme from *The Mighty Ducks*?" I ask.

"Yup." He grins happily at me. "Fitting, don't you think? It's a happy song. About . . . poultry."

"It's not about poultry."

"Sure it is. It's about the Mighty Ducks. Ducks are poultry."

"No, it's about winning." I shake my head. "And besides, even if ducks are, parrots aren't poultry. You eat poultry."

"True, but Polly barely escaped that fate."

He's smiling, so I know he's kidding, but I glare at him. "Meany."

"I wouldn't have eaten him. But after a week and a half of listening to him talk, Canis was about to rip him beak to tail," Jack says.

Canis is a mix of Labrador and pointer. He should have the words "bird dog" tattooed into his hide. I'm actually amazed Polly lived this whole time.

"Is Canis ready to be the only pet in your life again?"

"You'd better believe it." Jack sighs. "I can't wait. No bird-seed everywhere, no more screams, silent nights . . ."

"Christmas already, Jack?" Alisha says, walking up to the counter. "And here I thought Maya was the Christmas freak."

I giggle.

Alisha grins, looking around. "Looks busy. That's good," she says.

"It's a cold day. Everyone wants lattes," I say.

"Speaking of which," Alisha begins, "Jackie, will you make

me a cinnamon latte while Maya gets me the totals?"

"Sure thing, Alisha," Jack says, starting on her drink.

She leaves, latte in hand, a few minutes later. "See you later, guys."

"Bye," I say, turning back to Jack. "So, I went on a blind date last night."

He's right in the middle of sipping from his straight-up black coffee, so he ends up choking. "With whom?" he says, hacking.

"Some guy who scored an eight on the good-looking scale and a two on the personality scale." I sigh. "Half the time, we just sat there. Staring at our food. Fiddling with our enchiladas."

"Sorry." He starts laughing.

"It's not funny, Jack."

He clears his throat to stop the laugh. "Why did he not have a personality?"

I shrug. "I don't know. He just didn't. Apparently, he isn't around women much."

"He said that?" Jack takes a lady's order, and I start making her three to-go coffees.

"No, Travis did." I say this in a small voice while he's talking to the lady. "Anyway, change of subject, Zach is moving to town tomorrow."

"Thanks. Here's your change and your coffees," Jack says to the lady, handing her the drinks in a cardboard carrier.

She dumps her change in the tip jar. "Thank you!"

Jack turns back to me the moment she leaves. "Wait, what?"

"He's moving here tomorrow. I'm supposed to go to Mom and Dad's right after church so I can help them."

"No, Travis was at your blind date?" He's frowning.

I twist a rag around in my hands. "Well, it was kind of a double date *and* a blind date."

"Oh." He starts grinding a new batch of coffee beans.

I grab a filter to help him. "It was Jen's idea."

He opens his mouth to say something, but right then the phone rings. "I'll get it," I say.

The cordless is under the front counter. "Thanks for calling Cool Beans. This is Maya. Can I help you?"

"Is there a Jack Dominguez there?" Female voice.

"One sec." I toss the phone to Jack.

He clears his throat and then answers it. "This is Jack." I finish getting the new coffee batch ready, disguising my eavesdropping. It's not that often that Jack gets a call, period—much less from a girl.

He tucks the phone under his ear. "Hey, how are you? Yeah. Mm-hmm. They what?" he almost yells.

I jump.

"What did you tell them? What?! Oh, man." He covers his face with his left hand. "Mm-hmm. No, I understand. Bye." He hangs up, but his hand stays over his eyes. "Oh, no," he mumbles.

"What? What happened?" I'm hopping around him like a little spastic puppy. "What is it? What's wrong, Jack?"

He sighs and rubs his face before moving his hands. "They never showed."

"Who never showed?"

"Polly's owners."

My mouth drops open. "What do you mean?"

"I mean Polly is still at my apartment's office building." He groans now. "Man!"

Poor Jack! "What are you going to do?" I ask, popping the new coffee grounds in the coffeemaker.

"I don't know. Rebecca, the secretary, called the number I

gave her for them, and they said they weren't coming today, so she asked when they were, and they hung up."

I don't know what to do, so I grimace a half-smile at him. "I'm sorry, Jack."

"It's not your fault. Want a nocturnal parrot?"

"No. Sorry."

"Oh." He sighs again. "Nutkin, I need to go put her back in the apartment, so do you mind if I take off in a few minutes for about half an hour?"

"No, go do it. Sorry."

A man comes over for a refill, and I dispense a new cup of dark roast for him. I can smell our fresh-from-the-oven scones, and apparently he can too. "Here you go, sir." I hand him the drink.

"Thanks. What's baking?"

"Scones."

"I'll take one."

I ring him up and give him a warm pastry.

Jack unties his apron and goes into the back, coming back out a few minutes later. "I'll be right back, Maya."

"Don't worry about it. Sorry."

He suddenly starts laughing. "Will you stop saying 'sorry'?"

"Okay." I wince. "Sorry."

"Back in a minute." He leaves.

I wipe down the counter and look around the coffee shop. Nearly all the chairs are filled with people laughing, talking, reading, or busily typing away on a laptop. A group of Cal-Hudson college kids are sprawled out on the two couches by the fireplace, textbooks and notebooks scattered everywhere. I silently thank God I'm done with school.

Jen walks in right then. She's wearing form-fitting jeans and a soft gray wool sweater that spotlights her blue eyes.

"Hey, Maya." She comes up to the counter and looks around. "You guys are busy. Where's Jack?"

"He found out he's got a parrot."

"I thought he had a parrot."

I nod. "He got it back."

"Oh." She grins. "Can I have a small English Dusk tea?"

"Here or to-go?"

She sits at the bar. "Here."

I pull a huge red ceramic mug from under the counter and attach the strainer sack to it. I scoop the loose-leaf tea and dispense the hot water over it.

"So, what are you doing today?" I ask. I hadn't seen her yet today. By the time I got up and showered, she was on a run, and I was almost late for work.

"I'm about to go to the grocery store," Jen says, grinning at me.

"Aww, is that why you came in?" I coo.

"Yes, it is. What do you need?"

I dig around for a sticky note and write her a list. She takes the note, reads it, and then looks up at me. "Seriously, Maya?"

"What's wrong with it?"

"All of this is instant dinners and ice cream."

"It's cheap!" I say. "And I work out."

Jen just shakes her head and smiles. "Oh, gosh."

"Thanks for going to the store."

She nods. "Sure. What time do you get off?"

"Ten or so."

"Okay. Travis and I are going to dinner tonight, so I may not be home when you get back." She finishes off her tea.

Again? "How do you guys afford eating out all the time?" I ask.

"He's pretty well-off, Maya." She smiles all sappy-like. "He bought me—"

I hold up a hand, cutting her off. "Wait, let me guess. Tulips?"

My sarcasm is lost on her. "He's so sweet, isn't he?" she sighs. "Well, I'm off to the grocery store. Call if you need something not preservative-chocked."

"Ha-ha," I say, picking up her empty mug. "Thanks, Jen. Bye."

Jack walks up right as Jen is leaving. "Hey, Jack," she says.

"Hi, Jenny. Leaving right as I get here? That's nice of you," he teases and gives her a hug. "Hey, you know what you need?" he asks, one arm still around her.

She gives him a look. "What?"

"A companion. Company. A friend. Someone you can tell even your most horrible secrets to."

"I don't want a parrot, Jack."

He sighs and lets her go. "What if it were free?"

She shakes her head. "They're messy. And loud."

"What if I *paid* you to take her?"

"No thanks," she says cheerfully as Jack deflates. "I'm sure someone wants your parrot, Jack." She nods around the restaurant. "Maybe someone here does."

"Does anyone want a parrot?" Jack yells.

There is suddenly total silence. Everyone looks at him confusedly and then almost at the same time starts their happy chattering buzz again.

Jack shoves his hands in his pocket. "I'll take that as a no."

It's ten thirty by the time I get home and tiredly sit on the edge of my bed to take my shoes off. Cool Beans was busy until we finally shooed the last customers out so we could lock up and leave.

Calvin is hopping up on my lap for some attention, and I sleepily scratch his ears. "Hi, baby. It's been a long day."

I lie back on the pillows and yawn, covering it with my wrist. I glance to my left, and there sits my Bible.

How long has it been since I did my devotions?

I pick up the sticky-note-clad Book and frown. It's been a while. I close my eyes. I'm so tired right now; I could fall asleep in my coffee-scented clothing. Which is a big no-no because then my sheets smell like Cool Beans, and suddenly my work life and my home life are one and the same smell.

That's bad.

I put the Bible back on the nightstand. I'm so out of it that I wouldn't be able to learn anything right now anyway.

I find the remote to my little TV instead and flick on the Style Network. Changing into a pair of pajama pants and a cami, I cuddle under the covers and slowly drift to sleep, dreaming of dark-rinsed jeans and jewel-toned tops.

At exactly ten in the morning on Sunday, I fall into a padded folding chair, coffee and Bible in hand. I'm wearing jeans and a thick blue sweater since our cold weather front has been holding for the past few days.

"Morning, Maya," Andrew says, coming by.

"Hey, Andrew."

"Good week?"

I nod. "Decent."

He smiles and moves on to greet the next person walking in. I sip my coffee, looking around. Jack and Jen aren't here yet, and a group of about twenty people mill around, grabbing coffee and visiting.

I'm not very good at meeting new people. I get all freaked out about having to come up with small talk.

There's a guy I recognize from the past several weeks sitting two empty seats down from me. I've never talked to him. Guys are even weirder to randomly just go talk to. Then it looks like I'm coming on to him, which I'm not.

He must notice my fidgeting because he looks over at me. "Hey," he says.

Oh great. Now I have to talk back. Why am I so good at this at Cool Beans and so bad at it here?

He's looking at me expectantly. He's blond and cute, and that makes it even harder to talk normally to him.

I'm mentally going over the five points of meeting new people that Andrew told me when he asked why I never talk to people outside of Jack, Jen, and him.

I wrote it down on a sticky note at the time:

> *Five Points of Meeting New People:*
> *S — Say hi and your name.*
> *M — Mention interests.*
> *I — Investigate their interests.*
> *L — Laugh a lot.*
> *E — Exit, knowing you made a new friend.*

"Hi," I say back, wringing my hands nervously. "I'm Maya. I'm interested in coffee, chocolate, and snow, and I wish I could paint like Thomas Kinkade, and I'm curious what you like to do." I try to giggle casually, but it comes out like a staccato version of Cogsworth the Clock on *Beauty and the Beast.*

He blinks at me.

I rub my forehead.

"Good morning, everyone," Andrew says, the official opening of our Bible study.

Why did Andrew ever give me that list? It makes it worse!

Honestly, how hard is it to say, "Hi, I'm Maya. What's your name?"

I'm using both hands on my temples now.

"Headache?" Jack whispers in my ear, sliding into the seat next to me.

"Of course, you show up *now*," I hiss at him.

"What?"

"So, why don't we all quiet down and turn to James." Andrew is looking right as me as he says the words "quiet down."

I glare at Jack and grab my Bible.

Forty-five minutes later, Andrew prays and we're done. Honestly, I didn't hear too much of the message. I have to drive to San Diego right now to help Zach and Kate get their new house set up.

Mom sent me a text this morning that said, *Sweetie, it's raining so wear something warm.*

Swell. Moving in the rain.

I'm probably being really immature and selfish about this whole Zach-moving-back thing. I mean, maybe we'll get along just fine now.

"You're grouchy," Jack says to me.

"Sorry." I sigh.

"If either of us deserves to be grouchy, it's me." He points to his chest. "I called Polly's owners thirty-seven times last night before I finally got ahold of them, and you want to know what they said?"

"You get to keep her?"

"Yes."

"Don't sound so excited."

"A nocturnal *Amazona aestiva*. I have a Lab/pointer cross and a blue-fronted Amazon parrot. Does this sound like a future zoologist?" he rants. "No, I might as well have a goldfish."

"Sorry, Jack."

"I mean, one of my classmates last year had a capuchin monkey named Felix. A *Cebus apella*. Can you imagine?"

"Not really."

Jack is off in his own world. "He's learning so much about the primates; it's ridiculous. Capuchins are the most intelligent monkeys on the planet."

"You can probably find someone who wants a parrot," I say.

"I've talked to everyone."

I frown. "Don't get mad at me. You're grouchy, too."

"Sorry."

We both stand there.

"So," I say after a minute. "I actually need to go. Zach and Kate are moving in today."

"Sorry for getting mad, Maya."

"Me, too." I wave and give him a small smile. "See ya."

There's a huge Mayflower truck parked in front of a cute red-brick ranch-style house on the street Mom gave me directions to, so I'm assuming that's Zach and Kate's new house.

Calvin's curled up in a little ball on the passenger seat. Raindrops are pattering down on the windshield; my wipers are making a rhythmic *swish-swash* sound; and I'm fighting sleep myself.

Mom's standing in the landscaped front lawn in her obnoxiously bright orange raincoat. I can't help the grin. Zach and I have ragged on Mom about that coat since we were in high school. It makes her look like she's either working a crosswalk or blocking a construction zone, but for some reason Mom loves the jacket.

She waves as I pull up and park behind the truck. I shrug on my royal blue coat and pull up the hood. Calvin wakes up when the wipers turn off.

"Rise and shine, bud," I say, opening my door to the chilly, wet day.

"Hi, honey!" Mom yells.

"Hi, Mom." I wave and wait for Calvin to drag his lazy body out of the car. He squints at the rain and pauses. "Get out, Calvin."

He huffs his breath out but does as I ask. We walk over to see Mom.

"What are you doing?" I ask her.

She starts walking back to the garage. "I saw you driving up. I just helped Dad, Zach, and the movers take in the entertainment center. I'm waiting for them to come back outside."

"By 'help' she means told us what to do," Dad says coming into the garage in a black-hooded jacket and pulling on a pair of wet leather gloves.

"Hi, Dad."

"Hey, honey, how's it going?" He gives me a light side hug and looks down at my dripping beagle. "Hi, Calvin!"

My dog loves Dad. Calvin immediately starts wriggling all over, running for Dad.

"Where are Zach and Kate?" I ask.

"Inside," Mom says, pointing to the door leading into a huge laundry room. I nod and walk inside.

The house is gorgeous. Vaulted ceilings, creamy beige paint, white trim, and where there's not beautiful hardwood, there's plush carpet.

I hear Kate before I see her.

"Oh, be careful with that," she says, right before I hear a loud bang and an "oops" in a voice I don't recognize.

I follow the voices into the gargantuan living room. Kate's wringing her hands in frustration while Zach and three movers are muscling their very large, very ornate entertainment center into place.

I walk over and smile at her. "You okay, Kate?"

"Hi, Maya," Kate says. And then she shocks me so much I almost lose control of my jaw muscles. She leans down and wraps me in a hug. "I'm so glad you're here. I'm losing my mind."

I pull it together quickly and hug her back. The only other time I've hugged Kate was on her wedding day, and that was awkward because she was wearing yards and yards of white lace.

"What's wrong?" I ask.

She leaves her arm over my shoulders. She's five foot eight and at five two, I guess I make a good armrest.

"I hate moving. I hate it so much."

I've never seen Kate this unraveled. Her long, shiny choco-late-brown hair is in a ponytail; her jeans are worn around the edges; and she's wearing a T-shirt. She has on mascara but no other makeup.

I can't remember ever seeing Kate in a T-shirt, much less in hardly any makeup.

Zach grunts as he straightens from where he had his grip on the bottom edge of the entertainment center. "Hey, sis," he mumbles. He's wearing a sweatshirt and dirty jeans, and he rubs his rumpled hair, arching his back. "I'm too old for this."

Dad comes in then, hefting a matching end table. "You're too old for this?" he says, laughing. "Wait until it's your kid you're helping move in."

"I like the house, guys," I say, still admiring the paint job and the ceilings.

Kate looks around, relaxing for a minute. "Isn't it cute?"

I nod. "Very cute."

"Have you seen the kitchen yet?" she asks me.

I shake my head.

"Come on, I'll show you."

I follow her mutely. Who is this? Kate is not huggy nor is she chatty.

She should get stressed out more often.

She leads me into a good-sized kitchen with lots of beautiful, white-painted wood cabinets and light-colored granite counter-tops. All of the appliances are stainless steel, which contrasts nicely.

"I want to paint that wall a cranberry color," Kate says, pointing to the wall behind the cooktop. "I think it will add just the right amount of color to this room. What do you think?"

I nod. "I think that would look really nice."

"And I want to change our breakfast table out for a more bistro-style table in here." She nods to the little nook area. "You don't need a table, do you?"

"No, but my friend Jack just eats at his coffee table every night."

Kate grins. "Well, let him know he can have a real table if he wants one."

We rejoin the others, and I glance at Kate. That has to be the longest conversation I've ever had with her.

"Couches go there and there," Kate says to the perspiring movers, pointing.

"Katie, where do you want the bookcases?" Zach asks.

"Which ones? Medical books or fun books?"

"Medical."

She thinks for a second. "In the study against the east wall."

I have to hand it to my brother: He's got the whole Let-the-Woman-Design-the-House thing down.

I go back out to the moving truck and find Calvin nosing around the garage. "Are you all dirty now?" I ask him, looking him over.

"Roo!"

"Apparently." I shake my head. "Go play outside so you get cleaned off."

I climb up the ramp into the truck and look for something I can carry. While I have spent many years running, I haven't spent that much time working on my upper-body strength.

Mental note: Begin lifting weights.

I find a box of towels and carry that in.

Zach and Dad are setting up the mahogany bookcases in the study. "Maya, can you grab me a level? There's one on the fireplace mantel," Zach says to me.

"Sure. Towels?"

"Anything you don't know what to do with, put it in the guest room."

"Okay."

I find the level and take it back to him. "Here you go."

Zach looks up at me. "Thanks. Hey, how are things with Travis?"

"Fine," I say. *Confusing*, I think as I leave the room.

It's six thirty before we stop for dinner. Everything is in the house and the movers have left, taking their big truck with them.

Zach collapses on one of the sofas, laying his head on Kate's lap. "I'm bushed," he says. He winces and archs his back again. "Maya?"

I sigh and grin at him, pushing up my sweater sleeves and kicking off my shoes. "Come here."

He falls off the couch and lies on his stomach in front of the entertainment center. Gingerly, I step on his back, grabbing one of the shelves for balance. "If you make any mention of me gaining weight since I was fifteen . . ." I warn.

He makes a noise in the back of his throat right as his back cracks loudly. Mom jumps.

"Maya! Stop that! Zachary, do you have any idea what that does to your spine?"

"Mom, I'm a doctor," Zach protests into the carpet.

"I don't care. You're not using your brain."

Kate giggles on the couch.

Dad falls into the other one. "Well, Kate, you have a great house here. It's good to have you back in town."

"Oh, Maya, not by my neck."

"Sorry."

"Thanks," Kate says to Dad. "I like it."

Mom settles next to Dad. "I guess we can see how much my kids still listen to me."

"What?" I ask, grinning.

"Funny, Maya." Mom rolls her eyes. She reaches down and rubs a now-clean and dried Calvin.

"You don't mind him in here, do you?" I ask, worriedly.

"Are you kidding?" Kate says. She taps on her knee and Calvin trots over. "I love dogs. I told Zach that we have to get one now." She rubs Calvin's head. "Beagles are adorable. So are basset hounds. Do you know anything about bassets?"

"I've heard they're hard to train," I say.

Kate nods. "Are beagles?"

I shrug as best as I can, standing on top of Zach's spinal column. "Calvin wasn't too hard. It's all about consistency."

"Okay."

"So, what's going on with Travis?" Zach asks, voice muffled.

I dig my foot into the small of his back. "Nothing. He's dating Jen."

"Still hard for you, huh?"

"No."

Kate looks up from Calvin. "Zach, stop. She doesn't want to talk about it."

I step off Zach's back. "There. You're all popped."

He does a push-up to his knees and rolls his shoulders. "Ah. Thanks, Maya."

"What do you want to do for dinner, kids?" Mom asks.

"It's a good soup night," Kate says.

I nod happily. "Soup!"

"Agreed," Mom says.

Dad looks at Zach. "Apparently, we're having soup."

"We need to get another guy in here, Dad. We're outnumbered." Zach digs his elbow into my side. "Huh? Huh? That's up to you."

"Ow. See if I ever pop your back again."

"I'm sorry."

I make peace with the boys. "Fresh Choice? Then you can get whatever you want."

Dad nods. "Okay."

Mom's hungry. "Let's go then."

I sit down with my second bowl of clam chowder. Fresh Choice is nearly dead tonight, and I chalk it up to the weather because the chowder is delicious.

"Maya, how late is your coffee shop open?" Zach asks, digging into his second plate of salad.

"Depends on the night. Between ten and eleven."

He nods. "I think we might come by on Tuesday, then. One of the other doctors at the hospital has a house in Hudson, and he invited us for dinner."

I raise my eyebrows. "That's a drive."

"You do it every week."

"Yeah, but not every day. That would get old." I sip my soup. "Okay, good. You should come by — that'd be fun. You can see where I work."

I'm surprising even myself by saying this, but it's true. Something's changed with Zach and Kate today. Maybe it's pity for my situation with Travis. Or stress wearing down the normal reserves. Whatever it is, I like it.

Kate smiles at me across the table. "Drink recommendation?"

"Caramel cinnamon mocha. But it's not on the menu. You have to have special connections with the barista to get that drink." I point to myself. "It's the Maya Special."

Zach grins. "So, are you working Tuesday night?"

"I think so." I think I'm closing every night this week. Which is sort of sad. As much as I hate getting up early, Jack's right: It's very nice to be done by two.

And Cool Beans is very boring from about five o'clock on.

"Okay. Well, we'll see you Tuesday then," Zach says, all businesslike.

I smile.

CHAPTER TEN

I get to work at two on Monday. Lisa starts pulling her apron off when I walk through the door. "Hi, Maya!" she says, all chipper.

"Hey, Lisa." I smile. "How's it going?"

"Slow day," she replies, warning in her voice. "Hope you brought a book or something." She picks up a library copy of *Mansfield Park*. Lisa's going to school to be an English teacher.

"Jane Austen?" I ask.

"We're studying her right now." Lisa grins. "It's my favorite class."

"I'd imagine."

"Have a great day!" She hangs her apron in the back, grabs her purse, and leaves right as Jack is coming in.

"Bye, Lisa," he says to her. He walks over to the counter and looks around. "Wow. Three whole customers?"

Today is sunny and warm, and suddenly everyone wants slushes and Cokes instead of hot chocolate.

"Yep." I nod at him. "Exciting day ahead."

"Oh, joy. Did Zach and Kate get moved in okay?"

I nod again. "Yeah. They were really nice yesterday. Personable."

He pulls his apron over his head and joins me, leaning

against the counter. "That's good."

"They're coming in tomorrow night."

He frowns slightly. "Have I ever met Kate?"

"I don't think so."

"Well, good, I'll have to meet her tomorrow."

I start making myself a fat-free mocha. "What did you decide to do about Polly?"

"I put an ad in the paper."

"Are you serious?"

He walks over and grabs the complimentary paper we offer our customers. Spreading it out on the counter, he points to a classified ad.

PARROT — Free to a good home, blue-fronted Amazon. Talks. Friendly. Call Jack at (619) 555-4356. Desperate to find a home for her.

"Tragical," I say, shaking my head.

"If I don't get any calls today, I'm bringing her here tomorrow and trying to give her to a customer."

"Too bad she's not a cute little puppy. She might go faster if she were."

"Remember me talking about that internship at Hudson Zoo?" Jack asks, closing the paper and changing the subject.

"Yeah. Did you get it?"

He starts grinning.

"Yay! Good job, Jack!" I smile at him and give him a hug as he comes back around the counter. "When do you start?"

"I think I start in May. I still have a few more applications and things to fill out now. So, right after I graduate pretty much."

"Awesome!" I finish making my mocha and close a lid over it.

The door opens, and a very heavily made-up blond bombshell who looks about thirty walks in. She's wearing fishnet stockings, a charcoal gray pencil skirt, a black-and-white skin-tight sweater, and a glare.

I barely hold in my groan, but Jack's not quite as talented. He disguises it as a cough, though.

Oh, no.

"Mrs. Mitchell. Hi," I stutter.

Jen's mom is in town? Why did I not know this? I should always know these things.

"Good afternoon, Maya." Candace Mitchell is forty-eight years old, but I guess enough money can buy any age you want. She lays a perfectly manicured hand on the counter. "Jack."

"Hi." He waves, staying a safe distance away from her perfume.

Mrs. Mitchell looks at me. "Jennifer said that you would be here today. Is there any possible way you can make a decent cup of coffee?"

I smile politely at her. "Yes, ma'am. We are renowned for our coffee."

"I do not care that you are renowned. So is Starbucks, and their coffee is the most bitter, burned coffee I have ever tasted."

There's enough acid in Mrs. Mitchell's voice to melt away any unprotected skin cells. I subconsciously put my hand over my cheek.

"I'll give you a taste of ours," I offer meekly.

Jack's already got it for me. He's standing a few feet behind me. Close enough for moral support, far enough that he doesn't get singed.

Mrs. Mitchell's perfectly arched eyebrows raise just a smidgen as she takes the tiny tasting cup. "How can I possibly get enough to taste anything from this?" she grumbles but takes a sip.

She sets it on the counter with a huge sigh that racks her petite frame. "No one knows how to make good coffee anymore. It is not that hard. I make the best coffee on the East Coast, and it only takes good beans, a high-quality, nonbleached filter, and the right pH level in the water. I do not understand why that is so hard to comprehend!"

I take the empty cup from her. I'm hearing that song my mother always sang me when I was a little kid. Something about if you can't say something nice, say nothing.

I guess she doesn't know what to do with someone not responding to her rant because she makes another dramatic sigh. But really, what am I supposed to say? "Here's a free coffee that you'll hate"? I think not.

She sighs again, in case I didn't hear her.

"How long are you in town, Mrs. Mitchell?" I ask, pulling her focus from our awful coffee.

"Just until nine o'clock this evening. Jennifer is dating a new boy, and we all know how the last one turned out." She rolls her baby blue eyes. "It is better if I nip this one in the bud."

I wince. "Wait, what?"

"Travis Clayton? He works for an insurance company? He helps families with his company avoid being sued and such? What kind of a job is that?"

Actually, Jen told me Travis works for the protection part of the insurance company, and while, yes, he helps people avoid being sued by their neighbors if their house burns down and catches the neighbors' houses on fire, he also personally helps the families get back on their feet.

I have just about had my fill of Candace Mitchell. I glance at the clock. Two minutes and fifteen seconds. That's a new record, I think.

I shrug and answer her question. "It sounds like a normal job to me."

"Exactly. Normal is not something Jennifer should aspire to. We all know how Adam ended up." She opens her Marc Jacobs purse. "I am meeting them for dinner tonight."

"Oh."

One more huge sigh. "And I guess I will take one of those horrific cups of coffee."

I ring up her total.

She hands me a well-used credit card. "Good to see you, Maya. Though I do wish you would take better care of yourself. You will never catch a man looking like that."

"Here's your coffee," I say, stuffing my response into the side of one cheek.

She looks me up and down. "I am just trying to help. Surely you know that men prefer women with long hair, Maya. Not a short, out-of-control style like that. And you really should look into doing Pilates classes. It will do wonders for those hips."

"Bye, Mrs. Mitchell," I say, pointedly.

Rolling her eyes, she pops the lid on her coffee. "Good-bye, Maya. Jack."

She exits, leaving only the trace of her expensive musky perfume.

I rub my face, and Jack massages my shoulders. "Sorry, Pattertwig," he says. "She's not a nice woman."

"I don't understand how sweet, wonderful Jen can have a mother like that," I say.

Jack sighs. "Me either."

"Do you think she knows that her mom's going to crash her

date?" I ask through my hands.

Jack winces.

I grab my phone.

"This is Jennifer Mitchell, legal assistant to —"

I hang up on her voice mail. "She's not answering."

Jack is still staring after Mrs. Mitchell. "Just once I want to hear her use a contraction."

"It won't happen. I've spent three days around that woman before, and it never happened."

"Three *days*?" Jack is impressed.

"She came to visit and naturally stayed in our filthy apartment." I grimace, impersonating her. "Last time, she told me I needed to wear higher-quality clothing and lose about fifteen pounds."

Jack rolls his eyes. "Why? So you can look like her? I've met stair rails that have more curves than her."

I smile, hearing his unspoken compliment. "Thanks, Jack."

"How did Jen end up so nice?" Jack mumbles.

"She chalks it up to becoming a Christian freshman year at Cal-Hudson," I tell him. "You should ask Jenny about her testimony sometime — it's a good one."

A UPS deliveryman comes into the store with a dolly and three huge brown boxes. "Hi there," he says to me, holding out the little machine for me to sign. "How's your day going?"

"Fine." I sign my name and squint at the boxes. "Our slow day is over, Jack. Here's inventory."

"Great."

The UPS guy smiles at our enthusiasm — or lack thereof. "Best of luck with that." He slides the boxes off the dolly right behind the counter and leaves, whistling.

"What is all this stuff?" Jack asks, slicing open a box.

"Christmas stuff. Alisha told us last time she came that she was expecting a shipment. What kind of merchandise is it?" I try dialing Jen again. This time I leave a message.

"Hi, Jenny. Call me."

I look over at Jack, who is pulling coffee thermoses emblazoned with *Cool Beans* out of the box.

"These are kind of cool," he says.

"Beans," I finish.

"Funny."

It's six o'clock, and I still haven't gotten ahold of Jen. I've called her seven times, left four voice mails, and texted her three times, but she still hasn't responded. I'm hoping that means she's still at work and dinner got called off.

I slip my phone into my back pocket, lean on the counter, and look around the store. It's nearly empty. A cute redhead and a nice-looking guy are talking quietly on one of the couches by the fireplace. Jack's mopping in the back, and I'm lazily organizing the front counter area.

Mrs. Mitchell is not a nice person. She'll tell Travis to back off and that Jen's waiting for a Kennedy.

I sigh at a huge green mug.

On the one hand, then Travis would be single.

I blink and straighten.

What?

What is this? I'm turning into a psycho!

I hurriedly put the mug away. And just what would happen then? Jen and Travis break up, and he'd come running back to me? He doesn't even recognize me! And even if he did, what did I think would happen? We'd live happily ever after?

I've already thought that once.

By all intents and purposes, it was a "mutual" decision to break up. But really, it was him. He moved to Stanford; we were one year into the whole long-distance thing; and we were both getting frustrated.

"Pattertwig?" Jack breaks into my thoughts, and I startle.

"Yeah?"

"Can you come help me for a second?"

I follow him to the back, and he hands me the mop.

"You mop while I tip the shelves back," he says, grunting as he lifts.

I swoosh the mop around a few times, and he sets the shelves back. "Thanks."

"Welcome."

"You okay?" he asks as I walk back out to the front.

"Fine."

I get home, and neither Jen nor her mother is there. I'm breathing a sigh of relief at that last part but still worried about Jen. Calvin greets me at the door with a happy doggy shake.

It's dark outside and chilly, but I need the endorphins. *Legally Blonde* was right: They do make you happy. "We're going for a quick run," I announce to my little beagle.

"Roo! Roo!" he answers excitedly, lunging for his leash.

I change into workout pants and a T-shirt. As I tie back my hair, I grab a sticky note.

Reasons I Love My Mother:
1. She is motherly.
2. She cares about me as a person and what I like.

3. She never tries to make me be anything but me.

4. She is not necessarily in fashion all the time.

5. She not only uses contractions, she also uses fragments.

Then I send Jen one more text: *Your mom is in town. She's going to try to break up you and Travis. Just a friendly warning. Love you.*

"Ready, Cal?" I ask. I decide his hopping means yes, and we start for the door. I open it and see Mrs. Mitchell standing there getting ready to knock.

"Oh!" I say, startled.

"That is no way to greet a guest," she rebukes.

"Sorry. I just didn't expect to see you," I say. My whole body is shriveling up like one of those month-old apples in the fridge. Which reminds me that I need to clean those out.

"Well, are you going to make me stand outside, or are you inviting me in?" she snaps.

"Uh—"

She steps inside.

"I'm actually on my way out," I say. Calvin is cowering behind my right calf. "We're going on a run."

She stares at me. "Dressed like that?"

I look down. Black stretchy yoga pants, a plain white T-shirt, black hoodie, and running shoes. I'm not sure how this outfit can go wrong.

Apparently it can.

I can feel Calvin shuddering behind me, and I wince. Mrs. Mitchell stares down the little beagle. "What is wrong with your dog? Does he have a nervous-system disorder?"

"I don't think so."

Right then, of course, Calvin gets so panicked under her

glower that he makes a little puddle on the floor.

"Oh my gosh!" Mrs. Mitchell cries, like he just did his business in her lap or something. "What a horrible, disgusting dog! Why do you keep him in this apartment?"

I pick up my trembling puppy and carry him to the kitchen, setting him on the kitchen mat in front of the oven and rubbing his ears. "Shhh," I whisper. "The wicked witch can't hurt you, Toto."

I grab the antibacterial spray from under the sink and a bunch of paper towels. It's been about a year since Calvin made a puddle on the floor. Want to guess when the last time was?

Yup. When Mrs. Mitchell last visited.

"Are you waiting for Jen?" I ask timidly, sopping up the mess and spraying it down with Lysol.

"Is that not obvious? You might offer me something to eat or drink while I wait."

I sigh and straighten. "Did you want something to —"

"Ice water." She cuts me off and sits straight-backed on our squishy, slouch-only sofa. "And something decently nutritious to eat. I never ate this evening, and here it is, ten fifteen at night. My daughter has apparently forgotten every manner I ever taught her and never called to inform me where dinner was. And be sure to properly scrub your hands, young lady, before you touch anything edible in nature." She's scowling deeper than prebenevolent Scrooge but oddly has no wrinkles.

Creepy.

"Let me see what we have." Why couldn't she just get something to eat on her way to the airport?

The airport!

I dump the paper towels in the trash and pop back into the living room. "Didn't your flight leave at nine?" I nearly yell.

"Yes, it did. I never saw Jennifer, so I canceled my ticket." She grimaces at my purse and uses the nail of her index finger to push it farther away from her. "I am staying here until she gets her head on straight. I guess it will take longer than I thought. Do you ever clean?"

"Occasionally."

"You really should hire someone to do that. A clean house is an inviting house."

"I'll get your water." I go back into the kitchen. Calvin isn't straying more than a half step from my leg. Poor little guy. Mrs. Mitchell makes him nervous.

I grab my phone from my jacket pocket and text Jen hurriedly. *She's here at the apartment, and she's not leaving.*

I can't understand why Jen isn't answering.

"How long does it take to get a glass of water?" I hear from the living room.

I look at Calvin, and he whimpers. He's trembling, poor little guy. I can't be here by myself with this woman and my scared little dog. I send one more text, grab a glass, and fill it with water.

"Here," I say, handing her the water.

"My goodness, Maya, you do not have to be rude about it," she says airily, taking the glass. "Your mother did not raise you to respect your elders very well." She takes a tiny sip. "Now I suppose that your having something edible in this apartment is unlikely. . . ."

I sigh and kiss the thought of a nice, relaxing long run goodbye. Since Jen has recently joined the all-natural-food club, we probably have something. "I'll check," I say, going back yet again to the kitchen.

I open the fridge and freezer doors and find one of Jen's

Lean Cuisines. As far as nutritious food, the options are that, a frozen chicken breast, or a wrinkled-up apple. "How about a Lean Cuisine?" I yell.

"Fine. Whatever is nutritious is fine."

I pop it into the microwave and stay in the kitchen. Five minutes later, I pull out her pasta and dump it on a plate.

"Here you go," I say, handing her a fork and the plate.

She doesn't take it from me. "You expect me to eat on the couch?"

I jerk the plate and fork back and set it on the table. "Here you go," I say again, trying to inject some enthusiasm into my voice, but in the meantime sounding like one of those Animaniacs I used to watch on Saturday mornings when I was a kid.

"Oh," she says, settling into a chair. "Finally."

There's a knock at the door right as she starts to eat. I open the door and nearly crush Jack in a hug. "Thank you, thank you!" I whisper-yell.

"No worries," he whispers back, grinning. "Hi there, Mrs. Mitchell."

"Jack. You are here late."

He doesn't lie about his reason; he just doesn't give one. "Yep," he says.

She goes back to eating.

"Where's Jen?" Jack asks me quietly.

I shrug. "I don't know."

"She is not answering her cell phone." Mrs. Mitchell butts into our conversation. "Why you would carry a cell phone and not answer makes no sense to me."

Jack notices my outfit. "Going for a run?"

"Maybe later."

Mrs. Mitchell finishes eating and stands. "Well, which one

of you is going to go get my things?" she asks, pulling a set of keys with a rental company tag from her purse.

"Things?" I echo.

"My suitcase. My vanity case."

She's staying the night. I clench my teeth together so my prayer isn't audible. *Lord, seriously, why?*

Anytime Mrs. Mitchell stays the night, she doesn't just take the sofa bed like my parents do. No, she requires a "real" mattress. So, it's either Jen or I on the pullout in our own home.

If she were Jen's grandma or had some kind of back condition, I could understand the need for a real bed. I'd even support the idea and offer up my own room to her. But she's not Jen's sweet, adorable grandma; she doesn't have any kind of muscular condition; she's in better shape than both Jen and I; and if that isn't enough, she's not getting up and going to work in the morning. It would be a different story if we *offered* her the bed; then I'd be fine with it.

I grab for the keys. "I'll get them," I say, needing some air.

"I'll help," Jack adds, and we both book it outside. Calvin is right on my toes. I pull the door closed behind us and groan.

"Sorry, Nutkin," Jack says sympathetically.

"It's not your fault." I rake a hand through the scattered, tangled, curly mess that is my hair. "It could be worse; she could live in town."

"Good. Look at the bright side."

We walk down the stairs, and I click the keyless-entry button to find her rental. The horn honks on a silver Chrysler.

"If nothing else, she makes me appreciate my mom," Jack notes. "My mom may spend more time in the kitchen than she does doing anything else, but she always took care of us. We always had the best enchiladas and a great bedtime story."

Jack's mom is the best Mexican food chef in Southern California. I think at one point a major restaurant in San Diego was buying tortillas from her.

"I know; I made a list of what I like about my mom after I got home," I tell him, popping the trunk on the Chrysler.

"Maya and her lists," Jack says. "Still making lists of what you're learning during your devotions?"

"Not as much," I say offhandedly. I bite the inside of my lip. I feel guilty, but I just don't have time to read my Bible very often anymore. And when I do, I'm always distracted with this whole Travis thing.

I'll do it tonight, I promise myself.

In the trunk we find a suitcase the size of my washing machine and a cosmetic bag that could hold Calvin, and suddenly it hits me.

"Jack," I say, staring at the suitcase, "who brings a suitcase this big on a trip that is supposed to last five hours?"

Jack purses his lips. "Well, I barely bring a duffel bag for a trip that lasts a week, so I'm a bad person to ask."

I frown at him. "What do you do for clothes?" If he says he just wears the same thing every day . . .

"I bring an extra pair of clothes in my backpack and wash one while I wear the other. It works out well," he explains.

"Oh. Well, anyway, normal people do not carry a suitcase this big with them all the time." I rub my cheek. "Now my only question is, how long is she planning on staying with us?"

A cute little Taurus pulls into Jen's parking spot, and Jen climbs out, smiling. "Hey, Jack! Hi, Maya, what's going on? Did you get a new car, Jack?" She comes over excitedly. "It's nice!"

"Jen," I start.

She sees the suitcase before I can finish my sentence. "Oh.

My. Gosh." Her mouth is open as she stares at the designer leather mini-refrigerator-size box in the trunk.

Jack doesn't say anything, just wraps his arm around her shoulders. She's covering her mouth and leaning into him, eyes still on the suitcase.

"You didn't get my texts," I say quietly.

She starts digging madly through her purse and pulls out her cell phone. "It's off," she moans. "I forgot to turn it back on after my staff meeting this morning." She turns it on, and it makes a way-too-cheerful sound for this somber moment.

"Sorry, Jenny," Jack says, hugging her tighter. Apparently, he's decided his role in all of this is to constantly apologize.

"Six voice mails and fourteen texts," she mumbles. She closes her eyes and starts laughing, but it's humorless.

I exchange a look with Jack. Not sure what to do here.

"I'm sorry, Jen," Jack says again. Even Calvin is whimpering quietly in commiseration.

"This is about Travis, isn't it?" she realizes suddenly. One look at my face and she knows the answer. "I knew it was a mistake to tell her!"

Definitely, I think. "Probably," I say.

"Auuugh!"

"Easy, Jenny." Jack loosens his grip now that she's not leaning on him for support. She starts pacing, shaking.

I move out of her way. Her lips are moving, but no words are coming out. I'm trying to decide if I even want to know what she's saying or if she's praying.

"Amen," she growls. She inhales so hard that her whole body rocks. "Okay. I'm ready."

"Jack, Maya, for goodness' sake, how long does it take to get one suitcase and a vanity case?" Mrs. Mitchell calls from just outside the front door.

Jen's breath whistles past her clenched molars. "Hello, Mother."

"Jennifer? Is that you?"

"Yes."

"Come up here right now, young lady. I need to speak with you."

"Pray. Hard," Jen hisses to me as she stalks over to the stairs.

Jack muscles the suitcase out of the trunk of the car, and I pick up the vanity case. We follow Jen up the stairs and into the apartment. I close the door after Calvin, and we all face her mom.

Jack is a wimp. "Well, I'll be going," he says the second the suitcase touches the floor. He gives Jen another hug.

I just shake my head at him. He winks at me and leaves.

"Jennifer, we need to talk about this new boy you are seeing." Mrs. Mitchell sighs. "He is not good enough for you."

"Mother, I'm twenty-four years old. I'm perfectly capable of finding a guy by myself." Jen's voice is calm, but her hands are clenched together. She slouches into the couch, kicking off her heels.

Oh, good grief. I'm a wimp, too. I quietly signal to Jen that I'm going for a run and grab Calvin's leash. He follows me outside.

I clip the leash on his collar, and we go down the stairs. We start off at a good pace toward the park that Calvin loves. I like it because it's very well-lit at night.

We get back to the apartment thirty minutes later. I'm tired; it's eleven fifteen; and Calvin is dragging his feet up the stairs.

I unlock the front door and step inside. The apartment is

dark and quiet. The sofa bed is pulled out and occupied. I bite back a sigh and quietly go to my room.

After a quick shower, I change into flannel pajama pants and a T-shirt and climb into bed.

Glancing at the clock, I moan. It's eleven thirty. I don't have to work until noon again tomorrow. I look at my Bible and consider.

I'll do it tomorrow before work. I promise.

CHAPTER ELEVEN

I wake up slowly and yawn, looking over at my clock. Eight thirty. I sleepily climb out of bed, nearly tripping on Calvin, who's cuddled up in a little ball right next to my nightstand.

"Hi, baby," I coo.

He sighs and smiles, rolling onto his stomach for a morning rubdown. I oblige, but only because he's cute about it.

I brush my teeth and go into the kitchen, trying to run my fingers through my bedhead. No Jen. No Jen's mom.

I smile.

There's a note on the coffeemaker.

Maya—I took the day off, and I'm taking my mom to the airport. Will be back around eleven. Jenny

"Hooray!" I say to the coffeemaker. I pull out a big mug and pour a cup of steaming dark liquid in celebration.

I have approximately three hours before I need to leave for work. I sip my coffee and consider. Today's Tuesday, so Zach and Kate are coming by tonight. I'm really curious to see if the sweetness continues.

I carry my cup with me to my room to make sure my work clothes are clean and see my Bible.

Now's a good time to do it.

I pick it up and settle onto my bed. I wonder who won the debate between Jen and her mom last night about Travis.

He might be "normal" as far as Mrs. Mitchell is concerned, but Travis is smart. He always has been. When we dated, Dad said that Travis was going to have no problem securing a great job and advancing quickly just because of his intellect.

Apparently Dad was right.

I shake my head slightly. Back to the Bible.

I don't even remember where I was. I open it up to Acts 24, and verse 16 catches my eye. "In view of this, I also do my best to maintain always a blameless conscience both before God and before men."

I stare at it for a few minutes.

I roll my shoulders and clear my throat. I think I was in Philippians actually. I flip the pages and start reading in chapter 4, verse 15.

"You yourselves also know, Philippians, that at the first preaching of the gospel, after I left Macedonia, no church shared with me in the matter of giving and receiving but you alone."

Huh. Interesting.

I close the Bible and sip from my coffee. Maybe *What Not to Wear* is on.

I flick the remote.

Zach and Kate get to Cool Beans at nine thirty, right as I'm handing a large decaf French roast to a man carrying a newspaper.

"Enjoy," I say to him.

"Honey, it's quiet; I'm reading the paper; I have a cup of coffee; and there are no kids around." He gives me a weak smile. "This place is paradise." He settles into a chair by the window.

Zach comes over and sets his hands on the counter. "So this is Cool Beans," he says, looking around.

"Yep," I say.

"Neat." He's still looking around. Kate is quietly perusing the menu.

Okay, so apparently it was the moving that made her all nice.

They're both dressed up like they just got back from a Ralph Lauren show. Kate's wearing a knee-length flowing skirt in a beige color with a dark brown top, and Zach's once again wearing khakis and a sports blazer.

I fidget, pulling the sleeves of my black long-sleeved shirt down over my wrists from where they'd been pushed up to my elbows.

"Hi, Kate," I say.

"Hi, Maya." She smiles politely.

I point to Jack. "Zach, you remember Jack. Kate, this is my friend Jack."

Jack pauses from wiping down the espresso machine. "Hi, guys."

"Nice to meet you," Kate says.

"Okay, Maya, I want a cinnamon café au lait or whatever you said I should get," Zach says.

"Caramel cinnamon mocha," I tell him.

Jack grins. "Ah. The little-utilized Maya Davis special."

"Small, medium, or large?" I ask.

Zach squinches his face. "Mmm. Medium. To-go. Decaf."

"Wimp."

"Maya, it's nine thirty. I have to sleep tonight."

"But you have an hour drive," I point out. "You have to stay awake, right? That stretch gets real boring, real quick. Especially at night."

Zach taps Kate's shoulder. "That's why I married her. It's her job to keep me awake on long road trips."

Jack laughs. "How sentimental of you." He starts on Zach's drink.

Zach grins.

Kate is done reading the menu. "Can I get a small English Dusk tea? Also to-go, please. That's loose leaf, right?"

I nod. "Yeah."

"That's what I want."

I start making her tea. This is Jen's favorite tea, and I haven't talked to her all day, ever since the incident with her mom. She didn't get back home before I left to go throw away my chance at financial freedom someday (i.e., fill up my gas tank).

Jack hands Zach his mocha in a paper cup. "Here you go."

"Thanks."

Kate's tea is done a few minutes of silence later. "And there's the tea," I say. "Drive safely, you two."

"We will." Zach smiles at me. "Nice place, Maya. See you Sunday night at Mom and Dad's."

I barely keep back the sigh. "Okay." No more pajama pants, no more slap-happy game nights. Now I have to dress up to lounge in front of Mom and Dad's fireplace. Actually, not even lounging. Now, we're all sitting straight-backed on the sofas.

Jack rewipes down the espresso machine. "So, how's Jen?" he asks.

"I haven't seen her since you did. After you left, I went on my run."

Jack pauses. "You went on a run at ten thirty at night?"

"Yeah."

He frowns. "By yourself?"

"Well, I had Calvin."

He sets down the rag on the counter. "Maya . . . that's not safe."

"Jack, we live in Hudson."

"So? You don't know everyone who lives here." He sighs and runs his hand through his hair. "Just do me a favor and run before dark, okay? While Calvin is a canine, I don't think he'll be much protection."

I'm trying to take his admonishment for the concern it is rather than getting frustrated. "Okay."

"Or call me or something. I'll go run with you. Or you can take Canis. He's at least sort of intimidating. But good grief, Maya, think first."

"Okay, all right?"

"Good." He picks up the rag again. "You were saying about Jen?"

Appreciating the change of subject, I nod. "She slept on the couch and took her mom to the airport this morning. That's all I know." I look at the clock. "And she's probably out with Travis right now."

Jack frowns. "When you guys dated, was he so monopolizing?"

"Kind of."

"Not a good habit."

I shake my head. "Probably not."

Jack grabs a broom from the back. "Sorry to step on your independent streak earlier, Nutkin." He smiles at me. "I just get worried about you sometimes. Off driving back and forth to San Diego every single weekend, running around town with only little Calvin to protect you." He shrugs. "I just don't want to see you get hurt."

I smile back, letting him know all is forgiven. "It's nice of you to be concerned. Sorry for getting annoyed." Pretty much that means: Thanks, but leave my habits alone.

He starts sweeping. The guy with the newspaper and no kids is our only customer, and it is boring, boring, boring.

I yawn.

"So," Jack says, changing the subject, "Hudson Zoo called me this morning, and they've decided my internship is going to be with the reptiles."

"Oh, Jack, I'm sorry."

"Why? I love snakes! They have one of the rarest snakes in the world at the Hudson Zoo. Did you know that?"

"Um. No."

"It's a Northern Black Racer snake." He's so excited that he's beaming.

"Wow."

"You're not interested, are you?"

"I don't know," I say, pushing my hair behind my ear. "Does it crawl on its stomach?"

He rolls his eyes. "Yes."

"Does it eat mice and stuff?"

"Yes, Nutkin."

"Does it stick out its tongue?"

"Yes." He sighs.

"Wow!" I yell, startling the man with the paper and probably reminding him of home, because he gets up and leaves. "Oops."

Jack starts laughing. "Leave me alone."

I get home at eleven. Jack "dawdled," as my mother would say, during the cleanup, but I couldn't blame him. Now he has to go spend the night with a Zorro-quoting bird.

I walk in the door, greet a sleepy but happy Calvin, and drop my purse on the floor. Jen is half asleep on the sofa, curled up on her side with a blanket and a pillow. There's an episode of *I Love Lucy* on, the sound turned down.

"Hi, Jenny." I plop on the couch beside her feet. "How was your day off?"

She rolls to her back and rubs her eyes. "Hi, Maya. It was good. All I did was watch movies."

She's wearing her nice lounging-around-the-house outfit, which means she wasn't alone. Gray yoga pants and a royal-blue long-sleeved T-shirt. And her hair has been blow-dried today.

"Travis came over?" I ask.

"Yeah. He brought three chick flicks and some chicken soup." She smiles as she stretches. "The soup was disgusting. Travis is not a good cook."

"Guess you'll have to remember that," I say lightly, mostly because I did remember. One time, he attempted to barbecue steaks for us as a romantic anniversary dinner. He accidentally seasoned them with cayenne pepper instead of lemon pepper, and it was so hot I about had to cut my tongue out.

There's a brand-new bouquet of ruby red tulips on the coffee table. "He does know how to buy flowers, though."

"That he does." Jen smiles that same contented smile. Apparently, flowers are more important than culinary skills.

"So, what's going on? We never got to talk last night." I squeeze her sock-wrapped foot. "Are you okay?"

She sighs. "I'm okay. Mom hates Travis." She pauses and frowns. "Except she's never met him, so I guess she hates the *idea* of Travis. She thinks he's beneath me and my family." Jen rolls her eyes. "Like we're so much better than the whole population."

"Well, technically, your mom does look better than the majority of the population." I grin at her, trying to lighten the mood.

Jen covers her face. "Oh, gosh. Let's not even go there."

"Sorry. Anyway."

"Anyway, we had a talk last night." She purses her lips. "She doesn't understand at all. If she doesn't pick out the guy for me, he's not the right one."

"And you think Travis is the right one?" I ask slowly and in a small voice. My heart is hammering against my ribcage, and I sneak a deep breath.

She doesn't answer for a while, staring at the tulips, lightly twisting her bare ring finger. "I don't know."

I clear my throat. "Oh."

"I don't know, Maya. We've only been going out for what? Three weeks?"

"Around there." I nod.

"So much has happened, and I've seen him almost every day. . . ."

I concede that one. "True."

"And he's not like any other guy I've ever met. He's sweet and caring and dotes on me like I'm the most important thing in the world to him." She brushes a hand through her hair. "I mean, look. I had a bad night with my mom, and he came over with movies, dinner, and tulips. What other guy does that?"

I shrug rather than answer.

I have to tell her. I just have to. She's going to kill me for keeping it a secret this long.

"He makes me laugh harder than anyone else on the planet." She stops and looks at me. "Well, maybe not as much as you made me laugh when you got your wisdom teeth out last year."

I throw a pillow at her face. "I was on painkillers!" I yell.

She starts snorting and then giggling just thinking about my drunken behavior. "One minute you couldn't stop laughing about that scene in *While You Were Sleeping* where the paperboy wipes out on his bike—which isn't funny, and we weren't even watching the movie, by the way—and the next second, you were bawling huge tears over Calvin tripping on his ears." She's laughing so hard that she's shaking. "Remember?"

"No, I do not," I say, shaking my head. "I think you're making this whole thing up."

"Oh, gosh! And then Jack came by—"

"You can stop this anytime."

She snorts again. "And you started crying harder because he'd lost one of the buttons on his shirt sleeve—" She gasps, laughing too hard to breathe.

I just sit there, shaking my head. My only memory of having my wisdom teeth out is getting to have milk shakes for every meal and sitting with a bag of frozen peas tied around my head.

My mom came to take care of me, and I'm pretty sure she took a picture of the green pea headband and sent it to all of my extended family in our Christmas card last year. And the reason I found out about it was that my aunt wrote me back to say she's glad I finally found out the usefulness of vegetables.

I clear my throat. "Anyway, back to the topic at hand."

"Okay, okay." She takes a deep breath. "Anyway, he makes me laugh."

"That's a good thing," I say.

"And he's so cute and sweet and gentle and funny and—"

I cut Jen off before it becomes impossible to control my gag reflex. "Jen, maybe we should talk about the things that irritate you about him."

She frowns. "Why?"

"Just to keep my stomach happy."

Jen rolls her eyes. "Fine. Okay, I don't like how he rubs his chin when he's not sure what to do. It's annoying."

I had found that trait endearing, but okay.

"And I don't like how he always has to answer his cell phone because of his work."

"That would get old," I agree with her.

"And sometimes he grinds his teeth." She shakes her head. "That's so bad for your enamel, not to mention your temporomandibular joint."

"Your what?"

"Jaw muscle."

Why she couldn't have said that in the first place . . . I scratch an itch on my arm and nod. "Uh. Okay."

Then she sighs and smiles that same dreamy smile again. "But all of those things aren't really that big. We totally agree on our faith, on our politics, even on how often you should floss."

"Well, that last one is definitely make-or-break in terms of marriage," I say seriously.

"I know, right?" She grins. She goes back to staring at the tulips.

I watch her for a minute and then lean my head back against the sofa, thinking. This is weird — so very, very weird. It doesn't seem like that long ago that Travis and I were having these conversations.

Based on everything Jen says, she and Travis make a perfect couple. So why can't I see it?

I was so convinced I was supposed to marry him. Everything I read in my Bible, everything I felt when I prayed about our future marriage, everything I felt with him seemed so *right*.

"Well, just be careful, Jenny," I say, softly. "Sometimes things change when you least expect them." I stand. "I'm going to bed. Good night." I smile and walk to my room, leaving her staring quizzically after me.

Once I get to my room, I quietly close the door and sit on the edge of my bed, holding my face in my hands.

My Bible and pad of sticky notes are right there on the nightstand. I frown at them but pick up the pad of pink squares.

Reasons I Hate Adulthood:

1. You have to pay for car insurance.

2. You can't just cry and have Mom come fix everything.

3. You have to be responsible.

4. Just because you think God is leading you toward something doesn't mean that He is.

CHAPTER TWELVE

Andrew Townsend walks through the door of Cool Beans at exactly eight thirty the following evening. It's thirty minutes until Bible study starts, and I'm halfway done making a fresh pot of the dark roast for all of the caffeine-lacking twentysome-things about to invade the building.

"Good evening, Sister Maya," he says, slapping his huge hands on the counter.

"And yet another reason to be thankful for my family the way they are," I say sweetly. "You are providing me with lots of new ideas for what to say when we go around the table on Thanksgiving."

He points a finger at me. "You are not very nice. But you do make an excellent cinnamon vanilla latte, and I'll take one of those."

"Decaf?" I ask, even though I know the answer.

"Good grief, no. How would I ever make it through my lesson with the unleaded stuff?"

"I'll be sure to tell the people who do order decaf that not even the pastor can make it through his sermon without the caffeine."

He nods. "It's a fair warning. I'll bring a sign next time."

I start on his latte. "You know, some pastors actually have a time limit that they stick to."

"What's the fun in that? Sometimes I go long; sometimes I go short." He spreads his hands. "Variety is the spice of life, so they say."

I shake my head. "I disagree with 'They.'"

"Oh yeah?"

"Variety is confusing. What if everything changed all the time?"

He raises his eyebrows as he acknowledges the genius in my thinking. "I guess we'd have a lot of people with poor hygiene."

"What?"

"If everything changed all the time. We'd never find bathrooms. Or showers or toothbrushes or—"

"Okay, sufficiently grossed out. You can stop now," I say with a grin. Andrew is one of my all-time favorite people to banter with.

He grins back and plunks a wad of cash on the counter. "And no sunflower mug this time. I need a serious mug that says, 'I'm preaching about serious matters of the heart, soul, and mind.' Got it?"

I nod. "Got it."

"Good. I'm going to start destroying the nice layout you have created."

"Go forth and conquer."

He starts moving the chairs and couches into a U-shape—multiple rows, theater style—leaving the two tables with customers alone. They look at their watches, though, and decide to leave.

"You have a way of scaring off customers," I say, bringing his latte over to him.

"Well, I'm loud and large. Most people don't appreciate those two spiritual gifts," he says, grunting as he carries the couch over to the other chairs. And yes, he *carries* the couch up off the floor by himself. Andrew is a Viking.

"I thought spiritual gifts were like stewardship and hospitality and love and stuff," I say, following him over.

"You'd better go back and read your Bible again, Maya. It says the body of Christ is made up of many parts. I claim the mouth and the bicep."

He sets the sofa down and flexes. I roll my eyes and hand him the coffee mug. He just sighs at the big pink hearts all over the chocolate-colored mug.

"Maya . . ."

"What? You said you were teaching about the heart, soul, and mind. I picked hearts this week. Maybe you can have a mug with brains on it next week." I smile cheekily and leave him to finish with the chairs.

Jack's whistling as he sweeps the kitchen area. "Was that Andrew?" he asks.

"Yep," I say, yawning, preparing for a long night of making fifty different lattes.

"Did you give him another girly cup?"

"I did."

Jack grins. "You're so predictable."

"Well, we just decided that variety can be bad, so I guess that's a good thing." I smile.

Forty-five minutes later, there are thirty-nine people here. Andrew's candid teaching style is apparently becoming popular. Almost everyone ordered our advertised caramel hot chocolate or pumpkin cinnamon latte.

I'm running the cleaning cycle on the espresso machine. Jack and I are trying to clean as much as we can during the opening announcements, so we don't have to stay until late, late, late cleaning.

Travis and Jen are sitting next to each other on the sofa. Jen's cradling her tea, knees pulled to her chest. Travis has one arm around her, the other hand holding his straight black coffee.

Jack finishes wiping down the countertops. "Let's find a seat," he whispers right as Andrew finishes up with the announcements.

"So everyone try to be there Saturday night at the You-Can-Bowl, and we'll bowl our way to a great time."

Liz cracks up. No one else finds the joke that funny, probably because it wasn't.

I catch the almost imperceptible glance from Andrew toward Liz. Apparently, that little love affair hasn't been addressed yet.

I pull my apron over my head and go to the back to hang it up. Jack's grabbing our Bibles.

"Thanks." I smile at him.

"Welcome."

We find seats in the back. I try really hard not to stare at the back of Travis's and Jen's heads. But gosh, it's hard.

"Ladies and gentlemen, we are in a fascinating study of Proverbs." Andrew's voice booms across the little shop. He looks around. "Jack, will you please read chapter 12, verses 17 to 19?"

Jack nods. "Sure. 'He who speaks truth tells what is right, but a false witness, deceit. There is one who speaks rashly like the thrusts of a sword, but the tongue of the wise brings healing. Truthful lips will be established forever, but a lying tongue is only for a moment.'"

"Thank you, Jack." Andrew looks around. "Today we're going

to focus on the word *but*—not like those hind cheeks—and how it is used in every sentence we're looking at here. If you tell the truth, you'll do well, *but* if you don't, you'll have a life of misery, pretty much."

There are chuckles around the room, but I swallow.

Another lesson on being honest?

"Now here's a question," Andrew continues. "Is a half truth or just not disclosing the truth as bad as a lie?"

I squoosh further down in my chair.

"I think so," Liz says. "I think if someone asks you a question flat-out and you avoid answering, it's as bad as a lie. But I think there are also times when it's better not to say anything."

"Nice use of *but*, the word of the day," Andrew says.

She beams.

"And I agree with you. For example"—he morphs into rabbit-trail story mode—"my mother once dyed her hair the exact color of Welch's cranberry juice. Now," he says, over the giggles, "did I tell her that her hair made me thirsty? No. But when she asked me a few days later if I liked it, did I tell her yes? No. I said, 'Mom, your hair is the color of something that should be rich in antioxidants, and dead protein cells just aren't.'"

I can't help but laugh.

"Guys, here's another question. Where do we find real truth?"

"The Bible," everyone sing-songs like we're two-year-olds in Sunday school class.

"Right," Andrew nods. Now he's in charismatic preacher mode. "If you're not in the Word, breathing the Word, eating the Word, singing the Word, you will not be able to live according to the Word!"

I'm smiling but my stomach is pinching up in conviction.

Okay, God, I get it. I'll tell the truth about Travis, and I'll do my devotions.

Bible study is over, and Cool Beans is empty by 10:50 p.m. Andrew's muscling the couches and chairs back into place, and Jack's mopping the back area. I grab Hulk the Vacuum Cleaner and drag it out to the front.

"Oh, great. It's the eardrum buster," Andrew says, spying the vacuum.

"Sorry."

"Stop apologizing, Maya."

I set the vacuum down, plug it into the wall, pop the handle back, then stop right before I flick the on switch. "Andrew," I say, "I've got a question."

"Go for it," he says, sliding a chair under a table and turning to focus on me.

"Sometimes—not always, understand, but sometimes—I can do really well at having a daily devotional. But then other times, I have a really hard time focusing on what I'm reading," I stutter.

"Okay. You're human. And?"

"And how do I focus when it's hard to, I guess?"

Andrew points to the couch, and I push the Hulk's handle back into the locked position. I plop down on one end, and he takes the other end.

"Maya, focusing isn't as much about what's going on out here in our peripherals as what's going on in here in our heads," he says. "It's the same no matter what you're doing. I've seen people who can read with such intensity that they don't look up when there's a water-pipe explosion next door, but I've also seen people who can read only two words before they remember something they forgot to do."

I nod, not really getting where he's going with all this.

"It's the whole Mary and Martha thing, Maya," he continues. "If you're focused on what you need to get done that day or on something that's bothering you, you're not going to get anything out of your Bible reading. But if you focus on the words in front of you and pray for the ability to see beyond the page into how the words can make a difference in your life, you'll be able to get a lot out of it." He stops. "Make sense?"

"Um. Kind of."

"Try that tonight and let me know how it goes, okay?"

"Okay."

I go back to the Hulk and turn it on. The little pots with fresh-cut flowers on the tables are rattling as I drag the vacuum back and forth.

There's a note on my bedroom door when I get home to our dark apartment.

Maya—I am going to bed early to prepare for Calvin's 2:24 a.m. wake-up call. Please try to quiet him before I get up this time. Good night. —Jenny

"Surly," I say to Calvin, who's batting his tail on my comforter in greeting as opposed to getting up in a real nice-to-see-you effort. "It's nice to see you, too."

I change into a pair of sweatpants and a long-sleeved T-shirt. Grabbing my Bible, I plop on the bed.

"Okay, focus, focus," I say. Calvin noses my knee.

I open up to John 15. "These things I have spoken to you so that My joy may be in you."

Calvin sighs, and I look over at him. "What's wrong, baby?"

He wags his tail, so I guess he just wanted some attention. Well, my philosophy is: You have to show affection to gain affection. At least it is if you're a dog.

"In a minute," I tell him, going back to the Bible.

"Roo!"

"Hush."

He buries his nose in his paws and huffs his breath out.

I look back at the passage in John, but the words are not connecting with my brain. *Focus.*

I read a few more words. "And that your joy may be made full. This is My commandment, that you love one another, just as I have loved you."

Love one another.

Based on our conversation last night, I think Jen thinks she's falling in love with Travis. She's infatuated at least.

"Well, it's not like it's hard to fall into infatuation," I tell Calvin.

He squints at me.

"Well, it's not. Travis is a great guy. He's sweet; he's considerate; and he's definitely good-looking."

Calvin shares my sentiments. "Roo!"

I thoughtfully rub his ears. "I just wish I knew how to tell her, Cal. I mean, she should know about the past. I should tell her."

Calvin wiggles closer to my hand.

I give him a good rubdown this time. "How about you stay quiet tonight, huh? No more Wednesday-night nightmares, okay?"

He licks my hand in apology, as if to say, *I don't mean to.*

"I know."

I look at him and rub his ears one last time before I rake my hand through my hair. "How about ice cream?"

"Roo! Roo!"

"Come on, then."

I pad out to the kitchen and open the freezer. Calvin hops along behind me happily.

"Vanilla or mint chocolate-chip?"

Calvin plops on his rear end in front of me and cocks his head.

"You're right. No contest." I pull out the artificially colored green ice cream and find a bowl. When you think about it, mint chocolate-chip ice cream is kind of gross. They take perfectly good all-natural ice cream and inject it with this green dye just so you feel like you're getting a genuine mint taste.

I know the mint plant is green, but is the extract? And if it isn't, who decided that everything minty in nature should be green? The people who make Andes mints?

Wait a second. I look closer. A spoonful has been stolen from this ice cream! I whip my head around, looking for the ice-cream thief. Jen wouldn't have taken it — she's head over heels into this whole natural thing. Who else has had access to my freezer?

Mrs. Mitchell!

I shake my head. Well, well.

I scoop a hefty bowl, squirt some chocolate syrup on top, and grab a spoon. We head back to my room, and I plop on the bed and look at my Bible.

Lord, I'm sorry. I can't focus right now.

I spoon the ice cream into my mouth and reach for a sticky note.

Reasons I Cannot Focus:

1. Jen and Travis. Their names even sound good together.

2. I'm still freaked out by Mrs. Mitchell.

2½. Mrs. Mitchell stole a scoop of ice cream.
Nutritious food, my eye.
3. Jen is falling in love with Travis.
4. Travis is probably falling for Jen.

"It's a good thing, right?" I ask Calvin, who is salivating over my ice cream. I look at him for a minute and sigh. "What do you know? You're a beagle."

I just feel so . . . I don't even know the words. Guilty? Confused? Trapped in this fake ignorance of Travis?

And the truth will make you free.

"And hurt a bunch of people," I remind whatever part of my brain brought back that verse. "So, it's not all fun and games."

Jack keeps telling me just to sit Jen down and tell her. "Rip off the Band-Aid," he said earlier today. "Tell her you've wanted her to know for a while, but it just seemed awkward, and then you didn't know what to do."

I think I know my roommate better than that. She'll definitely get her feelings hurt. And then she'll do the whole quietly-wander-about-the-house routine while I beg for forgiveness anytime she comes within a three-foot radius. It happened when I accidentally ate the pie she made the first time her mom visited us.

I didn't know the pie was for her mom. There was not a note or anything on it. Just a freshly baked blueberry pie on the counter. Naturally, I assumed it was for us.

And this—this is quite a bit bigger than a pie.

Hi, Jen, did I mention that Travis and I looked at engagement rings, too? No? Oh, sorry, I guess I skipped over that part.

Yeah. I dip another spoonful of mint and chocolate and green dye #76. The best thing to do is to keep my mouth shut.

Jen doesn't know; Travis doesn't recognize me; and Jack will stay quiet because he believes it's my job to tell her.

It will all be better if I clam it up tight.

And the truth will—

"Wonder what's on the Style Network?" I ask Calvin, cutting off the voice and picking up the remote.

The meadow is green and frosted with dew, looking like a painting I saw not too long ago in a home-and-garden magazine. Jen looks around, a huge, thick, mattresslike blanket in her arms.

"Here looks good," she says to me, throwing the blanket on the grass. I sit down, hefting a cooler onto the blanket with me.

"Cushy," I say. The blanket is probably thicker than my sofa.

"Isn't it? What's for lunch?"

I open up the cooler. "Well, I brought a bunch of good things. . . ." I look inside and gasp.

Ten miniature frogs are hopping around inside the cooler.

"What?" Jen asks innocently.

"Oh. Nothing, nothing," I say, not wanting to alarm her. I look over her shoulder. "Oh, what a pretty forest," I say, unenthusiastically. The second she turns to look, I dump the cooler out.

"Yeah, it's great. Seriously, what are we eating? I'm starved."

I open the cooler, looking for something edible. There's a piece of lettuce, a cucumber, two Andes mints, and a bottle. I lift out the bottle.

"Green dye?" Jen reads the label. "Why are you bringing green dye on a picnic?"

I force a laugh. "Well, funny story." I put the bottle down, but the lid pops off and the dye splashes all over my face.

Jen screams, "Oh, no!"

I yelp, "Oh, gosh!"

"Your face is green!" Jen's voice started slowing down. "Your face is green! Yoooouurr faaace is greeeen. . . ."

"Roo!"

I jolt awake, nearly falling off the bed again but catching myself just as I'm sliding off the side. "Calvin!" I hiss.

He quiets momentarily.

"Hush!"

He jumps up on the foot of the bed and curls into a ball.

Falling back, I drift back to sleep.

My phone rings on Thursday right as I'm leaving for Cool Beans for my two o'clock shift. I glance at the caller ID.

"Hi, Mom."

"Hi, Maya. How's it going?"

I nod to my car as I unlock it. "Pretty good. You?"

"Good. Listen, I have a question."

"I figured." Mom never calls without a reason.

"What?"

"Nothing."

She sighs. "Anyway, do you remember the black sweater that I wore to your great-aunt's funeral?"

I climb in the car and squint out the windshield, thinking. "Um. No."

"It's long-sleeved, and I wore it with that black-and-white skirt?"

"Did I go to Aunt Josephine's funeral?"

Mom thinks for a minute. "Oh, wait. I guess you didn't."

"Then, no. I don't remember the top. What about it?"

"Well, now you're not going to be able to help me," Mom groans.

I back out of the driveway, tucking the phone between my shoulder and my ear. "Help you with what?"

"A co-worker of your dad's is having a retirement party, and I was wondering if that sweater was too somber to wear to it."

I can't help the smile. Sometimes, it's really obvious that Mom misses having a girl around the house.

"What did Dad say about it?"

She tsks her tongue. "Oh, you know Dad. He couldn't care less what I wear."

I grin. "True."

She sighs. "Okay, well, I guess I'll just have to figure it out."

I start driving toward Cool Beans and smile lightly. "Hey, Mom?"

"Yes, sweetie?"

"I miss you, too."

CHAPTER THIRTEEN

It's Sunday, and I'm walking out of church after listening to Andrew talk about something in James, I think.

Jack is right next to me. "So, what time are you going to your parents?" he asks.

"I'll probably leave around four."

"Okay. What are you doing until then?"

We get to my car, and I toss my purse on the passenger seat. "I don't know. Maybe watch a movie or something." I look up at the clear sky. The day is sunshiny, but it's cooler. Plus, Sundays are my favorite days just to chill in front of a good movie or a good book.

Jack nods. He squints as he looks back at the church. He looks nice today—straight-cut dark jeans, a white polo shirt, hair slicked into a sticky-up preppy style.

He starts biting his lip, and I frown.

"What?"

He nods toward the church. "Look."

Tim Watterby is standing there talking to a blond girl I've never seen before. Tim is probably the cutest guy I've ever met, but he's so darn self-conscious. He can barely say hello to a girl without either (a) bursting into a spontaneous retelling of his entire childhood in a very loud, uncontrolled voice or (b) getting sick and running for the bathroom.

It appears that this is an example of option *a*.

The blond looks interested at first, but after ninety seconds of anyone's mouth moving like that, I'd assume you'd get real tired, real fast.

"Poor guy," I say.

"He needs to relax." Jack shakes his head. "Some people just can't talk to girls."

"Well, girls are pretty scary." I roll my eyes. "I just don't get it."

Jack looks at me. "Get what?"

"Why guys are so intimidated by girls."

Jack laughs. "You're kidding, right?"

"No."

"Pattertwig, girls are way intimidating."

"Not me," I say. "I'm not intimidating."

"Sure you are," he disagrees.

"Jack, I'm five foot two, and my idea of self-defense is Tae Bo," I say, making a fist with my hands. "That's laughable, not intimidating."

He rolls his eyes. "Not in that way. . . . It's more like . . ." He moves his hands around, searching for the right word in the air. "I don't even know how to say it."

I watch Tim for a minute and then look at Jack, who is back to watching Tim. "I have eaten an entire bag of Cheetos in one sitting. Is that intimidating?"

"Novice. That's all I've got to say. Novice."

I purse my lips. The blond girl waits for Tim to breathe, then interjects a hasty good-bye.

Poor Tim.

Jack sighs for him.

"I can score six holes-in-one on Harvey's Miniature Golf course," I say.

"Doubtful. I'd have to see it to believe it."

"I can tell what color M&M it is with my eyes closed," I try again.

Jack nods. "Okay, okay! You're intimidating. Happy?" I grin at him. He laughs again and slings an arm over my shoulders. "So, you need to kill a few hours? Let's go get lunch and then go golfing. I need to see this putter in action." He fakes a golf swing.

"You'll get killed. Are you sure your ego can handle the humiliation?"

Jack pats his chest. "Nutkin, my ego has handled more humiliation than the average soul and emerged even stronger because of it."

I roll my eyes. "Whatever. I'll see you there, loser."

After Jack and I finish lunch, we head for the golf course. Jack is right behind me the whole way. I can't help the grin. My dad is the king of miniature golf. He had us on those fake lawns as soon as we were old enough to stand by ourselves. I hit my first hole-in-one at the age of three.

Jack doesn't stand a chance.

"Okay," I say, fifteen minutes later, golf club and neon pink ball in hand. "We'll play by who gets the most holes-in-one. Deal?"

"You're going down, Davis. It's a scientific fact that men are more suited toward golf than women." He tosses his blue ball up in the air and catches it.

"Words aren't tasty, Jackie. Don't make me make you eat them," I say. "Hole one!"

I march over to the first hole. There's a big elephant with his trunk blocking half the drive. The hole is straight behind him.

"Ah, the ever-popular *Elephantidae*," Zookeeper Jack says. "Ladies first."

I plop my ball on the green, squint at the path, and tap it lightly.

"Too soft," Jack says right away.

The ball bounces against the trunk, hits the edging on the green, rounds around the elephant, and falls gently into the hole.

I clear my throat. "I believe that counts as one."

Jack scratches his head. "I might have misspoken earlier. See, when I said golf was for men, I meant the kind without a large Asian mammal between me and par."

"Too late, Jack. Hit the ball."

He hits it too hard. The ball careens into the trunk, whacks against the edging, and does a clean hop over the opposite side's edging and starts rolling down the hill to the river running through the whole course.

"Dang it!" Jack takes off after the ball.

I grin.

By hole number six, I'm winning four to one. Jack saunters over to the zoo animal of choice for this hole, a giant mom giraffe and her two babies.

"And here we have a *Giraffa camelopardalis*," Jack says, patting the mom's side. "In Middle English times, it was called a 'camelopard.'"

I laugh. "You need to know all this why?"

"Because when I'm the director of the San Diego Zoo, some little kid is going to ask me why the giraffe has spots like a leopard and a face only a mother could love." He grins.

"And your answer will be?"

"Because God made them like that. Why else?"

I nod slowly. "And it has taken how many years of school for you to learn that? Couldn't you have just read Genesis?"

"Enough, Nutkin. You're just jealous that you don't get to work with such amazing mammals every day. Try to hide your envy of me."

I laugh. "Whatever happened with Polly?"

"She's still on my porch, still quoting *The Mask of Zorro*. Only now, it's all the bad lines."

"Well, she is on your porch. I'd be upset if you left me on your porch."

Jack grins at me. "I'll keep that in mind. I don't think I'd have as hard a time getting rid of you. You're cuter than Polly."

"Aw, I think that was a compliment!" I coo. I line up my putt and gently strike the ball. It rolls right between the two unrealistic giraffe babies and drops into the hole. "Yet another sinker," I say.

"You're cheating."

"Am not. You cannot cheat at miniature golf."

"Can too. You could drop it in."

I point at my club. "Then I am obviously not cheating."

"Maybe my golf ball is dented." He starts inspecting it, turning it in the sun.

"Come on, you big whiner, hit the ball."

He sets the blue ball on the green and putts it too softly. It stops rolling halfway to the hole.

"I believe that's five to one," I say. We start walking to the next hole.

"So Zach and Kate will be at dinner tonight?" he asks.

"Yeah."

"Don't sound too excited."

"I'm trying, Jack, I really am. I do love my brother. They just make normal everyday conversation so much harder."

"Like how?"

"Like, I don't know how to explain it." I set the pink ball down. "It's like everything just gets awkward and stilted. I want to say it's because we're still not used to Kate being there, but conversation with Zach has always been a little hard. He's a super smart doctor, and I'm a barista." I shrug. "Not that Mom and Dad care, but I do."

Jack smiles sympathetically. "Not like this helps too much, but I like you as a barista."

I tap the ball for another hole-in-one. "Thanks, Jack."

"I hate you as a golf player, but I like you as a barista."

I laugh.

At three forty-five, I turn in my club to the man in the stripy suit and grin at Jack. "Thanks for the afternoon. That was fun." In all, I got ten holes-in-one. Jack got three.

It's a new record—for both of us, I think.

"I'm glad you had a good time." He rolls his eyes. "I'd say the same, but I think I need to go home and soak my self-esteem now."

I smirk. "Told you." I look at my phone and see the time. I still have to change clothes and pick up Calvin, plus the hour drive. "Well, I should get going. I'll see you at work tomorrow. We're opening this week, right?"

"You got it."

"Okay. Bye, Jack." I smile and wave, starting toward my car.

He has a sad expression on his face as he waves. "See you, Maya." He heads to his car.

Well, in all honesty, I did warn him I'd beat the snot out of him, so I'm not too concerned about the forlorn look on his face. It just makes me smile more as I drive home to pick up Calvin.

I get to Mom and Dad's a little after five. Dad is out front, watering his favorite tree.

I park in front of the house and wave. "Hi, Dad!"

"Leave the car running, sweetheart."

I do as he says, half-annoyed because I'm twenty-four but half-smiling because Dad equates my car being in good shape with him still taking care of me. I guess it's a father-being-pro-tective-of-his-little-girl type of thing. But all of this protective-ness just means I have no idea how to do anything on my car because Dad always does it. What if I stall out in the middle of a desert someday? Never mind why I'm in a desert, but I'd be stuck there.

Zach and Kate's Hummer is in the driveway already. I hop out, popping the hood. Calvin hurries out after me, running for my dad.

"Hi, Calvin!" He rubs the dog's ears. "Hi, sweetie," he says to me. "How's it running?" He lifts the hood and looks at the Jeep's innards.

"Fine. Seems to be running just fine."

He swipes his finger on some post-rain sludge. "Kind of dirty down here, Maya."

"Well, it's been raining," I say defensively.

"Hmm." He leans further under the hood, his head and

shoulders disappearing. I stand there for a minute. "You can go on in. Tell your mom I'll just be looking at the Jeep for a few minutes," he says.

"Okay."

Calvin opts to stay with Dad, and I walk into the house. I immediately smell a pot roast, and I hear Mom talking. I find her, Zach, and Kate all in the living room. There's no fire going in the huge fireplace, and Mom's not wearing sweatpants. Zach's got on khakis and a button-up, and Kate's wearing a skirt.

I guess we're not lounging in front of the fireplace playing Cranium tonight. I tuck away the disappointment. Most Sunday nights I drive home still giggling over Dad acting out something stupid.

"Hey, guys," I say.

"Hi, sweetheart," Mom says, giving me a hug. "How was the drive?"

"Uneventful."

"That's good to hear," she says. She smoothes my curls away from my cheek.

"Hi, Zach. Hey, Kate."

"Hi," they say together.

Mom looks at me. "We were just talking about Zach's new position at the children's hospital."

"You like it?" I ask.

"I love it. My supervisor is very helpful, and the cases are challenging. I've got a couple of surgical procedures already lined up for next week."

I nod. "Cool. Kate, did you find a job?" Kate has been applying all over San Diego for any lawyer openings.

She starts nodding. "I think so. I have a second interview tomorrow morning at eight."

"Nice."

"Mm-hmm."

I look at Mom, who is still playing with my hair. "Hi, Mom," I say, relaxing into her touch.

"What did you do today, Maya?" she asks.

"I went to church, and then Jack and I went miniature golfing."

"Fun."

"Yeah."

The conversation lapses, and I hold back a sigh. It might be a long evening. My back pocket buzzes, and I pull out my cell phone.

It's a text message from Jen. *I'm going out with Travis tonight, so I might be home later. Just didn't want you to panic.* ☺

Funny.

I put my cell phone back. We've moved on to discussing gas prices—the go-to topic if there's nothing else to talk about. It's probably because no one likes them, so everyone can agree.

Mom pulls on a pair of mitts and opens the oven to a steaming roast surrounded by potatoes and carrots.

"Mmmm," I sigh. "This is why I come home every week."

"Thanks. I miss you, too." Mom smirks.

"And for the wonderful company," I quickly add.

"Too late." Mom slides the roast onto a pot holder on the countertop. "But I'm glad you like the cooking."

"Definitely beats instant dinners."

Zach shakes his head. "Do you know the sodium content in those?"

"Probably high." I snag a steaming carrot. "Good thing I'm still so young and fit," I say, batting my eyelashes.

"Maya." Zach puts on his doctor voice.

"Uh-oh," I sigh.

Mom grins at me.

"A diet high in sodium is the number one cause of high blood pressure, which leads to a whole bucketful of other health issues."

"Thank you, Dr. Davis," I say.

Mom saves me. "Maya, go call your father for dinner."

"Okay." I head for the garage and find Dad wiping off his hands with an oil-stained rag. "Dad, dinner's ready."

"Thanks, Maya. I just finished changing your Jeep's oil, so you should be set for a few months."

"Thanks, Dad!" I smile. "I was planning on going by Jiffy Lube later. . . ."

He shakes his head. "Those guys just don't do as good of a job."

I grin.

He finishes on his hands and wraps an arm around my shoulders. "Things are going okay?"

I shrug. "Yeah."

He nods. "Good. I know I'm not the most attentive, but how are you doing with Zach back in town?"

I give him a small smile. "You're observant."

He squeezes my shoulders. "Well, I did watch you two grow up together."

"That you did."

"And I just want you to know that even though he's back in town, we'll try our best to keep Sunday nights the way they were."

I wrap my arm around his waist. "So, can we play Cranium tonight?"

He laughs. "Think it's time Kate saw the real Davis family?"

"I think she can handle it. Besides, she's married now. There's no turning back."

He walks inside with me. "Sounds good to me then."

I get home at ten thirty. I park in front of the apartment complex, grab my purse, and nudge a sleeping Calvin. "Wake up, bud. We're home."

He sleepily follows me out of the car and up the stairs. Right as I get to the top of our stairs, Jen's car pulls into her spot. I wave and leave the door open for her.

She walks in as I dump my purse on the kitchen table and turn on the lights.

"Hi, Maya." She smiles. She takes off her long overcoat and hangs it in the closet. She's wearing a cranberry lacy dress and gold heels. Her hair is falling over her shoulders in beautiful curls.

"Dang, girl," I say, nodding in appreciation. "You are dressed to kill."

She curtsies. "Why, thank you." She frowns at my jeans and navy blue sweater that I still have on from church. "I thought you went to your parents?"

"I did."

"Dressed like that?"

"Zach and Kate are in town now."

"Oh," she says in understanding. "Got it."

"How was your date?"

She sighs. "Amazing."

"That bad, huh?"

"Maya, he's so wonderful. He's charming and funny and handsome and generous. He's the best thing that's ever happened to me."

I force a smile and sit on the couch, preparing for another Travis dish. I have to get up in about seven hours to open at Cool Beans, so my day tomorrow is looking less and less cheerful.

Jen plops on the opposite end of the couch. "But we've already gone over this before," she says, surprising me. "What did you do today?"

"Well, after church, I went golfing with Jack and then —"

"Wait a second," she interrupts, waving her hands. "You went *golfing*? With Jack?" A very annoying smile spreads across her face. "Oh."

"Okay, first off, it was miniature golf, and I kicked the daylights out of him; I won so bad. And second, what's the big deal? Jack's one of my best friends."

"Nothing, nothing. No big deal," she sing-songs.

I sigh and rub my cheek. Apparently, we are still in the "Why Can't Everyone Be as Happy as Us?" stage but at a much higher level. I'd rather be set up with another no-personality package than have Jen start trying to match me up with Jack.

Match me up with Jack? I bite back a laugh. Even the thought is ridiculous. He's my best friend and one of the greatest guys I know.

"Jenny," I say in a barely disguised friendly warning. "Don't even go there."

"Why not? Jack's fun and kind and already understands all of your weird quirks."

"Weird quirks? What weird quirks? I don't have any quirks."

Jen rolls her eyes. "Please, Maya. What about getting a bowl of ice cream at one fifteen in the morning? Or writing every single thing possible down on a sticky note that you'll probably never read again because there's a layer of notes as thick as my hand all over your desk?"

"Those aren't weird."

"We haven't even gotten to your dog. He howls every single Wednesday night; he does Pilates, for goodness' sake." She shakes her head. "See, Jack knows these things, and he still likes you!"

I hold up both hands. "Okay, stop. I love Jack. But I don't love him like *that*. At all. Got it? He's a terrific person, and I'm sure that God has someone amazingly special picked out for him. But it's not me." I sigh. "I want to feel something like you feel with Travis. Jack is one of my favorite people, but I don't feel all squishy inside like I"—I cough—"like *you* do with Travis."

"Well, if that's how you feel."

"It is."

"Then I'll leave you alone. But Maya," she says, leaning closer, "think about everything that Jack means to you. You tell him everything. Just don't take it for granted."

"I don't." Suddenly I have the worst craving for ice cream. I get up and head for the freezer. "I just don't think it's anything more than friendship." I grab the new container of caramel-fudge ice cream and start shoveling it into a bowl.

Jen watches me in silence from the couch. "I didn't mean to upset you."

"I'm not upset." I grab the chocolate syrup.

"Yes, you are."

"Jenny, I'm not."

She sighs. "Maya, what's wrong? For the last month you've been sulking around all depressed. You hardly smile half as much as you used to. It's like you're . . ." She looks away.

"Like I'm what?"

"Like you're not telling me something. What's wrong?"

I nearly wince as she nails the truth.

"I know you're not dealing with Zach moving back very

well, and you never talk to me about it. Is that it?"

I shrug.

She rubs her hands through her hair. "I know I've been preoccupied with Travis, and I'm sorry. I haven't been a good friend."

The guilt is coating my throat so thick I can barely muscle the ice cream down. I sit back down on the couch and shake my head. "Don't be sorry. You're a great friend."

She scoots closer to me. "What's going on? I watched you this morning at church. You barely heard two words Andrew said."

"I heard more than two words," I say defensively.

"Yeah? What did he teach on?"

"James."

"What in James?"

I look at her. "So I was a little distracted."

"Maya, I recognize that you and Zach have this whole sibling rivalry going on, but his moving back cannot be the end of your walk with God. I mean, have you ever thought maybe that's why you're not happy?"

Irritated, I lick my spoon. What gives Jen the authority to tell me what's wrong with my life? Everything was just fine before she had to go and start dating Travis. Even though I barely see him, I still have to hear her dish about him all the time and picture him falling in love with her blond adorable self.

Not that I blame Travis entirely. Jen is an amazing, wonderful person. She's funny; she's smart; and she's head over heels in love with God. She's beautiful.

A far cry from weird, quirky me, right? Me, who can barely make it through a day without my bowl of frozen creamy sugar. Me, who spent how many years trying to be the perfect girl for

Travis Clayton, only to find out right after Christmas five years ago that not only was I *not* the perfect girl, but no matter what I did, I could *never* be her. Me, who had finally, *finally* moved on . . . And then God had to go and make Travis fall in love with my very own perfect roommate.

I freeze, spoon halfway in my mouth.

Oh, God. She's right.

Not about Zach, obviously, but about the end of my walk with God. I'm so angry and I never even really confessed to it . . . until just now.

Seriously, God, why?

I was head over heels in love with Travis. When we broke up, I thought it would be okay. He was at Stanford; I was in Hudson. We'd never have to see each other again. You would think that an all-loving God would be sensitive to this and not allow him to start dating Jen.

Jen pats my leg. "Just think about it, Maya. You've got an early morning, so I won't keep you up. Good night. I love you." She leans over to give me a hug. I smell her flowery perfume.

"Night. Love you, too."

She goes into her bedroom and shuts the door. Calvin is dead asleep next to the love seat. The apartment is quiet. The only light is the one over the kitchen table.

I sit there quietly for a long time.

CHAPTER FOURTEEN

Monday morning does not start well.

It's another rainy, overcast day. I ended up getting about four hours of sleep because I couldn't fall asleep for a while.

I block a yawn and push through the door of Cool Beans. The lights are already on, and Jack's whistling by the coffee grinder.

I pull off my hood and wince at the frizzy curls that are exploding out of my head.

"Good morning, Pattertwig." Jack smiles from behind the counter. "You look a little tired."

"Mmm." I sit on one of the bar stools and lay my forehead on my arms. "I didn't sleep very well."

He slides a mocha across the counter. "Here. Drink up."

I take it and hold it between both hands. He turns and keeps working on the coffee, still whistling. I think it's a Chris Tomlin song.

"Thanks," I say, sipping. The mocha is the perfect blend of espresso, smooth chocolate, and cream. He even added a touch of cinnamon. "This is great."

"Well, I am a professional." He grins at me. "Why didn't you sleep well?"

"I don't know." I rub my face. Yet another lie. I sigh. "Okay, I do know."

He gives me an understanding look. "You don't have to tell me, Nutkin."

"It's this whole thing with Travis and Jen. I feel so guilty that I can't even think about anything else." I rub my forehead.

He finishes with the coffee and turns to look at me. "Maya," he says, one of his rare uses of my name, "this is probably too personal, but . . ." He rubs the back of his neck.

"What?"

"Well, when was the last time you had a good long talk with God about it?" He winces. "That's really personal. Don't answer that."

I smile. "You're one of my best friends. You're allowed to ask." I take another sip of my mocha and stand, going over to toss my purse and coat in the cabinet and get my apron. I'm stalling, trying to figure out how to answer his question.

On the one hand, I just got mad at God last night about all this. On the other hand, I haven't been able to have a good devotion since any of this happened.

Andrew always says that a good devotional time is not God's responsibility, it's ours.

"So, did you recover from the miniature-golf embarrassment?" I ask Jack, pulling on my apron and changing the subject for a few minutes.

He looks at me as I come back to the front and sticks out his tongue. "There was no recovery period needed, Nutkin. You got lucky."

"Right." I roll my eyes. "You got creamed."

He just sighs. "You know, I thought you were joking about the hole-in-one thing."

"Well, I wasn't. My dad is a golf nut." I smile at him, kneel on the floor, and start checking the inventory in the small fridge out front. Alisha will be by sometime today or tomorrow for the list, so it's best to have a head start on that for her.

He finishes with the dark roast and moves on to grinding the medium roast, our house blend. If I weren't such a fan of dark coffee, I'd love this blend. It's super smooth and has these subtle nutty overtones. It's a great dessert coffee.

"Hey, Jack?"

"Hey, Pattertwig."

"Have you ever had to tell someone the truth after a long time of keeping it from them?" I ask slowly.

He gives me a weird look. "I'm sure I have."

"Did they take it okay?"

"You mean, do I think Jen will take it okay?" He smiles gently. "Just tell her, Nutkin. You're going crazy."

"I just don't want to hurt her."

"I know. But hasn't it been worse with her not knowing?"

"Well. Kind of."

He raises his eyebrows. "Kind of? Please tell me you're kidding."

"Well, yeah, it's been harder for me, but it's been easier for her. You know Jen. If she knew I had dated Travis, she never would have kept going out with him." I shrug, checking the expiration date on the milk.

"Lame excuse."

I look up at him.

"Nutkin, if Jen liked Travis so much and had known you'd dated, don't you think she would have just cleared it with you and moved on?"

"Well . . ."

"I think you're just scared to tell her now." He turns the grinder on. "Why are you so scared anyway?" he asks over the chomping noise.

I look through the heavy-whipping-cream containers, checking dates.

I tried for four years to be the most perfect girl out there for Travis. Then I found out, as much as I had tried, his ideas apparently changed, and I wasn't the perfect girl anymore.

I pick up an expired cream container and straighten up.

I guess Jack notices I didn't answer his last question because he suddenly grins at me. "Oh, did I tell you the good news?"

"Finally heard back from your application to be a backup singer for the Temptations, huh?"

He grins wider, recognizing the reference to his secret wish in the second grade. "No," he says. "Polly found a new home."

"Aww, all by herself?"

He ignores me. "A guy called yesterday and wanted to give Polly to his wife as an anniversary present." He sighs. "I'm just praying it won't be the last anniversary present he gives her."

"Jack!"

"What? She's a nocturnal parrot, Pattertwig. *Nocturnal.* As in, not a whole lot of romance is going to be happening after dark. I'm thinking this doesn't make for a happy marriage."

I laugh for the first time that day. "Did you tell the man that?"

"Yeah. Well, not the part about ruining marital bliss. Just the part about her talking through the whole night. He thought it sounded endearing."

"Endearing?" I wrinkle my nose. "Did he actually say that?"

"He did."

"I haven't heard that word since the last time I watched

Anne of Green Gables."

Jack shrugs. "Maybe he's a fan of Anne."

"Maybe." I dig through our five-pound bags of coffee, making notations for each blend we have. "Is it time to turn over the sign?"

Jack looks at the clock. "Yup."

"I'll do it." I set my notepad down on the counter and walk over to the windows. I raise the shades and flip over the Open sign. I stare out the windows for a second. It's a "blustery" day, as Winnie the Pooh would say.

Jack's looking out the windows, too. "Lots of lattes today," he mumbles.

"We've been having a major cold spell." I smile. "Maybe we'll have snow this year!"

Snow in Hudson is about as likely as finding water in an unopened Coke can.

"Maybe," Jack says, kindly not destroying my pipe dream.

Our first customer comes in a couple of minutes before seven as I step behind the counter. "Good morning," I call to the nice-looking lady dressed in a black business suit.

"Good morning," she says. "Can I get a medium cinnamon soy latte? To-go, please."

I ring up her total, and Jack starts making it. "And let the day begin."

I look at our whiteboard as I pull my apron off at two o'clock. Jack and I have kept track of the drinks we've made with hash marks up there.

In all, we made thirty-six lattes and fifteen coffees.

"Not bad." Jack whistles when I tell him. He finishes

running the automatic cleaner on the espresso machine and takes his apron off as well. "No wonder the smell of milk is making my head hurt."

I grin. "Maybe you could take this zoology in a new direction toward dairies."

"And maybe I won't."

"You could spend your life researching cheese instead of the mating habits of monkeys. I think it's a good trade. I could be a cheese taster. I like cheese."

"This is just a guess," Jack says, clocking out, "but I think there's more to cheese research than tasting it."

"I'll be the taster in charge of Havarti. I like that one."

We walk out together. I wave at Lisa, who has her apron on and is already helping a customer with yet another latte.

"Bye, guys!" she calls.

"See you, Lisa." I smile.

We push through the door, and Jack stretches by the driver's side of his car. "Mmm. I need a nap."

I squint at the fuzzy gray sky. "It's a good napping day."

"I can't take a nap. I've got a fifteen-page paper due tomorrow afternoon on the molecular genetics of the *mammalia* circulatory system."

"Sounds insanely interesting."

"It actually is." He smiles. "And I'm giving Polly to her new owner in an hour, so I should go clean out her cage." He gives me a light hug across my shoulders. "I'll see you later, Maya. I'll be praying for you with this Jen and Travis thing." He slides into his car.

"Bye, Jack."

He waits until I get into my car and put it in reverse before he drives away. Jack's like that though. Always the gentleman.

I get home, and Calvin greets me at the door excitedly.

"Hey, baby," I say, giving his face a rubdown. "Did you sleep in today?"

"Roo!"

"Good boy!"

It's about two fifteen and Jen will probably be at work for another three hours. I wander into the kitchen and open the fridge, looking for something to snack on while I start a load of laundry.

I grab an apple and head to my room. I look at my Bible lying on the bedside table and frown while I chew.

It's my responsibility, not God's. Andrew's words are floating through my brain, and I sit on the edge of my bed. Calvin hops up beside me, greedily eyeing the apple.

"Careful, kid, that's what caused the Fall," I say, absently patting his head.

I reach for a sticky note.

> *Reasons I'm Having Trouble with My Devotions:*
> *1. I feel guilty about Jen and Travis.*
> *2. There seems to be a block between me and God lately.*
> *3. I never feel comforted reading the Bible anymore,*
> *only convicted.*
> *4. It's way easier to see what's on the Style Network.*

"See? There are actual reasons," I tell Calvin.

I pick up my Bible and thumb through the Psalms. They are supposed to be the comforting chapters, right?

"For my iniquities are gone over my head; as a heavy burden they weigh too much for me." I blink at Psalm 38:4.

Okay, then. Apparently David felt the same way I do at one time. I take another bite of the apple, thinking.

If I tell Jen that I kept something like this from her for the past month, she'll be very hurt. She'll be upset that I didn't feel like I could tell her. She'll blame me, herself, and Travis, and everything will just be a big, ugly mess.

If I don't tell Jen, she won't be hurt; she won't be mad; she'll stay happy; and everything will be great.

But, apparently, keeping my mouth shut is causing problems with my relationship with God.

I glance at Calvin. "Doesn't it say to confess your sins to *God*?"

He looks at me and then the apple. Not much help.

I chew quietly. So it stands to reason, then, that if I confess my sin to God, everything will be fine. Jen doesn't need to know; my conscience will be clear; and we'll all live happy, healthy lives.

"Lord," I say, feeling awkward. "I'm sorry I didn't tell Jen about Travis. I should have told her in the beginning, but I didn't because . . ."

I sigh. Why didn't I just tell her?

Because you didn't want to share that torch.

"I didn't tell her because a part of me still wishes I were with Travis. *Wished.* Wished, Lord. Past tense. That part is . . . uh, over. Please forgive me. And please take away this guilty stuff in my stomach. I promise I'll always tell the truth from now on. And just so You know I'm serious, I'll stop watching the Style Network and start having devotions every night again."

I nod. "Amen."

There. I breathe a sigh of relief. I confessed; God knows; and I'm not watching the Style Network every night anymore.

Things will all get back to normal now.

"How sweeeet it is to be loooooved by yooou!"

"Jack, please!" I finish squirting a healthy dose of whipped cream over a double-shot large mocha for a tiny teenage girl who needs more calories.

She giggles at Jack's off-key sing-along with Michael Bublé playing over the speakers in the store.

I hand the infatuated sophomore her drink and turn to Jack. He's been singing for the past two days. I can take Jack's voice for about two hours before I start digging in my pocket for a bobby pin to scrape out my eardrums.

At my last count, it had been fifteen hours.

Let's put it this way: Jack Dominguez is not the next American Idol.

"You don't like my voice?" he asks sadly.

I wince. "Well, compared to what?" If we're comparing his singing to an air horn, then yeah, I love his voice.

"Michael Bublé?"

"Um."

He pouts, but I can tell he's faking.

"Sorry, Jack. Michael wins."

He grins. "At least tell me I beat him in looks."

"You beat him in looks."

"Well, thanks!" He beams.

I shake my head. "It is ridiculous that giving a parrot to some poor unsuspecting couple makes you this happy."

"She's no longer my problem. I sent her off with a wave and a song."

"No, there was no *a* song. *Endless* songs." I rub my forehead.

"You know, if I didn't have such a secure self-esteem, you'd be seriously damaging it, Pattertwig."

"Could you maybe just whistle for a few minutes? Or better

yet, let Michael sing while you make coffee quietly?"

"Ouch." He rubs his heart. "That stings."

"Sorry."

He's quiet for all of three minutes. Michael's rendition of the Motown classic "How Sweet It Is" ends, and Frank Sinatra's "Fly Me to the Moon" begins. There's the happy chatter of twenty-some-odd people visiting over lattes and MixUps.

"In other wooorrdsssss, please be truuuuee!"

"Jack!"

He starts laughing. Two girls sitting at the bar giggle. A grin slips out in spite of myself.

He grabs my hands and starts whirling me around behind the counter in a fifties-inspired swing dance. "Fill my heart with soonngggg," he sings, haphazardly twirling me past the espresso machine.

I'm giggling now. The big-band music finishes, and he catches me by the sink. The people sitting at the bar and at the few tables right by the counter start clapping.

"Thank you! We'll be here all week," he says, bowing. "Go ahead, Maya, take a bow."

I roll my eyes and laugh, trying to catch my breath. "Get away from me."

He spreads his hands to the people. "Come back next week for our Polka Fever festivities."

I snap a towel at him. "You are insane!"

Alisha walks in then, looks at everyone laughing and Jack bowing, and shakes her head. She smiles at Jack. "I take it you're sleeping better now."

He grins happily. "Yup."

"Welcome back. It's nice to have you coherent again."

"You might want to remind Maya of that," Jack says.

Alisha looks at me as I hand her an americano.

"He won't stop singing," I tattle.

"Didn't I tell you no singing in here when there're custom-ers?" Alisha teases.

He shrugs. "I guess I forgot."

"I'll let it slide this once." She sips her drink. "This is perfect. Got the inventory list for me, kids?"

We go over the list and sales figures, and she picks up our time cards. "Lovely," she says, putting her sunglasses back on her face. "Maya, have a good day. Jack, behave."

"Yes, ma'am."

She grins.

Jack turns to me after she leaves. "So, you're doing better."

I nod. Last night before I went to bed, I opened my Bible and read all about burnt offerings in Leviticus. And while it hon-estly wasn't that interesting, it made me keep thinking about this whole idea of giving up stuff. So, I kept my promise and didn't turn on the Style Network. Even though I missed a brand-new episode of *How Do I Look?*

"I confessed everything," I tell him in a quiet voice, so all the customers don't overhear.

Jack's eyebrows raise. "Wow! How'd she take it?"

"No, not to Jen. To God."

He gives me a look. "Wait, so you confessed everything to God. What about Jen?"

"Well, it says confess your sins to *God*, so I did. And I gave up watching the Style Network, and I'm going to read my Bible instead."

"Uh-huh." Jack clears his throat. "So, that's it?"

"Yep."

"No more anxiety?"

I shake my head. "Nope."

"No more guilt?"

"Well, eventually there won't be any." That's what I decided anyway. No more guilt, no more confusing feelings about Travis. It's all a matter of deciding to move on. Right?

"And you gave up watching the Style Network," he repeats. "How does that fit into this?"

"Well, it doesn't really. It's just my way of showing God that I'm serious."

"Nutkin. I'm not a theological genius or anything — "

"Yeah?"

"But I think you might have a sort of skewed view here."

"Do you think I should give up TLC, too? I debated it, but I really like Stacy and Clinton."

He shakes his head. "How about you talk to Andrew about this tonight at Bible study?"

"About what?"

"Just the whole 'giving up stuff to compensate' thing." He touches my shoulder. "I think he'll probably be able to help more than me."

I shrug. It makes sense to me. I'm not explaining it to Jack very well, apparently. "Okay," I say, just to pacify him. I walk over to the register to greet a new customer. "Hi there."

"Hi. A small coffee, please."

I'm wandering the aisles of our local grocery store at five thirty that night. Norah Jones is playing softly over the speakers, and I can hear a mom shushing her kids in the aisle next to me. I've got a bag of Calvin's dog food in the basket, and now I'm staring at the cereal section.

COOL BEANS

Remember when there were only like five different kinds of kids' cereal and all of them were advertised on the cartoon channels? I gape at the fifty different kinds of sugar-filled, colorful cereal that all claim to be part of a healthy breakfast.

Right.

I pick up a box of Mini-Wheats and decide that's healthy enough for me.

"No, Wayne, I told them that our clients' cases have the *utmost* privacy, not *at most* privacy."

Harried voice, talking about clients, the word *Wayne* — it couldn't be anyone but my lovely roommate in the next aisle over.

I push my basket around the corner to go say hi and stop right before she sees me.

Jen's not alone. Travis has a small carrying basket in his left hand and Jen's hand in his right. Jen's rolling her eyes at him as she talks to her boss.

"Yes. Yes, Wayne. Okay. All right. Yes. I'll see you tomorrow." She hangs up with a groan. "I'm sorry," she sighs to Travis.

He gives her a gentle smile. "Don't worry about it, sweetie. Is he okay?"

"Is he ever okay?"

He laughs. She smiles and scoots a little closer to him. They stop and face the pasta section.

"What sounds good for dinner, babe?" Travis asks, pulling her close and kissing her temple.

We are still in a grocery store, right? Not a gazebo in the park?

"Mmm. Fettuccine?"

"Good choice. Maybe with chicken and some fresh vegetables?"

"Sounds perfect," Jen says, smiling into his eyes.

I silently slink back into the cereal aisle as he leans down to kiss her. I make a face. Good grief. Do people really want to see someone make out in the pasta section? I think not. Unless it's *Lady and the Tramp*, I think kissing parties should avoid pasta.

Never in my life have I heard asking about fettuccine with chicken as a prompt to pucker up. Maybe it's the new pickup line. "Hey, do you like fettuccine?"

Lord, help me remember. No guilt, and Travis is history! He can kiss whomever he wants. Still . . . it's hard not to remember what it was like. . . .

I put the Mini-Wheats back. Tonight requires something serious.

I fill the cart with a box of Cocoa Puffs, a bag of marshmallows, Oreos, peanut butter, and a rental copy of *My Best Friend's Wedding.*

I wait until Jen and Travis have checked out before I approach the cash register.

"Bad day?" the lady asks me.

"No."

"Sure." She tells me the total. "Enjoy your evening."

"Thanks." I grab my sugar-laden bags and head to the car. Bible study starts in almost three hours. That gives me plenty of time to go have a bowl of cereal and start the movie, especially since Jen is apparently otherwise occupied.

I get home, greet Calvin, kick off my shoes, and pour a bowl of chocolate.

Reasons I Am a Fan of Chocolate:
1. It is full of antioxidants.
2. It has whatever those chemicals are called that induce a happy feeling in your brain.

3. They have proven that people who eat a small daily amount of chocolate are better off physically, mentally, and emotionally than people who don't.
4. Um . . . it tastes good.

Popping the movie in, I settle down with Calvin on the sofa. I have one bite in my mouth, and we've just watched Julia Roberts review a restaurant's odd-looking food.

"That looks gross," I tell Calvin, pointing with my spoon.

"Roo!" he agrees.

My phone rings right as I finish slurping the last of the milk out of my bowl. I push the pause button on the DVD remote. "Hello, my loveliest mother," I say.

Mom laughs. "Okay, so you either don't answer the phone well, or you answer it so well that it makes me think you want something from me."

"Only your unconditional love, Mommy."

"As long as you don't repeat puberty, I can probably promise that."

"Well, thanks." I roll my eyes at Calvin.

"What?" Mom protests. "You have to remember how horrible you were as a thirteen-year-old."

"As a matter of fact, I don't."

"You must have mentally blocked it because you were terrible. Everything made you burst into tears, and poor Zachary couldn't even walk through the room without something being hurled through the air at him."

I gape at Calvin. "Okay, that part I do remember! He definitely deserved every single one of those things being thrown at his head. He was mean. It wasn't my fault my acne was so bad."

Mom laughs. "The bad part about having a boy and a girl

four years apart like you two are. You both went through puberty around the same time."

"Someday I might forgive him."

"Anyway, I didn't call to talk about you throwing things at your brother."

"Okay." I let Calvin lick the Cocoa Puffs remains out of the bowl and push stop on the remote, settling in for a long conversation.

"It's Zachary's birthday on Monday, so I think we should celebrate it on Sunday since you're coming for dinner." Mom gets all giddy. "It will be his first family birthday party since he left for college!"

I take the bowl back from Calvin before he licks through the ceramic. "Okay, sounds good."

"Now. What are you getting him for his birthday?"

I frown. "Um. Probably the same thing I've gotten him for the last eight years."

"What?"

"A card."

"Maya," Mom chides, "you can't be more creative? This is a big birthday. This is the last time he has the word *twenty* in his age."

I scratch Calvin's ears. "So, what should I get him?"

"Actually, I already have an idea for you."

"I figured."

"Funny, Maya. No, I think you should give Zach a gift certificate for a massage. He's been complaining for the last week about his neck hurting."

"Doesn't he work in a hospital? Couldn't they take care of that for him?"

Mom ignores me. "And if you want to splurge a little, you

could give him a whole day at the spa."

I make a face at Calvin. "This is Zach we're talking about, Mom. I cannot picture him in a spa, and I'm not sure I want to."

"But it's *so* relaxing. I think he'd love it."

"Mom."

"Okay, he wouldn't. But he would if he'd let himself."

I laugh. "I know what to get you for your birthday. So what are you getting him?"

"Your father and I got him an engraved stethoscope."

"I thought you got him that for graduation."

"No, for graduation, we got him an engraved briefcase."

"Oh. Nice." I glance at the clock. "Well, I'm not sure what I'll get him then. But I actually need to get ready to go to Bible study."

"Okay, sweetheart. Well, we'll probably meet at that steakhouse we always went to when you were a little kid."

"Sounds good. Love you, Mom."

"Love you, too. Have a good night."

I hang up and pull on a pair of sneakers. Calvin starts hopping around excitedly, running for his leash.

"Aww, baby, we're not going on a walk."

"Roo!"

I take the leash from him and have him sit down, trying to explain. "It's Wednesday. I have Bible study."

He cocks his head at me.

"Bible study," I say, louder. "I have to go."

"Roo?"

"Like every Wednesday night. But how about we have a bowl of ice cream together when I get home?"

"Roo! Roo!"

"Okay." I smile and rub his ears. Like owner, like dog. Ice cream can cure just about anything.

Jack is pulling into the parking lot right as I do. "Hi again, Maya." He grins, climbing out of his truck.

"Your face has to be killing you after all that smiling."

He grins wider. "My cheeks are kind of sore. Nothing like Canis's, though. He's so happy, he can't stop singing."

Once again, like owner, like dog.

I wonder if there's a legal limit of how many times you can think that in one evening. If not, there probably should be.

He follows me into Cool Beans. Lisa and my other co-worker, Rachel, are busily making lattes.

"Want anything?" Jack asks.

"Mmm. Nah. I'm fairly close to the lethal limit of caffeine consumed. I should probably pass."

"Suit yourself." He goes to the counter. "Hey, Rachel. Can I get a decaf caramel cinnamon latte?"

Ooh. That sounds good. I lick my lips, thinking about the gooey caramel topping, the creamy milk, the slightly roasted taste of espresso. . . .

"Sure thing, Jack," Rachel says. She starts foaming the milk, and the espresso machine begins whirring.

Resist, resist . . .

I clamp my hands together. "I'm going to go find a seat," I say in a hoarse voice, heading for the row of chairs in the back of the room. If you can take yourself out of the place of temptation, it always goes better.

I find a couple of chairs, lay my Bible on one, and drop my jacket on the other to save them.

"Evening, Maya."

"Hi, Andrew."

I squint at the oversized Viking and frown. "Did you iron your shirt?"

He shifts in his almost-crispy button-down. "Why?"

"And what's with the dark-rinsed jeans?"

"What?"

I point. "And you're wearing *loafers*," I over-enunciate. "What happened to your Pumas? And your carpenter jeans? And your wrinkled polo shirt?"

He sighs. "What's with you being all overly observant?"

"I did have six cups of coffee today."

"Oh." He gapes. "That's bad for you."

"Probably. It smelled good."

He grins.

Jack comes over holding two to-go cups. "Here," he says, handing me one. "Wipe the drool off your chin."

"Jack!" I pop the lid and inhale the sweet scent of caramel and cream. "Thank you! You didn't have to do that!"

"Yeah, really. You didn't have to do that," Andrew says. "She's had a more-than-healthy dose of that drug already today."

"Decaf," Jack whispers to Andrew.

"Boys, I'm hyped up on caffeine. I'm not deaf."

Jack takes a swig of his drink and looks at Andrew. "What's with the dressing up today?"

Andrew rolls his eyes. "You guys act like I never look nice!"

"Um. You don't," I say.

"Well, thank you, Maya, that's very sweet."

"It's true," I say, matter-of-factly. "You never look awful, but you don't usually look this good."

"I look good?" He straightens his already cracklingly straight shirt. "Thanks," he says, smiling.

I glance at Jack, who's grinning behind his coffee cup. "Okay. Who's the girl?"

Andrew physically brushes aside my question. "Don't be ridiculous, Maya. Anyway, it's time to start the study." He leaves us and heads toward the front of the circle of chairs, sofas, and tables he created.

I move my Bible and sit in my chair, cradling my coffee with both hands. "So, who's your bet?" I ask Jack, pulling my jacket onto my lap so he can sit down.

He sits and looks at Andrew, frowning as he thinks. "Tough call. I have a hard time picturing Andrew with any girl."

"Jack!"

"What? He's just kind of rough around the edges."

I think about that one. "True. But still, he probably wants a girlfriend as much as the next guy."

"Okay, everyone settle down," Andrew yells across the little coffee house. The crowd disperses to find their seats, taking their Bibles and legal addictive stimulants. "Welcome back to the book of Proverbs."

Jen and Travis duck in right then. Jen falls into the chair next to me; Travis is right beside her. "What did I miss?" she whispers to me.

"Andrew ironed his clothes," I hiss back.

She straightens in her chair and stares at him. Scrunching back down, she leans over. "Who's the girl?"

I try to hide a giggle behind my cup.

"So, if everyone would quiet down and turn there . . ." Andrew continues, glaring at me and Jen.

I smile an apology and flip open my Bible.

Travis stretches his arm around Jen's shoulders, and they

settle in for the study. I scoot over an inch or two so his hand isn't resting on my shoulder. Can anyone say *awkward*?

I look at Jack, and he's watching me. He gives me a comforting wink.

"All-righty, Proverbs chapter 14 please. 'A truthful witness does not deceive, but a false witness pours out lies'" (NIV).

I hold in a sigh. Is it just me, or is Proverbs kind of repetitive?

Andrew looks up. "We talked about this subject of honesty in a lot of detail last week, so I'm not going to go over it again. I just want to say, for those of you who weren't here, that honesty is not the *best* policy. According to this," he thumps his Bible, "it's the *only* policy, like my mom used to say." He looks around. "We discussed how a half-truth or just not telling the truth is the same as a lie."

I hold my coffee cup tighter.

"And I want to talk a little about the word *witness* in this verse." Andrew looks around. "What are you witnessing for? Christ? Yourself? Your desires?"

My hands are clenched so tightly around the coffee that the lid pops off with a *thoink!* It clatters on the floor. "Oh!" I say, without thinking.

Andrew, along with the rest of the Bible study, turns to look at me.

"Sorry," I say, picking up the lid. I clear my throat. "Um. Go ahead."

Andrew gives me a weird look, but keeps teaching for the next forty-five minutes on the rest of chapter 14.

When the study ends, about half the people leave and half stay and mingle. Jack takes my empty cup and goes to throw away both of ours. I look at Jen, but she's busy talking to Travis about the lesson.

"I think he's so right," she says. "Especially about that witness part—it's so easy to forget that it's not just when we're sharing the gospel that we're witnessing."

Travis is nodding. "Yeah, I agree."

I stand and start toward the counter to talk to Lisa, but I get sidetracked when I see Andrew close his Bible and make a beeline for a certain cute redhead who has been dimpling up around him for the past year.

"Hi, Liz," Andrew says, grinning nervously.

"Great lesson, Andrew." She smiles.

"Oh. Thanks," he says in a rush.

I clamp my mouth shut to keep from saying "Awww!" out loud. How cute is this? I've never seen Andrew so nervous in my whole life.

Liz looks adorable and still way too beautiful to be interested in rough and dirty Andrew, but then again, he did iron tonight, didn't he?

Jack comes over. "What are you grinning at?"

I point to Andrew and Liz.

"Oh," he says slowly. "I think I know the reason that iron finally got pulled out of the box." He laughs.

"What a predictable goofball. Why is it that when guys meet a girl they like, they immediately shower more often?"

"You'd prefer we didn't?" Jack asks, grinning.

"No, I'm just saying it's predictable. You might as well wear a big sign saying, 'I Like You.'" I look up at him. "Have you ever done that for a girl?"

"Showered?"

"No, just cleaned up a lot."

He thinks about it. "Yep."

"How old were you?"

"Seventh grade. Her name was Allison, and she was my

neighbor down the street."

I grin. "It didn't work out?"

"No, she ended up going to an out-of-state college the next year."

"College?" I gape at him. "Gosh, Jack. Have a thing for older women you never told me about?"

"Come on, Nutkin. It was the seventh grade. With all those hormones floating through their systems, junior-high boys could have a crush on a Muppet."

I laugh.

He grins at me. "What are you doing now?"

"Talking to you."

"I meant, now that Bible study is over?"

I shrug. "I promised Calvin I'd share a bowl of ice cream with him, but he doesn't typically have a great memory, so I'm not really tied to that plan."

Jack frowns. "Calvin eats ice cream?"

"He loves it."

"That's not necessarily the best thing to feed a dog, Pattertwig."

I brush aside his concern. "Calvin has been building up an immunity to frozen sugary milk since he was a puppy."

Jack laughs. "Okay then. Well, want to change out the company and go with me to Dairy Queen?"

"I don't know. Can I get a dipped cone?"

He pretends to think about it. "Maybe."

"Then I'll maybe go."

Dairy Queen is open until midnight, but based on the crowd there, I think they'd save money closing earlier. The two lonely

employees almost break the Blizzard machine in their excitement about having actual customers.

"Hi!" one of them bursts. "Welcome! We're glad you're here!
Do you want ice cream?!"

Jack almost takes a step backward. "Uh, yeah."

"Great!"

I smile at the guy. "Can I have a chocolate-dipped cone with
sprinkles, please?"

"Of course you can," the guy says. "Choco-dip for the lady,
and for you, sir?"

Jack glances at the menu. "An Oreo Blizzard, please."

"Done and done." He tells us the total.

I reach for my wallet tucked in my purse, but Jack beats me
to it. "Oh, no you don't, Nutkin," he says, handing the man a
ten-dollar bill.

"Jack, I can afford ice cream."

"But you can't afford my wrath, so just let me pay."

I smile. "Thanks, Jack."

We sit with our sweet treats at a table in the far corner a few
minutes later. Jack looks over at me.

"So, how's it going with the whole Jen-Travis thing?" he asks.

No beating around the bush with this guy.

I lick my chocolate-covered delight in a cone. "Well. Okay."

"Have you told her?"

"I told you, Jack. I don't need to."

"I was just wondering if you'd changed your mind."

I shake my head. "No. Not really."

He shrugs. "It's up to you. I'd just really encourage you
to tell her. You'll feel better; she'll know what's going on; and
I think it would make your devotions better than you said
they are."

I take another bite quietly.

He tactfully changes the subject. "So, Liz and Andrew, huh?"

I grin. "Finally! She's liked him for how long?"

He thinks about it. "I don't know. When did she first start coming early to Bible study? And you want to talk about men being obvious. . . ."

"Okay, girls are obvious, too."

"Some girls anyway."

I carefully lick off a mouthful of sprinkles. "Hey, Jack?" I say around them.

"Yeah?"

"Do you think it's as blatant to Liz and Andrew as it is to us how obvious they're being?"

Jack swallows a spoonful of creamy Oreos before he answers. "Probably not. It never is as obvious when it's happening to you."

"Why is that?"

He shrugs and looks at me. "Maybe you're not paying as close attention."

Makes sense. I nod. "You're probably right. I mean, when it's happening to you, you're so freaked out that I don't think you're really focused on the other person's actions as much as yours, you know?"

"Or maybe you're just not thinking about them in that way."

"Kind of like Andrew at first, right?"

"Right."

I pause, halfway through a lick. "Wait a second!"

"What?"

"What if he likes her just because I pointed it out to him?" I gasp.

Jack looks at me. "I wouldn't think so. I bet he just never considered Liz as anything other than a nice girl until you pointed her out to him."

I grin smugly. "Good thing they have me."

He shakes his head. "Oh boy."

"Thanks again for the ice cream." I bite into the cone. "When does your internship at the zoo start again?"

"May 1."

I finish the cone and wipe off my fingers on a napkin. "Wow. That's a ways away."

"It'll give Alisha plenty of time to find a replacement."

I stop and stare at him. "Replacement?"

He looks up from his Blizzard. "Well, yeah. You didn't think I'd still be able to work at Cool Beans, did you?" He looks at my face. "Oh, you did. Nutkin, I'm sorry."

"No, I just didn't think about you leaving." I frown, feeling like he just said I was getting a replacement best friend.

He watches me for a few minutes. "It's not like we'll never see each other," he says gently.

"I know, but it will be weird." It won't be every day anymore. I clamp my hands together in my lap. I don't know why I hadn't thought about this before. It makes sense. And it's what he wants to do. Jack's wanted to be a zookeeper since the third grade. On Career Day, he drew a picture of himself taming an elephant. Of course he's not going to be serving coffee for the rest of his life.

"Nutkin?"

I blink and look at him.

He touches my arm softly. "You okay?"

"Yeah! Yeah," I say a little quieter, seeing as how the Dairy Queen guy jumped at my first answer. A vivid picture of what happens when you consume too much ice cream, I think: You get all jumpy. "I mean, of course we'll see each other."

He grins at me. "Of course." He nods.

I hold up my pinky. "Pinky promise?"

He laughs.

We walk out to our cars a while later, and I shrug into my jacket. It's not cold, but it is as crisp as it will probably get in Hudson this winter.

"Well, I will see you tomorrow at some horrible hour in the morning," I say. I reach for a hug. "Thank you. Tonight was fun."

He pulls me in, and it's a long, comforting hug. It's nice, and it's exactly what I need after this week.

"Night, Maya." He smiles at me and opens my car door for me. "Drive carefully."

"Thanks, I will." I climb in and wait for him to turn his ignition before I drive out of the parking lot.

I get home, and Jen's car is there. I walk up the stairs and open the front door, yawning.

Jen flicks the TV remote to turn it off and stands as I walk inside. "There you are!" she says. "Do you have any idea what time it is? Bible study ended two hours ago! Where have you been?"

"I just went to get ice cream with Jack. Why are you yelling at me?"

She sighs. "I'm not yelling. I just got concerned when you didn't show up right after the study, and I'm really . . ." She grabs her forehead and falls onto the couch.

"Jen?" I sit down beside her, pulling my coat off and wrapping an arm around her. "What's wrong? Are you feeling okay?"

She growls, rubbing her temples.

"Jen?"

Dropping her hands, she turns and looks at me. "Oh, Maya." She says my name at the end of a long sigh.

"What? What's wrong?" Panic is grabbing my chest with both hands. What if she found out? What if Travis finally recognized me at Bible study tonight? What if she's mad?

She inhales harshly and weaves her fingers together, staring at the blank TV. "He told me . . ." She starts slowly and then stops.

"He told you?" I gasp. "What did he say? I meant to tell you earlier, Jen, I promise, I just didn't want to make you upset."

She looks at me. "What are you talking about? You knew?"

My hands are shaking now. *Dang it!* Me and my big mouth. I take a deep breath, trying to appear nonchalant. "What did he tell you?"

She breathes again before saying it in a near whisper. "He told me he loved me." Then she bites her bottom lip and giggles lightly. "He loves me? Oh my gosh!" She stands, shaking her hands. "I didn't . . . It sounds so *different* saying it out loud!"

Jen starts squealing, and that causes Calvin to come running from the bedroom. I just focus on breathing for a second.

Oh, God, Jack was right. I close my eyes briefly with my prayer. *I have to tell her.*

I look up, and the smile on her face has enough wattage to light a hundred Christmas trees.

I'll tell her tomorrow.

"That's so great!" I say, forcing a smile and standing to give her a hug. "I'm so excited for you!"

Tomorrow.

CHAPTER FIFTEEN

I don't sleep well at all.

Aside from Calvin's 2:24 a.m. wake-up howl, I had four separate dreams of Jen kicking me out of the apartment, swearing never to be my friend again, not ever speaking to me after I told her, and then finally I dreamed we were licking Tootsie Pops and she hit me on the head with hers when I told her and it got stuck in my hair.

I woke up with my hand caught in my curls.

My alarm buzzes, and I moan at the still-dark room. *God, I don't want to get up today.*

If I don't get up, I don't have to tell her.

I sigh and rub my face, throwing off the covers. She won't be up when I leave, so I'll have to tell her when I get back.

I shower, get dressed, and eat quietly. Cocoa Puffs aren't helping this morning, so I reach for the sticky note pad.

Reasons I'm Afraid to Tell Jen:
1. She'll be hurt.
2. She'll probably get mad.
3. She may not want to be my friend anymore.
4. What will Travis think?

I carefully pocket the sticky note, not wanting this particular one to end up in the wrong hands. I glance toward her closed bedroom door and swallow. Tonight. I'll tell her tonight, despite the reasons I wrote down.

Calvin stumbles into the kitchen to tell me good-bye, and I rub his little ears. "Bye, Cal," I whisper quietly.

I get to Cool Beans a little early. I unlock the front door and walk into the cold, dark building.

Brrr.

The first thing I do is turn on the fireplace. There's instantly a warm glow flickering over everything, and the shivers running down my back start to stop.

Have I mentioned how much I hate opening?

The lights are on, the furnace growling, and I'm halfway through grinding the dark roast when Jack walks in. "Morning, Nutkin." He yawns, flipping the sign to open a few minutes early.

"Hey."

"How was the rest of your night?" He comes around the counter and pulls off his jacket.

"Long. You?"

"Short. I went right to bed." He grabs his apron and comes back. "Why was yours long?"

I finish the dark roast before I look at him. "He told her he loves her."

He blinks. "Who did? Travis?"

"Yeah."

"Wow. He doesn't waste time."

I shake my head and pour the medium-roast beans into the

grinder. "Nope."

"How'd she respond?"

I pause the grinder. "Actually, I don't know. She squealed a lot with me."

"Favorably, then, I'd assume." Jack grins.

"Jack, I have to tell her."

He knows this, because he's been telling me this since the beginning, but he gives me a sympathetic smile and a long hug. "It'll be fine, Pattertwig."

"Doubtful. But she needs to know."

"When are you going to say something?"

"After she gets home from work."

He nods. "Good plan." He looks at my expression and smiles comfortingly. "It will be okay," he says again, giving me another hug. "Hey."

I look up at him.

"I'm proud of you, Pattertwig. I know this is hard."

Our first customer arrives with an order for thirteen different drinks, mostly lattes. Then our normal business crowd comes in to get their caffeine fix before work. So, our conversation is pretty much finished for the next thirty minutes.

I take my lunch break at eleven thirty. There's a voice mail on my phone, and I check it as I'm driving to Panda Express.

"Hi, sweetheart." It's my mom. "I guess Zach's on some kind of health kick thing, so we're not going to the steak place on Sunday. We're going to go to that salad place instead. Call me back."

That salad place?

I frown and call her back. This is California, land of fruits and nuts. There's some kind of healthy salad place on almost every corner.

"Hello?"

"What salad place?"

"Hi to you, too." Mom sighs. "Honestly, Maya . . ."

"Sorry. Hello, Mother."

"That's better. The salad place next to the mall? Lettuce Eat? Or something corny like that. . . ."

I squint, thinking. "Caesar's Palace?"

Mom pauses. "Yep! That's the one."

"I thought Zach hated that place." I park at Panda and walk in. The hairnetted bald guy sees me, sees my phone stapled to my ear, and sighs.

"That was in high school."

"But now it's his birthday dinner?" I look at the man. "Can I have the two-entrée plate with the orange chicken and the Beijing beef?"

"What?" Mom says.

"Fried rice or chow mein?" the man asks.

"Hang on," I say to Mom, but the man thinks I'm talking to him.

"Miss, there are people behind you."

I point to the phone. "I meant—never mind. Fried rice. No, chow mein. Can I have half and half?"

"Healthy," I hear Mom mumble.

"We're having salad on Sunday," I tell her.

"We do not serve coffee, miss," the man says.

"One meal doesn't cancel out another," Mom says.

"What?" I say to the man.

He points to the soda fountain. "Only sodas. No half and half. No coffee here."

Meanwhile, my mom is yelling. "ONE MEAL DOESN'T—"

"I heard you!" I say to her.

"Then why did you ask for half and half?" the man growls.

"Half *rice*, half *chow mein*."

He nods and slams two big spoonfuls on a plate. "Anything else?"

"No. I mean, yes. A small drink, please."

I pay and sit at a table. Men in hairnets look really mean when they get mad. Maybe it's the lack of dignity.

"Maya?"

"Hi, Mom."

"So the Dressing Room sounds good to you?"

I pause halfway through pouring the Mandarin sauce on my rice. "What?"

"The salad place?"

I blink. Mom has issues with names. Obviously. "Oh. Yeah, it sounds fine."

"Okay. Five thirty."

I nod, then remember I'm on the phone. "Right. Bye, Mom."

"Bye, sweetie."

I hang up and dig into my steaming Chinese food. This is the epitome of comfort food, and I can barely hold back a moan of sheer pleasure.

Okay. Down to business.

Jen, I have something to tell you. I think about that and shake my head. Too "end of the world."

So, Jen, a funny thing happened about a month and half ago. Nah. It's not so funny.

Jen, Travis and I went to look at rings before. Bad idea. She'll think it's for her.

There's a lady sitting at the table next to me who's giving me a weird look. I finish a mouthful of the amazing Beijing beef and look over at her.

"How does this sound?" I ask. "Jen, I'm sorry I never told you, but Travis and I dated all through high school."

She shrugs. "Who's Travis?"

"Jen's boyfriend."

"And Jen is?"

"My roommate."

Her eyes widen. "And how long have they been dating?"

"About a month and a half."

"Oh, wow." She gives me a harder look now. "And you never told her?"

"Tonight I'm going to."

She tsks. "I'm glad I'm not you. Sounds fine, kid." She gets up with her empty tray and leaves.

Helpful lady.

I finish eating, check the clock on my phone, and jump up. I'm due back at work in five minutes.

I get home at two forty-five. Hopefully Jen will be home a little after five, and we can finally have our talk.

I have it all planned out. Jack helped me figure out exactly what to say. I rub an ecstatic Calvin's ears and practice the speech on him.

"Jen, I'm really sorry that it has taken me so long to tell you this, but I didn't want to upset you. And then when he didn't recognize me, it just made it that much easier to not say anything. But from sophomore year in high school to the summer before my sophomore year in college, I dated Travis. I know you're probably mad at me for not saying anything, but I really just didn't want to get in the way of you two."

Calvin cocks his head at me.

"I'm just practicing. What do you think?"

He sighs. Not a good sign.

"Want to go on a walk?"

That gets him excited.

I go into my room and change into my Cal-Hudson sweat-shirt and running shoes. I try to pull my hair up into a ponytail, but once again, it's not behaving very well. I give up and leave it down.

"Ready, boy?"

We get back home about an hour later. I shower, then mind-lessly watch Emeril Live teach us how to cook a mushroom and pepper flat iron steak. I look at the clock on the VHS/DVD player. It's five o'clock.

Any minute now.

My nerves are taking over my stomach, and I try to focus on Emeril to distract me. It feels like someone's using that meat tenderizer he's showing the audience how to utilize on my esophagus.

"So then we're going to add a little salt. Bam! Bam! Bam!"

Everyone in the live audience laughs and applauds. I wonder if there's applause signs so they know when to clap. I would never know when to clap. I can honestly say I've never even thought about clapping for someone throwing salt on something.

Calvin's ears perk up right as I hear someone's heels on the metal steps outside, meaning that Jen is home.

My heart is beating so fast that I can hear the echo in my left ear.

The door opens, and she comes in, looking tired. Her hair is back in a ponytail, which means she didn't have the best day at work.

Swell.

"Hi, Maya," she says. She drops her thirty-pound briefcase filled with all of Wayne's files on the floor, and it makes a hollow-sounding thud. Then she falls into the reclining chair. "Mmm. This is exactly what I need. What a day!"

"What happened?" I ask, trying to practice the same moves that the Incredible Hulk uses when controlling his blood pressure. *In through the nose, out through the mouth. One, two.* Wait, I think that's my Pilates instructor. Never mind.

"Oh, gosh," Jen says, covering her eyes with her right hand. "What didn't happen? One of our biggest cases decided to reassess the value in every piece of furniture that they owned so they could split their belongings fairly, which means we had to delay their court date until March. Wayne lost a custody case this morning, so he was Oscar the Grouch the rest of the day. And, on top of that, we got a new administrative assistant who managed to shred all the paperwork she was supposed to file and file all the paperwork she was supposed to shred." Jen groans. "Oy."

I'm not super observant, but I'm thinking this isn't the best time to tell her that Travis and I used to sketch drafts of what our future house would look like. I sneak a deep, ragged breath while she's staring at Emeril saturating the steak in a little extra-virgin olive oil.

"Sorry, Jenny."

"It's not your fault, Maya." She kicks off her shoes. "Just please say we have no place to be tonight and we can spend the whole evening on our couch watching *Fools Rush In.*"

Okay, so here's the new plan:

1. Watch the funny movie with Jen.
2. Feed her lots of foods filled with calming qualities — chocolate, cake, Cocoa Puffs, and macaroni and cheese.
3. Once she's doped up on carbs and enjoying the fluffy after-movie feeling, spill the beans.

I nod. "Okay. Sounds like a plan to me."

"Great." She pushes herself out of the chair. "I'm changing into pajama pants. What do you want for dinner?"

"I'll make dinner," I say, jumping to my feet. "You change."

She gives me a weird look. "Okay. Thanks, Maya. I've never seen you so excited to cook."

"I've just watched thirty minutes of Emeril Live showing us how to properly grease a cast-iron stove-top pan. I'm in the cooking mode. Plus, it's a movie night. That means we get to eat fun food. Not this splinter-laced, moss-covered-bark cereal you've been eating."

She laughs. "Well, thanks for describing it so appetizingly." She pauses on her way to the bedroom. "You know that's not his last name."

"What?"

"Live. His name is not Emeril Live."

"Oh." I blink at her. "Yeah, I know."

She grins. "Just checking. Thanks for making dinner." She disappears into her room.

"You are welcome." I head for the kitchen and open the pantry door. Luckily, my trip to the grocery store restocked us enough that our junk-food meter is reading moderate to high. It's sad when you can't trust your own best friend and roommate to contribute to this cause.

My phone buzzes in my back pocket. It's a text from Jack.
Have you told her yet?

I quickly write him back. *After I get her all placid from a movie.*

Within a minute, there's another text.

You are the only person I know who uses the word placid *in a text message.*

I grab a box of mac 'n' cheese and find a tub of premade sugar-chocked cookie dough in the fridge and a quart of vanilla ice cream in the freezer. I start the water boiling in our big saucepan.

Calvin's trailing my steps, and I look down at him, holding up the box of pasta. "Thank God for preservatives and fake cheese," I say.

"I don't think God created preservatives," Jen says, coming into the kitchen in bright pink fleece pants with stars and hearts littered all over them. She's wearing an oversized white T-shirt and braiding her hair.

"Then thank you, Kraft."

She laughs. "Pathetic." She points to the living room. "There's a new Emeril show on, and now he's making mushroom provolone chicken with asparagus and crème brulee."

My mouth starts watering. "Oh . . ."

"Makes mac 'n' cheese seem pretty sad, huh?"

I swallow and shake my head. "No! Not sad. We are young and poor. We can only afford the boxed dinners, thanks to Wayne's temper tantrums and stingy Cool Beans tippers. Yet despite all this, we manage to keep our bank accounts open and our taxes paid, whether or not we eat real food!" I hold the box to my chest dramatically. "We will survive! We will prevail!"

"Shut up," Jen says, taking the box away from me. "You are not allowed near this stuff anymore. What is with you?"

I bite my bottom lip, hoping she hasn't noticed the nerves shaking my hands. "Nothing."

She rips the top off the box and dumps the noodles in the boiling water. "I can't believe this is all we're eating for dinner," she gripes. "Where's the protein? Where's the vegetables? Where's the omega-3s?"

"Here's the ice cream," I say, holding up the container like I'm a more-clothed version of one of those women on *Deal or No Deal*.

She shakes her head at me. "Maya."

"I found cookie dough, too." I will win this woman back from the dark side if it takes every last breath in me.

She thinks about that one, stirring the noodles. "What kind?" she asks in a small voice.

"Chocolate-chip." I smile. "And I even have a package of pecans. We'll add the protein."

She is still wavering, but I can see the fight leaving her eyes. "Well, okay." She keeps stirring. "Cut it with the victory fists, Maya."

Sheesh. Ruining all of my fun.

Forty-five minutes later my bowl is empty and stained with fake cheese. Matthew Perry is halfway through trying to win the heart of a pregnant Salma Hayek, and I glance over at Jen.

She's giggling at something Matthew said, and I smile. See? This was a much better plan than springing the news on her right when she walked in the door after a long day at work. Now she's rested and happy.

"When do the ice cream and cookie dough come out?" she asks.

"Right now." I gather our bowls, dump them in the sink, and grab two more, the tub of dough, and the cardboard container of ice cream. You'd think Dreyer's could splurge on plastic containers given how much its ice cream costs.

As I scoop the ice cream, I listen to her giggling in the living room.

I suck my breath through my teeth. *In and out.* All is good. *Lord, help me please.*

The movie ends nearly another hour later. The ice cream is gone; the remaining cookie dough is looking kind of squishy; and Jen is curled into a little ball on the last couch cushion.

"That was nice," she says, her words running together in a contented *mmm* sound.

"Yes, it was," I say, fingers trembling. Must do it.

The muscles in my chest are constricting, and I take a deep breath. "Jenny . . ."

Right then, the doorbell rings.

Auuugh!

Jen frowns and sits up a little bit. "Are you expecting someone? It's almost ten."

I walk over to the door and peek through the little peephole. It's Travis.

Of course.

Dang it! I clamp my mouth shut on my words and look at her. "It's Travis."

She gasps and looks down at her movie clothes. "Hang tight for just a minute. I'm going to go change!" She's up and gone, bedroom door slamming before I can protest.

I close my eyes. I can't just leave him out there.

I open the door. "Hi."

He looks at me, hands shoved deep in the pockets of his coat. "Hi, Maya." Then he blinks and his mouth drops open.

Oh, Lord, please say he's not recognizing me now.

"Maya?" he says, small voice, ducking his head a little bit as he looks at me. He's staring at me with a mix of amazement and shock.

I just look at him, sucking my breath in. "Hi, Travis."

"Maya Davis?" Still in shock. He hasn't moved from where he is standing on the front porch.

"Come inside," I say quietly. "It's cold."

I shut the door after him. He's standing there, staring at me, eyes wide, mouth wide. I'm curious how long he can hold it until he starts drooling.

"Is it really you? You look . . . different," he stutters. "A lot different."

"Lost some pounds and some hair," I say, nodding slightly. I look up at him. "You haven't changed at all." Same smile, same eyes, same athletic confidence.

"Your hair is brown." He's blinking repeatedly. "Oh, gosh. I never even . . . How did I miss seeing you? When did you recognize me?"

I clear my throat. "Um. When I first saw you again."

"Are you serious?" he gasps. "And you never said anything?"

Aye, there's the rub, as Shakespeare would say. I shrug. "I should've."

I can hear Jen banging around in her closet, probably looking for clean clothes.

Travis's eyes get even wider, which I didn't think was possible. "Jen . . ." he breathes. "Does she know?"

I shake my head so fast my neck cramps up. "No, and I was

just getting ready to tell her when you came over," I say, massaging my throat.

"Oh, man." He starts fiddling with his class ring, which means he doesn't know what to say. "I don't even know what to say!" he bursts out all of a sudden.

"Shhh!" I frown at him. "I still haven't told her."

"Well, we need to!"

"I'm going to! I've been waiting for the right time, which was just now until you showed up!" I close my eyes and let my breath out. "Sorry."

He smiles slightly at me. "Same little fireball."

I try to hide the wince. It's too easy to be standing here looking at him and remember everything that happened between us. The silence is so deafening; I want to cover my ears.

"So . . ." he says awkwardly, after a few minutes. "How have you been?"

I can't help the giggle. He cracks a grin.

Jen comes out right then. "Hi, Travis, I didn't know you were coming over." She walks over to him and gives him a quick hug. She's changed into form-fitting, boot-cut jeans and a cranberry red sweater. Yeah, she looks like she was just lounging around the house.

"You didn't answer your cell, and you'd told me you were having a rough day. I brought you these." He digs in his pocket and comes out with a bag of M&M's.

He drove all the way over here to give her a bag of candy? Gag me now.

Jen doesn't find it so revolting. "Awww, Travis! Thank you!" She's puckering up, and I take my cue.

"Well, I'll just, uh, figure out if this is growing any forms of salmonella yet," I say, swiping the cookie-dough tub and heading for the kitchen.

Jen doesn't even notice my exit. Travis gives me a *What do I do?* look.

Do not say anything, I mouth.

He frowns at me and then smiles at Jen. I hightail it to the kitchen.

Dang it, dang it!

I slam the cookie dough on the counter and grab my forehead. *God, what do I do?*

Travis is the epitome of honesty. It's both a virtue and a curse. Virtue when he says you look beautiful because you know he means it. Curse when he won't use a line like "it's not you, it's me" to break up with you because he feels the need to tell you exactly why it's not working out.

Sometimes, there is such a thing as being too honest.

I hear muffled voices, and then the front door opens and closes, leaving me all alone in my apartment. They're leaving.

Closing my eyes, I lean against the refrigerator.

He's going to tell her.

Lord, is this payback for not telling her right away? You bring him in right as I'm going to say something?

I walk out to the living room. Calvin is lying down, head on his paws in front of the couch.

I grab my phone and push the speed dial.

"How'd it go?" Jack answers.

"I just opened my mouth to tell her when Travis walked in, and, of course, that's when he recognized me, and now he's gone with Jen, and I never got to tell her!"

"Whoa, breathe, Nutkin." He pauses. "He recognized you?"

"Yes!"

"It's about time," Jack says, disapproval in his voice.

"Jack. What am I going to do? He's going to tell her, and God's obviously trying to teach me a lesson."

"Don't panic. Just talk to her when she gets home." He lets his breath out. "And God isn't vindictive, Nutkin."

I sigh. "Okay."

"All right? Chill out, Pattertwig. Everything is going to be fine."

"Okay."

He makes a noise deep in the back of his throat. "It's late. Wish we had tomorrow off. Okay. Wait for her to get home, and just tell her and get it over with. This isn't healthy."

"Okay."

"Text me when it's over. I'm going to bed. Night, Nutkin."

"Night, Jack."

I hang up and start pacing. Back and forth across the living room. Calvin watches me for the first few minutes before lifting his head and yipping at me.

I glare at him and move to pacing the hallway outside my door. "Dumb dog."

"Roo!"

"This is my house!"

"Roo! Roo!"

I send another glare his way and go into my bedroom. I flounce on the bed and stare at my nightstand. Now's a good time for a Bible reading, right? Maybe a nice comforting psalm.

I open to the New Testament instead.

"Do not lie to one another," Colossians 3 yells at me. "Whatever you do in word or deed, do all in the name of the Lord Jesus, giving thanks through Him to God the Father."

"Okay, I get it!" I say to my ceiling. "I was trying to tell her! You couldn't have held him back for, like, another ten minutes?"

Silence.

I shake my head and close the Bible.

Calvin slinks in then, all contrite and downtrodden. I look at his lowered gaze and oversized silky ears hanging almost to the floor and feel bad.

"Come here, boy," I say quietly, patting the bed.

He hops up and lays his head on my lap. "Sorry," I say, rubbing his soft fur. "I'm not mad at you."

He licks my hand in apology.

I finger his ears, and he sighs and closes his eyes. All is well in Calvin's world, it seems.

Wish I could say the same. My best friend is about to find out I've kept a huge secret from her for the past month and a half; I have to spend Sunday night in complete awkwardness with Zach and Kate again; and God has apparently given up on responding to me.

I close my eyes and wait for Jen to get home.

CHAPTER SIXTEEN

She doesn't get home until nearly midnight.

I hear the front door open as I'm finishing off the rest of the cookie dough, lounging on the bed watching the Style Network, trying to pass the time and stay awake.

"Jenny?" I call. I put down the spoon and walk out into the living room. Jen's wrapped in a huge oversized jacket that is not hers but, based on the faint cologne scent, Travis's. She's not looking at me.

I stand there quietly. "Jen?"

"I'm tired, Maya." She gives me a brief look. "We'll talk tomorrow." And then she goes into her room and closes the door with an almost imperceptive click.

I think I could almost squeegee the guilt off my face.

Jack walks into Cool Beans at six twenty Friday morning and holds his phone out to me. "No text," he says. "Therefore, I assume it isn't over."

I'm tempted to put my face in the coffee filter I'm holding. "No," I moan.

"What happened?"

"Travis told her. Based on the look on her face, I'm assuming he told her everything. She came in, said she was tired, and went to her room. That was it!" I slam the filter into the machine.

"Easy, Nutkin."

"Jack." I sigh. "She looked hurt. I should've told her the first night. You were right."

"Well. That's no surprise."

"Jack."

"Sorry, Pattertwig. Okay, listen. Everything is going to be just fine. Give her a little time to digest it and then talk to her about it."

I nod. "Okay."

"In the meantime, don't take out your rage on the coffee-maker. They do break, you know."

I look at him, and he smiles and wraps me up in a hug. "It'll be okay. By tonight, you guys will be back to being same old, same old."

I nod into his shirt. He lets me go and washes up for the day, pulling his apron on when he's finished at the sink.

"Hey, Jack?"

"Yeah?"

"What do you do when God doesn't answer?"

He blinks at the deep theological thought so early in the morning. "What do you mean?"

"I mean, I've been praying about this and asking God to take care of this whole thing, but He doesn't answer."

Jack frowns. "Maya, God doesn't just take care of things for us. You have to do something, too."

I start measuring the dark roast into the grinder. I'm going with our signature African roast. It's the smokiest, blackest, deepest beans we have. It's a good somber-mood coffee.

I'm quiet as I think about what Jack just said. It sounds an awful lot like that saying "God helps those who help themselves," which Andrew spent about thirty minutes disagreeing with last Sunday morning.

"God doesn't help those who help themselves," he'd said. "Before we're saved, God helps those who confess that they *can't* help themselves. And after we're saved, God blesses those who bless others."

I look at Jack. "What?"

He starts on the medium roast. "It's like a story my mom used to tell me when I was a little kid. There was this kid who decided that he would be obedient to God by sitting on a couch and not moving for the whole day so he wouldn't get in trouble. But he was being disobedient because God calls us to have faith and actions." He sighs, looking at the coffee beans while he thinks. "It's James, right? I think James said that faith without works is useless."

I turn on the grinder, and the little shop is filled with the reverberating noise. It finishes, and I pour the grounds into the filter, turning on the machine.

Words to think about.

Jack gives me a hug good-bye at two. "Text me," he says again, climbing into his car. "I'll see you on Sunday."

"Okay."

It is quiet the rest of the day. I'm consumed thinking about Jen. What will she say? What does she think? What has Travis told her?

My phone rings right as I close my car door.

"Hi, Mom," I say tiredly.

Long pause. "Maya?"

"Yeah?"

"Sorry, I was just taken aback by the greeting. I wasn't sure it was you at first. I'm so used to being called 'Hey' or something like that."

I turn the key in the ignition. "And people ask me where I get my flair for the dramatic. They've obviously never met my mother." I back out and start toward home.

"Funny. So, what did you get Zach?"

Reverse course. I start driving toward the only shopping mall in Hudson. "I'm on my way right now," I say.

"Oh. So, what are you going to get him?"

"I don't know yet. We'll see what looks good."

"Call me when you find something. And don't get a stethoscope. We already got that for him."

"Yes, Mom."

"Okay. Bye!"

I hang up and park in front of the mall. Zach is probably the pickiest person in the world, save for maybe the California fiddler crab, who is supposedly the pickiest thing on the planet. I guess they go through 106 males before they decide who they are going to mate with. I know some married friends who might have benefited from that same wisdom, but I digress.

There's a little gift shop here called Fábrica De that sells all kinds of useless things no one really needs but everyone gives for people's birthdays.

I walk in and am immediately confronted with a huge floor-length magnification mirror.

Oh my. I had no idea my hair looked so awful today. I pull the elastic out of my hair and quickly swipe it back into a tighter ponytail. The annoying little ringlets that aren't long enough to fit in the band immediately fall right back by my face and around my neck.

I step forward and peer at my reflection, blown up to ten times my size, staring at the individual pores on my face.

Well. Apparently Grandma was right. I should have been using sunscreen all these years.

"Can I help you, ma'am?" A girl about my age is standing there with a little name tag on.

Wow. If the knowledge that, yes, I do have sun damage isn't bad enough, now someone my own age is calling me ma'am.

I don't like this store.

"I'm looking for a present for my brother."

She nods. "We do specialize in unique gifts."

Read: Useless.

"What does he do?" she goes on.

"He's a doctor."

"Have you considered an engraved stethoscope?"

"I wouldn't live through his birthday dinner. My mother already got him that."

She motions for me to follow her to the back of the store. "Over here are our medical birthday collections. We carry an incredible assortment of black leather and genuine silver accented supplies perfect for any up-and-coming doctor."

She points to a few shelves stocked with black leather. I pick up a paperweight and gape at the price tag.

"Fifty-five dollars?" I gasp. I show her the two-inch-by-two-inch leather box with a silver stethoscope pin glued on it. "Isn't that a little steep for something you can't use?"

"That's a paperweight, ma'am."

I'm going to strangle her if she calls me *ma'am* one more time. I'm twenty-four years old, for goodness' sake!

"Have you ever used a paperweight?" I challenge her.

She gapes at me. "Not personally, no," she says after a minute. "But I know lots of people who love to receive them as gifts."

There are address books, day planners, iPod covers, and Bluetooth cases all in the same black leather with the little stethoscope.

This is just a side note, but doesn't the word *stethoscope* remind you of a dentist and not a doctor?

I pull a black-leather-and-silver frame from the shelf. There's the standard picture inside of the flawless-looking couple smiling effortlessly at the camera, like they just happened to be caught in that perfectly posed position.

I'd like to see that couple in front of that magnification mirror. I rub the leather. It's a nice frame. Zach could put a picture of him and Kate in there for his office. I turn it over and look at the price. Thirty bucks is still steep for a frame, but maybe this will make up for the past eight years of only getting him a two-dollar card.

"Okay. I'll take this," I say.

She rings me up a second later. I pay her while she wraps my frame in several layers of paper.

"Have a good day!" she calls.

"Thanks," I say, being careful to bypass the mirror.

I get home, and Calvin is lying just inside the front door, head resting on the Pilates DVD. He perks up when I walk through the door.

"Roo! Roo!" He starts a happy dog dance, nosing the DVD around.

What a weird dog.

"Hang on, Cal," I say, stepping around him. I glance at the clock. It's a little after three, so I have two hours to kill before Jen gets home. I look at his hopeful little brown eyes and sigh. "Okay, we can do Pilates." Maybe it will calm my nerves.

"Roo!"

"Let me change."

I go into my room and put Zach's present on the dresser. I notice my Bible, lying where I slammed it down last night.

I look at it and inhale.

"Cal, you're going to have to wait a few minutes."

I pick up the Bible and settle on the bed.

"Lord," I say quietly, closing my eyes, "I'm long overdue for this, I know."

Suddenly, there's a hard plastic box in my lap. "Roo?"

I look down and see the perky smile of the Pilates instructor and Calvin's long pink tongue.

"Cal, not now, bud." I rub his ears and move the slobbery DVD off my jeans.

"Roo?" He hops into the spot vacated by the DVD and sticks his nose in my face.

This is not going to work. I scrunch his cheeks in my hands. "Okay. I've got to go for a little bit. I'll be back later."

If I'm going to talk to God, I'm going to have to get away from all these distractions.

Right then my cell rings.

Of course.

I look at the caller ID and frown. "Hi, Zach."

"Hey, Maya. How's it going?" His voice is fuzzy, so he must be calling from his Bluetooth.

"Um. Fine. How are you?"

"Good. Listen, I'm on my way home from the hospital, but

I was thinking about you and that whole thing going on with Travis and your roommate and was just curious how it was going."

I frown deeper. Since when did Zach become the caring brother? "Um. Not so well, actually."

He tsks. "I'm sorry to hear that, Maya. Want to talk about it? I have a half-hour drive, and it'll probably be longer because traffic is ridiculous."

I glance at Calvin, who huffs and settles next to me on the bed, head on his paws, seeing his visions of Pilates going out the window.

"Uh, well——"

"And you don't have to. I just remembered that you didn't want to talk about it in front of everyone when we were moving the other night. And I know that your roommate is your best friend, so I just thought you might need someone to talk to who isn't emotionally involved."

"Wow, Zach! I'm so impressed!"

"Well, my birthday is coming up. I'm expecting an embossed 'World's Best Brother' laptop case."

I roll my eyes, but I hear the smile in his voice.

"Funny, Zach."

"Thanks. So what's going on? Did you tell her? Jen, is it?"

"Yeah, Jen. Um, well, not exactly."

"So she still doesn't know?"

"No, she knows." I rub my forehead and spill the story. "Travis came over last night and finally recognized me. He told Jen."

"Oh. Wow."

"Yeah."

"How'd she take it?"

"How do you think she took it?"

He whistles. "Tough luck. Sorry, kid." He pauses, and I wince, waiting for the condemnation. "I guess you could've told her earlier."

"Thanks, Zach. That's helpful."

"Sorry. I'm just saying though. You kind of brought this on yourself."

"I know."

"It's like when you were in the third grade and never did that bug project and then were shocked when you got the F."

I gape. "That was not my fault! I was sick for two weeks with mono, and Mrs. Dexter never told me about the bug project. The F never went on my record. Mom went and talked to her."

"Okay, bad example."

I take a deep breath. "So, what should I do?"

"I don't know. You're asking me? I don't think I've ever even met your roommate."

"True."

There's a minute of silence.

"Let's talk about something else," I say. "How's the new house?"

"It's great. It's got its little quirks like every other house, and that actually reminds me: I need to stop by Home Depot and pick up a washer for the kitchen sink." I hear his blinker turn on.

"How's Kate?"

"She's good. She told you she had a second interview with one of the law firms near the house, right?"

"Yeah. How'd it go?"

"Really well. They offered her a job."

"That's great!"

"Hey, Maya, I'm going to duck inside Home Depot, so I'll

let you go. I hope things clear up with Jen."

"Thanks for calling, Zach."

"See you Sunday night, kid."

I hang up with Zach and look at Calvin, who's sleeping with his head on the Pilates DVD. Glancing at the clock, I grab my Bible, jacket, and car keys.

I've been to the spot I'm thinking of only one other time. It's just outside of San Diego, but the hour drive is well worth it. I found it completely by accident. A traffic accident deferred everyone off the highway one weekend when I was driving for some alone time, and I drove right into it.

Calvin lifts his head. "Roo?"

"Keep sleeping, boy. I'll be home soon."

The drive goes by fast. I'm going the opposite direction of traffic. I have the windows cracked, and I can smell just a hint of salt in the air. My radio's turned to the local Christian station, but I couldn't tell you who's singing. I haven't been thinking about it.

Last time I drove this was nearly five years ago. My hair was blond; I had big streaks in my makeup from crying the whole way here; and I hadn't picked up the running to stay on the thinner side yet.

I pass the Mexican restaurant on the left and the rocky crags on the right. The road turns into a dirt and gravel parking lot, but if you follow it around, there's a tiny service road that leads behind the rocks to the most gorgeous, unobstructed view of the ocean there is.

I check the clock. It's a little past five, which is perfect. I'll catch the sunset.

I park right behind a white chain gate blocking auto access

to the ocean and turn off the car.

Everything is completely quiet.

I scoot my chair away from the steering wheel, incline it back a few inches, and stare out the windshield.

Four and a half years—has it really been that long since I was here? I rub a hand through my short, curly hair. Yup, must be.

Travis had been late getting to my house that night. Again. I remember pacing in front of the door, getting more and more mad.

Long-distance relationships don't work.

And it's not like we didn't try. High school graduation was both the happiest day of my life—because I was finally done with the meanest calculus teacher on the planet—and also the worst day of my life—because it meant Travis and I were going separate ways come September.

"We'll be fine," he'd said over and over that summer. "I'll call you every night. We'll talk; we'll watch movies over the phone. The semester will fly past."

On our last day together, he gave me a huge teddy bear and a white-gold bracelet. "This is for you to hug anytime you need one," he said, handing me the teddy bear. It smelled like his cologne. He put the bracelet on for me. "And this is for you to look at anytime you need to know how much I miss you and love you."

If anyone had been listening, they probably would have needed one of those little bags the airlines keep in the seat-back pocket.

I wore the bracelet twenty-four hours a day; I cuddled with the bear every single night; and I had absolutely no nightlife waiting for his calls.

But, like I said, long distance doesn't work.

Stanford is even in the same state as Cal-Hudson, but that didn't seem to make any difference at all. Phone calls started out regular. Every night at nine, my cell phone would buzz, and Travis would be saying, "Hi there, gorgeous!" And we'd talk for two hours.

Then midterms came, and the phone calls moved to every other night. And Travis would greet me with a "Hi, beautiful" before we compared how much more difficult our professors were this year than in high school. The talks lasted an hour or less.

And finals? I remember walking to Cool Beans—during the preemployment days—to study and not even knowing when our last conversation had been. He called right after his last final and said, "Hey, Maya." It took fifteen minutes before we were both completely out of stuff to talk about. My days consisted of school, homework, talking to my mom on the phone, and driving home for the weekends. His days, on the other hand, were filled with school, football games, football practice, and then cramming in the homework until past midnight every night.

And while I was sitting in the exact same pew in the exact same church every weekend next to my parents, Travis was using Sundays to sleep in since he'd been working so hard during the week and played a football game every Saturday.

Our list of things we had in common was getting smaller.

We only had to make it to Christmas.

I squint at the beginnings of the sunset, clutching my Bible in my hands. I remember praying my heart out, *God, just help us make it to Christmas break.* I knew that as soon as we saw each other again, everything would fall into place once more.

How could it not? I loved him; he loved me. We *had* to still have stuff in common.

He had a bowl game two days before Christmas, and I wanted to go so bad. How romantic would that be? Me, wearing a scarf and hat in the Stanford colors, sitting in the stands next to his parents, cheering him on at his last freshman football game? Running onto the field after they won, kissing him on the fifty-yard line?

I know. Reaching for the airline bags again.

Instead, my aunt Jamie and her boyfriend Kyle came into town, and I got to have pre-Christmas dinner with them. So, I sulked at the dinner table and waited for the phone call saying he was finally on his way home.

And waited. And waited.

I called him—no answer. After the game had been over, according to the radio, for five hours, I finally called his mom's cell phone. They were on their way home, making a stop by the emergency room because Travis had gotten hurt.

I saw him the next day. He was all doped up on pain meds, and his right leg was in a cast and propped up on his parents' couch.

"Hey, Maya," he said, all groggily, "Merry Christmas."

It was awkward.

The sunset is in full color now, and I squish further back in my seat, watching it.

I think we more pretended we weren't changing than actually believed nothing had changed. I pretended to be interested in his football games and prelaw studies, even though the semester without a reference to a first down or a penalty was probably the most refreshing fall I'd had. And I could tell he didn't care that much about my English classes or my wanting to move into an apartment instead of the dorm so I could get a beagle.

The Sunday after Christmas, he skipped church again, this time blaming it on his leg. I blamed it on his lack of initiative but gave him the benefit of the doubt.

We hung out a lot, but we never really talked. We watched a lot of movies, saw a lot of high school friends. Everything had that weird, ominous feeling about it—like we had all become different people, but no one wanted to own up to that fact.

The last day before I was heading back to school, I went over to his house for dinner and a movie. It was one of the rare cold days in San Diego—I remember that.

Travis had been switched to a flexible cast. He answered the door without his crutches. "Hey."

"Hi."

Dinner was quiet. We ate with his parents, and while his mom and I tried to keep the conversation going, Travis didn't have much to contribute. I think I suspected right then what was coming.

He ended it right after dinner had been cleared and his parents had left the room. "Maya, I don't think we should date anymore."

Just like that. Blunt, honest. Exactly like Travis.

I knew we were going to break up, but just hearing it hurt. I managed a quick "okay then" and left.

"I'm sorry, Maya," he called after me.

I went back to school the next day and stumbled through the first week of classes. Every time my phone rang, I ran for it, hoping it was him.

I rake a hand through my hair, watching the darkening sky. I guess it was a month before I finally realized we'd broken up. He didn't call once during that month, though I'd heard from his mom at church that he'd found a good church he was getting involved with out in Stanford. Life felt empty.

So one night when I was on my way back home for the weekend, there was a huge traffic accident on the highway, and everyone was diverted off onto the side roads leading to San Diego.

Which is what brought me here. And where I cried for a good two hours, parked in this exact same spot.

"Oh, Lord," I sigh. I look around at the complete lack of people around me, the endless ocean in front of me, the rocky cliffs beside me.

"I screwed up," I say.

I think that if the Bible spoke in the current vernacular, it would say something like *Uh, DUH, Maya.*

"I ignored You and Your Word. I lied to Jen. I haven't been acting too lovingly toward Zach. And I've complained the whole time to Jack."

I rub my fingers over the soft leather cover on my Bible.

"And I never let go of Travis."

Aha!

There it is. Finally out in the last few streaks of daylight. I take a deep breath and look out the windshield again. "It's not like You didn't make it obvious that he wasn't the one for me, either. I'm just hardheaded."

And stubborn.

"That too."

The sky is brilliant — reds, pinks, oranges all mixed together on a canvas worthy of awards, sparkling off the rippling water.

"And I've been . . ." I swallow. "Jealous of Jen with Travis." What a horrible word.

Funny how much better I can hear that still small voice when all those distractions are gone.

Which is why you never told her.

Right then, I remember a lesson that Andrew did one Wednesday night a few years ago. "Tonight, we're talking about guilt," he'd said. "Everyone thinks of it as a bad thing, but I want you to see it instead as a pathway to getting back on track with God."

He'd walked us through Psalm 51.

I turn there, the pages flopping.

"Be gracious to me, O God, according to Your lovingkindness; according to the greatness of Your compassion blot out my transgressions. Wash me thoroughly from my iniquity and cleanse me from my sin. For I know my transgressions, and my sin is ever before me."

I point to the words. "This, God. This is what I want."

Andrew had said that when our sin is always before us, it blocks our view of God. "Confess your sin; get rid of that wall," he'd shouted at us.

"God, I'm sorry," I say. "I kept the truth from Jen, and I never really let go of thinking that Travis was the one. And help me with my relationship with Zach, please. It's not very good."

I look over, and a verse in Psalm 52 catches my eye. "I trust in the lovingkindness of God forever and ever."

Maybe that's the root of this. Trust.

"And help me to trust You."

Amen.

I drive away feeling content for the first time in five years.

CHAPTER SEVENTEEN

I end up in Zach's neighborhood a few minutes later. How, you ask?

Well, I drove there.

I park in front of his house and stare at the lit front window. This does not necessarily mean that they're home. Zach is one of those people who wastes electricity in order for it to look like they're home.

So people like me can sit on the street wondering, I guess.

I climb out of the car and up their front steps and lightly tap on the door. I feel weird. I've never been over to anyone's house without calling first, especially not Zach's.

The door opens a second later. "Maya!" Kate says, surprised and with good reason. I do live an hour away.

"Hi, Kate," I say.

"Are you okay?" she asks, immediately ushering me into the living room and sitting me down on the sofa. "What happened? Is everything all right? Zach! Maya's here!" she shouts.

"What?" His voice is laced with panic. "Is she okay?"

I really need to visit these people more.

"I'm fine," I say loud enough for Zach, who is racing in from the hallway, to hear. "I was just in the neighborhood and thought I'd come see what all you've done to the house."

They both tower over me as I sit on the sofa, arms crossed over their chests, still looking panicked.

"You live an hour away," Kate says to me, showing off those logical reasoning skills that got her into law school.

"Yes." I nod.

"And you're okay? Any pains anywhere?" Dr. Zach says. He not-so-nonchalantly lays his hand on my forehead.

I push it away. "I'm fine!"

Back to the crossed arms and towering gazes.

"So," I say, brightly, dropping my hands in my lap, "what all have you done to the house?"

Kate slowly turns her head and looks at Zach, shrugging.

"We hung a few pictures," Zach stutters.

"Great!"

Now they are blinking and towering over me.

Having enough of the towering, I stand, but it doesn't help much. I really need to look into some good quality heels like they're always touting on *What Not to Wear*.

"And we, uh, bought a new bed for that guest room," Kate says.

"Cool," I nod. "Very cool. Now your parents can stay with you," I tell Kate.

"Mm-hmm."

Zach frowns. "Okay, Maya. Enough. What's going on?"

I look at them both. "I just took a long drive and watched the sunset and had a long talk with God. And I realized that you guys and I have never really been close. Which has been mostly my fault," I say quickly. "And since you are living back in San Diego, I feel like we should at least work on it." I grin at Zach. "I mean, you figure God put us in the same family for a reason, right?"

"Or so Mom and Dad tried to tell us in high school," he says, grinning back.

I roll my eyes. "Right. And Kate, you got stuck in the middle of this sibling rivalry, so I've never really known you very well." I wave my hand at their ornate yet homey living room. "For example, you are a fabulous interior decorator."

"Thanks." She smiles.

"Come on, Maya, don't you think 'sibling rivalry' is a bit strong?" Zach says. "I never rivaled you. Just the age difference, the lack of things in common . . ." He shrugs.

I have to smile at the honesty.

Kate points to the sofa. "Zachary, you and Maya sit. I'm going to go make us some coffee, and we're going to find stuff we have in common."

Okay, weird. "I didn't mean for this to be a long thing," I say.

"No, seriously. Sit," Kate commands.

I sit.

"Decaf, please, dear," Zach calls after her.

"Old man," I say to him.

He waits until Kate is out of earshot. "This is how Kate's family deals with conflict. They sit; they drink coffee; and they 'share their feelings.'" He sighs.

"Weird."

"You're telling me! One time, Kate's mom had an issue with me always getting paged while I was at their house, so we had to have a thirty-minute discussion on how I'm a doctor and that's why I need this pager." He pats his jeans pocket.

I squint at him. "Every time you went over there it went off?"

His eyes immediately narrow, too. "Kids can get sick very quickly."

"And apparently in a timely fashion."

"Maya."

"Zach." I grin. "New subject. Quick, think of stuff we have in common so we can pretend we were talking about that when Kate gets back so I'm not here all night."

"See? That's the spirit." Zach smiles a goofy smile.

"Our last name," I say. "We've got that in common."

"For now," he nods.

"Considering the lack of prospects, for *a while*," I add.

He thinks for a minute. "We both like spinach artichoke dip."

"And watermelon." I make a face. "When you're not spitting the seeds at me."

"I think you deserved every one of those seeds," Zach says. "Growing up, you were a brat."

"That was only during puberty! And you weren't the sweetest kid on the block, either," I protest.

Kate comes in carrying a tray with three cups and a coffee-pot on it. "So, how's it going?"

"He called me a brat," I say, faking the attitude.

"Oh yeah? Well, she called me 'not sweet,'" Zach fires back and then laughs.

Kate just sighs.

I get home about eleven. We finished the third pot of coffee at ten, and when Kate found out I never had dinner, she warmed up leftovers. So I feasted on pork loin, asparagus spears, and homemade bread.

Much better than instant Bertolli.

And we decided to have dinner once a month, just the three

of us. Considering my culinary skills (yes, warming up frozen dinners is a skill; I know people who burn them), Kate and Zach voted for me to drive to their house, and they'll take care of the cooking.

There's the flickering glow of the TV in our apartment as I climb the stairs, and I take a deep breath.

Okay, Lord, help me get this out.

My stomach's curling in a painful pretzel twist. I try to remember the psalms I read tonight and the peace I felt. Another deep breath.

I open the door, and Jen flicks off the TV. She stands from the couch. "Hi."

"Hey." I close the door behind me, and we stand there in the dark. I turn on the table lamp.

Her arms are crossed over her chest. Her eyes look red-rimmed. Now my stomach's doing a churro twist.

I really hurt her.

She clears her throat. "You were gone for a while."

Nodding, I drop my purse on the floor. "I went over to Zach and Kate's."

Her eyebrows raise, but she doesn't question it.

I let my breath out. "Jen, we need to talk."

She nods and sits right back down on the sofa. "Yes, we do."

I sit opposite her in the reclining chair and fold my hands together, nervously. "Jen." I clear my throat. "I lied to you."

She nods but doesn't say anything.

"I never meant *not* to tell you about Travis." I squint, remembering. "I was just so shocked when I saw him that I couldn't think. And then when he didn't recognize me . . ."

She's still nodding.

"It made it easy to try to forget the past."

Again, more nodding. I'm taking this as a good sign.

"And I didn't want to hurt you."

She stops the bobblehead movement and looks at me. "Did you . . . do you still have a thing for Travis?"

Long silence. I look at my hands, at the wall, at the door, finally at her. "I did," I say quietly.

"I see."

"Not anymore," I say quickly. "He's all yours. You can have him. I just never . . . I don't think I ever . . ." Fumbling for the words, I close my mouth and stop for a second.

"You never?" Jen asks in a small voice.

"He broke up with me," I say a minute later. "But . . . I don't think I ever . . . broke up with him."

She frowns. "What?"

I wave my hands. "Do you remember when you broke up with Adam?"

Small smile here. "You mean when Jack broke up with Adam for me?" She grins wider.

I smile, too. "Um . . . yeah. Gosh, he was a horrible person."

"Maya, he wasn't a horrible person."

"He made you cry!"

"Therefore he's horrible? Maya, every single Hallmark commercial makes me cry!"

This is true. I've seen her curled up on the couch, sniffling into the throw pillow as some little kid's grandparents first hear him say, "Merry Christmas."

She gives me a look, and I acknowledge she's right. "Okay."

"Anyway," she says, "about breaking up."

I nod. "Right. So, when you broke up with Adam, it took him like six months to really come to grips with the fact that you'd broken up, right?"

"If you mean it took him six months to stop calling me every day, then yes."

"So, it's not exactly the same, but when Travis broke up with me, I didn't really believe him at first. We'd been going out for so long, and then just to have him completely out of my life . . ." I shake my head. "I think I always held on to the option of Travis." I pause. "You know what I mean?"

"Like it could still happen someday?"

"Yes."

She nods. "Go on."

"So when he first walked into Cool Beans," I count the points off on my fingers, "one, I was shocked because I hadn't seen him in five years. Two, I was shocked he was dating you. And three, I was super shocked that he didn't even recognize me."

"I asked him about that," Jen says quietly.

"What'd he say?"

"Apparently, you were blond." She quirks her head at me. "I just don't see it."

"That's a good thing. It wasn't a good look." I shrug. "I'm sure he was so focused on you that he never even really looked at me."

She curls her knees tighter to her chest. "That could be it, too."

I look at her for a minute. "And then when I didn't tell you right away . . . it just got harder and harder to say something and easier to keep it quiet."

"Easier?" She stares at me. "You've been acting really weird lately. You've been jumpy and nervous all the time, and I just thought it was because it's getting closer to Christmas, and Zach moved back to town, and you'd been drinking more mochas than normal."

I bite my lip, much as I hate that action. "Okay, so it wasn't easier."

"I would say not. Why didn't you just tell me?"

"Jenny," I say, looking her square in the eyes, "what would you have done? If the first night, I went to you and said, 'Jen, you're dating my old boyfriend'?"

She laces her fingers together. "I would have said, 'Thank you for telling me.'"

"You lie!" I shout. "You would have said, 'Oh my gosh, we're never going out again.'"

She chews her lip, thinking. "Okay, you're probably right."

"I'm definitely right."

She sighs and buries her head in her hands. "When did everything get so complicated?" she moans.

I watch her for a second. "Jenny," I say almost whispering.

"Yeah, Maya?"

"I'm sorry."

She lets her breath out and then looks at me. "Thank you." Her eyes are getting more shimmery in the lamplight, and I know what's coming.

"Jen. Jenny," I soothe, getting out of the recliner and moving to the couch. I rub her shoulder as the first tear trickles out.

She blinks rapidly, trying to keep them in, but the droplets just fall faster. "Sorry," she mumbles, using her shirtsleeve to wipe them away.

"No, I'm sorry!" The backs of my eyes start to sting.

"I don't even know why I'm crying." She sniffles.

My first tear makes its way down my cheek. I wrap both arms around her now, and we rock a little bit, tears flowing.

"I'll never lie to you about anything ever again," I promise.

"I'll never date another one of your ex-boyfriends," she

half-laughs, half-cries.

I wipe my face, grinning. "That shouldn't be an issue. He's the only one."

She giggles, reaching for her tear sponge, aka, the throw pillow. She smashes it against her face, sniffling.

Disgusting. "I'll get us the Kleenex." I grab a box from the kitchen and rejoin her on the sofa, handing her a tissue.

"Thanks." She blows her nose and lets her breath out slowly. "So."

"So." I blow my nose as well, swiping at the last few tears.

"What do we do now?" she asks.

"What do you mean?"

"I mean, is it going to be awkward for you if, uh, if Travis and I keep dating?" She asks the questions slowly, not looking at me.

She really likes this guy.

I smile.

"Not at all," I say, shaking my head. "That's where I went tonight."

"Travis's?" She frowns.

"No, no." I shake my head quickly. "I went to that overlook near San Diego I told you about one time."

She squints, trying to remember.

"It's not important. I went and . . . talked with God for a while."

"Yeah? How'd it go?"

"Better than it has in a month and a half." I look at my hands, twisting a clean Kleenex around in them. "I never really forgave God for what happened."

"What?"

"I mean, I never really trusted Him with my relationships.

I've got to work on that."

Jen rubs my hand. "We both do."

"Yeah."

We quiet, leaning back against the couch. I drop my head on Jen's shoulder and we both sigh.

"Are we okay?" I ask softly.

She wraps her arm around me and pulls me in for a long hug. "We're better than okay."

I smile into her shoulder. "Yay."

She laughs.

Right then, Calvin trots in. He's still carrying the Pilates DVD. "Roo!" he barks, dropping it on the couch beside me.

Jen laughs harder. "Your dog is ridiculous!"

I giggle. "He just likes working on his core. Right, bud?" I rub his ears.

"Roo!"

She stands. "I'm getting ice cream."

"I'm right behind you."

We both sit down with huge hot-fudge sundaes a moment later. "So, I don't know how this works. Are we allowed to talk about Travis?" I ask.

Jen licks her spoon. "Heck, yeah! I want to know what drove you insane about him."

I swallow, thinking. "His obsession with football."

She shrugs. "I guess he's over that now because I don't see it."

"Oh, gosh. Consider yourself blessed."

She grins. "What else?"

"He always told a story beyond the point where it needed to be told," I say.

Jen starts laughing.

"He still does it?"

"Oh, Maya. So the point of this one story was that he was late to an important meeting he had because he went to the grocery store. But he went into *so* much detail!" She giggles. "The tomatoes weren't very ripe, and the celery looked as wrinkled as his grandma precosmetic surgery. . . ."

"His grandma had cosmetic surgery?" I gasp.

She nods. "Better skin than I've got," she says.

"Oh my gosh."

"It took him thirty minutes to tell me he was late."

I grin. "Okay, your turn."

"He's always extremely courteous, but sometimes he's overly so," Jen says. "I mean, I have lifted a grocery sack or more in my lifetime, but if I even look like I'm about to pick one up, he flips out and gives me this long lecture on a guy's responsibilities."

"He could never get that I liked daisies," I say.

"Did he bring you tulips?"

I sigh.

She grins. "Works out well for me, then."

I pull out a generous spoonful of warm fudge and creamy vanilla. "I'm sorry if things were awkward between the two of you because of this."

She shrugs. "It wasn't that bad. He told me that you guys started dating in high school, things got pretty serious, and then you broke up freshman year of college."

"That about sums it up."

She carefully eats a spoonful of dripping ice cream before asking her next question. "Did you ever think you'd marry him?"

"Yes."

She nods. "That is probably why it took you so long to get over him."

"Yeah." I think about it for a minute. "What about you?"

"What about me what?"

"Do you think you could marry him?"

She blushes and says nothing.

"Uh-huh," I say. "Your poker face is awful." I look at her. "Take it slow, Jen. It's only been a month and a half."

"And we'll change the subject now."

"I'm just saying."

"Hey, who wants to do Pilates?"

"Roo! Roo! Roo!"

I don't get into bed until two forty-five. I moan and fall flat on my stomach into the sheets. My eyes are closed, and my cheek is buried into my pillow when I hear it.

Beep!

Ugh.

Beep!

What is that? I push myself up and look around the room. It's not my alarm; it's not my carbon-monoxide detector that Dad bought me.

Beep!

It's my cell phone. I grab it and lie back down with another groan. The too-bright screen reads, "3 New Text Messages."

Nutkin, just curious if you talked to her. Let me know. —Jack

Hey, just wondering what's going on tonight. I'm praying for you. —Jack

Six hours, no response. Now I'm getting worried. Call me when you get this, night or day. —Jack

I squint at the clock, my eyelids not quite open wide enough to see clearly.

I push the speed dial and close my eyes.

"Maya?" he answers.

"Is two forty-five considered night or day?" I mumble.

"Are you okay?"

"I'm fine. I talked to her; we had ice cream. I even drove to San Diego tonight and saw Zach and Kate. We had coffee."

He laughs, his voice deep from being woken up, I guess. "So, I'm taking the ice cream and the coffee to mean something like breaking bread?"

"What? No, we didn't break bread. We had ice cream." I make sure I enunciate this time. I put my hand over my closed eyes. Sleep. Sleep is what I need.

He laughs again. "No, breaking bread like an act of . . . you know what, never mind. So, everything's good then?"

"Mm-hmm." I'm trying to decide if I'm really on the phone or if it's the start of a dream. I can feel my breathing start to regulate.

"Okay. Well, thank you for calling and telling me. I've been praying for you."

"Mmm. Okay. Thanks. Good night." I roll over, snuggling into the covers, and I'm out before I even finish moving.

CHAPTER EIGHTEEN

Ten thirty, Saturday morning.

It's still not late enough after our teary ice-cream fest, but oh well. I'm standing in the kitchen in my pajama pants, T-shirt, fluffy slippers, and bathrobe staring at the cereal cabinet.

"Hey!" I yell. "Where's the Cocoa Puffs?"

Jen comes out of her room, hair done, makeup halfway done, still in her pajamas, carrying an eyeliner pencil. "We're all out."

"I had half a box left!"

"I had them for dinner last night." She gives me a warning look as she says it, and I keep my mouth shut.

Well, she was kind of upset last night.

The only other cereal in the cabinet is some leaves-and-honey cereal. I pick up the box in disgust.

"Try it," Jen says cheerfully. "You might like it."

I pour a bowl and gag at the swirling granules of pollen clouding the air around me. "Yuck." I look at her. "And what are you doing all pretty at this hour of the morning?"

She dimples. "Travis is taking me out to breakfast."

"Swell! Can I come?" I smile nicely. Breakfast out means pancakes.

"No." She returns the smile.

I pour milk on the cereal, and it immediately turns gray. Not chocolatey like Cocoa Puffs, not purple like Froot Loops, but gray like death.

"Yuck."

"Don't knock it before you try it," Jen sing-songs sweetly. She watches me, grinning, from the edge of the kitchen.

I dig my spoon in and pull out a round chunk of cement. I say a prayer and stick it in my mouth.

Eiegh!

"Gross!" I yell as soon as the compacted bark has slid down my throat. "What is this?"

"Oh, maple twigs, wheat germ, dried cauliflower, and raisins, all food-processed." She starts laughing hysterically. "Thanks for not telling me about Travis!"

"Jen!" I gag, wiping off my tongue with the edge of my bathrobe.

She's laughing so hard she's crying now. "Okay, that made everything all better." She swipes under her eyes. "Wow. Your expression was priceless!"

"I hate you."

"I love you, too." She grins at me. "Cocoa Puffs are above the sink." She waltzes back into the bedroom.

I empty my bowl in the sink, still gagging.

The doorbell rings, and I hear Jen gasp. "Dang it, he's early!" Then, the inevitable. "Maya, can you get that?"

I look down at my robe and pajamas. Then I look at Calvin, who is sleepily stumbling into the kitchen and smile. "I told you the bra when the roommate is dating was a necessity." I had put one on first thing this morning.

Apparently, my strict rules about such things have not been wasted.

I tuck my curling-out-of-control hair behind my ears and scuff to the front door. Travis is standing there with—what else?—a huge bouquet of tulips.

"Good morning," I say, tucking the robe tight around me. "Jen's still getting ready."

"Hi, Maya." Travis smiles.

Jen comes out right then. "Sorry, I'm ready now." She grins at Travis.

"You look beautiful," he says to her, and he's right.

"Aw, thanks!" She kisses his cheek lightly and looks at me. "I don't know when I'll be back."

"Have fun, guys!" I wave. The awkwardness is about to kill me, but I'm playing it cool. It's not like you can be extraordinarily cool in a bathrobe and fuzzy slippers, but I'm aiming for marginally cool. Sort of like lettuce cool as opposed to ice-cream cool.

After putting the flowers in a vase, Jen walks out the door, and Travis smiles at me before he closes it. "Bye, Maya."

"Good-bye, Travis."

It takes two bowls of Cocoa Puffs to wash the taste of ground-up nature out of my mouth.

I read my Bible over breakfast, figuring that I won't be able to concentrate afterward with that gross aftertaste in my mouth. I've started reading through James. If any book is about the practicality of living a Christian life, it's James.

"But if any of you lacks wisdom, let him ask of God, who gives to all generously and without reproach, and it will be given to him," says the first chapter.

God, give me wisdom today. I've been trying to focus on

praying about what I read in my devotional throughout the day. I read one verse every morning, and it's a little easier to remember than the long chapters I used to read.

I look at Calvin. I've put on a pair of fleece pants depicting Santa and his reindeer, a white T-shirt, and a black hoodie.

"So," I say, rubbing his silky ears, "it's just you and me, bud."

He sighs.

"You could be happier about that."

He just raises his little eyebrows and looks at me. We could go for a run, but it's cold outside, and I don't feel like changing clothes again. And running around an apartment complex in Santa and Rudolph pants just isn't a very good idea.

Neighbors and all that.

I rub his ears again and get up from the table. It's almost eleven thirty. I decide to wrap Zach's present so I'm not doing what I usually do when driving to San Diego for a birthday: wrapping the gift while driving the interstate. I've gotten some pretty nasty looks from people.

The doorbell rings right as I find the pink-polka-dotted wrapping paper—the only kind in the apartment—and Zach's picture frame.

It's Jack at the door.

I open it confusedly. "Hi."

"Nice pants," he greets me. "You never answer your cell phone."

I frown. "Oh," I say, remembering, "it's on silent because it was beeping weird last night, and I couldn't sleep." Calvin trots over and starts licking Jack's pant leg.

"What are you doing?" Jack asks, looking at the wrapping paper. "Is it Jen's birthday?" He reaches down and gives Calvin's ears a good massage.

"No, it's Zach's. Remember? Tomorrow night?"

"Pink polka dots?" He gives me a look. "I thought you made peace last night."

I nod. "I did."

"Trying to start up the war again?"

I roll my eyes. "This happens to be the only wrapping paper we own."

"And I guess buying new paper never occurred to you." He grins.

"Then I'd have to change pants."

He concedes with a smile. "True."

"Thank you." I sit down cross-legged in the middle of the living room with the tape and scissors next to me. "What are you doing here?"

He sits on the couch, and Calvin's right at his feet. My dog loves Jack. "Nothing really. Just seeing what you were up to."

Calvin really does need to be walked. A daily walk of forty-five minutes or more is the key to a successful family pet. Or so claims the Dog Whisperer. "As soon as I finish wrapping this, you can go on a walk with me and Calvin," I say.

Jack smiles. "Sounds great. As long as you change pants."

"Hey!" I protest. I stick one leg out. "It's Santa and his reindeer. See?" I'm fully planning on changing before we leave, but you don't diss Santa right before Christmas. Everyone knows what that gets you in your stocking.

"Nutkin, it's a month before Christmas."

"So?"

He sighs.

I fold the paper over the frame and use my elbow to hold it closed while I reach for the tape. I tear a piece off with my teeth.

Jack makes a sound in the back of his throat. "Do you

need help?" he asks.

"No tank you," I say and immediately regret talking with a piece of tape between my lips. It flops over and sticks to my bottom lip.

Swell. Now I have to either let go of my perfectly creased-into-place paper or figure out a new way to get the tape out of my mouth.

I carefully lean over the package and try to use my chin.

Jack is crying he's laughing so hard. "Maya, stop," he says when he takes a breath. He gets down on the floor with me and holds the paper for me while I pull the tape off my lip and chin.

"It is not that funny," I say.

"Sure it is," he disagrees. "Oh, Pattertwig, you're not seri-ously going to —"

I stick the tape on the package, and he gags.

"What?" I say.

"You just choked on that piece of tape, and now you're using it on his present?"

"Yeah. So?"

"So? He's a doctor. The fewer germs he's around, the better. Spitting all over his present isn't going to help."

"I happen to be feeling just fine, thank you." I whack the back of my hand on my forehead. "See? Normal temperature."

He grins as I finish putting the tape on the present.

"Okay, I'm going to go change pants," I say, standing.

"After all that grief you just gave me?"

"I never said I wasn't going to change. I just don't think it's a smart idea to talk badly about Santa this time of year."

"Oh, Maya," he says, rubbing his head.

I pat his shoulder. "You'll be okay." I run to the bedroom, carrying the present with me. Finding a pair of worn jeans and my running shoes, I pull them on and grab Calvin's leash.

"Cal! Let's go, bud!"

He comes running, sees the leash, and goes ballistic. "Roo! Roo!"

"Settle down, boy. Sit!"

He plops his little bottom on the floor, and I clip on his leash. "Ready?" I ask Jack.

Jack nods at my choice of clothing. "Much better."

"Not as comfy, but it works."

We start out at a good pace toward the park a few blocks away. It's a little chilly, but the sun is shining and the sky is clear.

Calvin's going at a happy trot, sniffing the air like he's tracking one of the Lost Boys from *Peter Pan*.

"So everything is back to normal with Jen?" Jack asks, hands shoved deep in the pockets of his jeans to protect them from the chill.

"I think so. It was a little awkward when Travis picked her up this morning but not too bad." I think the robe probably played into that.

"Good." He nods. "I'm sure everything will be just fine then."

"Yeah."

We lapse into a comfortable silence, and I squint at the park ahead. I usually let Calvin off his leash when we get there, and he does a few laps around the grassy field, checking out all of those intoxicating smells.

"You should've brought Canis," I say.

"Should've." He nods.

We get to the edge of the park, and I unclip Calvin's leash. There's hardly anyone here—an elderly couple is walking the perimeter at a slow pace, and way in the distance by the sports courts it looks like a pickup basketball game is going on.

Calvin's tail is wagging nonstop as he starts trotting a little ahead of us. We are barely shuffling forward. The day is gorgeous. Cold but beautiful.

"So, Maya," Jack says.

It's one of the few times he's used my name, so I know something's up. I stop and look up at him. "What's up?"

He looks at me, briefly meets my gaze, and then looks away again. "I'm glad things are better with Jen," he says flatly.

"Oh." Hasn't he already said this? "Me, too."

"Yeah."

Silence again. I watch Calvin sniff at the elderly couple from a distance and smile. Good. He's learning something. Last time we came to the park during an afternoon, he nearly bowled over a man who looked like he could drop from a stroke at any moment.

I hear Jack clear his throat. "Pretty day," he mutters.

"That it is."

I'm trying not to get weirded out. Jack's never this quiet. Maybe he's mad at me about the whole Jen and Travis thing. I think about that and decide no. He's known about it too long to get mad now. Plus, he'd just tell me he didn't like what I was doing, not play this whole quiet game. I watch Calvin's bobbing tail for a minute before I choke back a gasp.

Wait a minute! What if all this stuttering and silence is because now the intern job is taking him out of state, and he doesn't know how to tell me?

I wince, trying not to panic before he tells me. What will I do without Jack? No one else talks to me like he does. He knows more about me than anyone else and he's still my best friend — that says something about his friendship.

My heart's beating really fast, and I wring Calvin's leash in my hands. What if he's moving to the East Coast or something and can't even come back on the weekends? Who will I talk to every day?

"Maya," Jack starts again. He stops walking and waits for me to turn around. I'm still twisting the leash in a big knot around my fist.

"Mm-hmm?" I mumble, not looking at him.

If he even mentions the words *New York*, I'm going to cry.

"We need to talk," he says quietly.

I close my eyes. Here it comes. If he's not moving, he's considering it. The only other time he's been this serious with me was when he told me he was leaving Cool Beans for that internship.

"Nutkin?"

"Why do you want to move?" I burst. "Hudson is so beautiful! I mean, look at this weather! Could you get this anywhere else?" I try to motion to the gorgeous fall day, but the leash is tangled around my hands. "Ouch."

"What?" Jack says.

"I just don't understand why you want to leave," I say quietly.

"Maya, I'm not moving."

I finally look up at him. "Really?" I grin. "Good! Gosh, don't scare me like that!" I try to hit him in the arm, but again the leash stops me.

He looks confused. "Did I mention anything about moving?"

"No, but you were all serious and quiet, and I just knew it was bad news." I sigh. "If you're not leaving, it can't be that bad. What do you want to talk about?"

He looks at my immobile hands and shakes his head. "How could I move? I'm not sure you'd stay in one piece without me," he says. He unknots the leash off my hands and sticks it in his pocket.

I nod, feeling the adrenaline start to fade and my heart begin to beat normally. I inhale deeply. I overreact too much. It's not good for my adrenal system.

"I'm not moving, but we still need to talk," Jack says.

I squint up at him. "Okay."

He lets his breath out and puts one hand on my shoulder. "Maya. We've known each other for a long time," he says in a rush.

"Uh-huh." I nod. What if he's sick?

There's goes the pounding heart again.

He's still talking. "And I know that this is always awkward, and there's a chance it won't work, and you'll probably be upset at me for saying this, but I need to."

Okay, so he's not sick. He's got a crush on one of my friends. I frown.

"Saying what?" I ask.

He takes another deep breath and reaches for my other shoulder.

"Maya . . . I like you."

I look at him, waiting for more, but he doesn't elaborate. Just stands there with both hands on my shoulders, looking at me.

"I, uh, like you, too," I say confusedly. He's my best friend; you'd think he'd realize this would imply I liked him a little bit.

He shakes his head. "No, Nutkin. Not just . . . not just as a friend." He swallows.

I blink. "What?"

"I like you." He squeezes my shoulders lightly and then pulls his hands away. "I think you're beautiful. I like how you always try to do the right thing, and when you don't, you feel bad about it constantly. I like how you laugh at yourself and then make fun of me. You're my best friend, and I can tell you anything." He smiles and lightly touches my cheek. "I've, um . . . I've felt this way a long time."

I stand there frozen. The adrenaline is back, but this time it's making me stand perfectly still instead of fidgeting.

I blink a few times, clearing my vision. This is Jack, right? Jack, the kid who traded lunches with me in the second grade? The one who ruined my favorite pair of work shoes with a bowl full of frosting? The guy I tell everything? *Lord, what do I do?*

One thought starts to make it through the muddle.

This is not a good idea.

I start shaking my head. "Jack, what —"

"I know, I know. I didn't mean to spring it on you."

"I mean, you're my best friend; I mean, what if we —"

"Maya, do me a favor," he says quickly, cutting me off. "Think about it; pray about it. I know it's weird." He smiles a short smile at me. "I've been praying about it for a long time. I can wait a few more days. I'm going to San Diego this afternoon to see my family for the weekend, so I won't be at church. I'll see you at work on Monday."

And then he leaves, walking quickly across the grass like I'm going to start pelting him with something.

Calvin's sniffing some bush about ten feet away, so I sit down where I am and just gape after Jack's disappearing figure.

What just happened?

God give me wisdom, I pray as I clip Calvin back to the leash and head for home a little later. *Wis-dom, wis-dom, wis-dom*, the word reverberates with each step I take.

Okay, pros and cons.

On the one hand, I care about Jack more than most other people.

On the other hand, I've never thought about him like this before.

Where is a sticky note when I need one?

I hurry home, dragging a now-lethargic beagle behind me. I'm praying the whole way. This isn't like accepting a date with some guy I've never met before. If Jack and I start dating and we break up, our friendship is over. I know everyone claims you can still be friends, but let's face it. That only worked with Ross and Rachel, and that was because the name of the show was *Friends*.

We get home, and I run up the stairs to the apartment, let Calvin inside so he can collapse in front of the sofa, and scramble for a sticky note. Might as well start with the bad side.

> *Reasons I Should Not Date Jack:*
> *1. He's my best friend.*
> *2. He's my co-worker.*
> *3. He knows too much about me already.*
> *4. After finally letting go of Travis, do I really want to jump into another relationship with a whole different guy?*
> *5. And what if I ruin the relationship with Jack like I did with Travis?*

I pull that note off and start on the next one.

> *Reasons I Should Date Jack:*
> *1.*

I sit there for a long time.

God, what do I do? I pray again.

Jack obviously cares about me. Even before this whole park fiasco, he has always been concerned about how my day has been, how my devotions are going. And he was very sweet during the Jen and Travis drama.

Apparently, he's felt this way a long time. Why did he decide to tell me now?

And the biggest problem . . .

The biggest problem is that things will never be the same between us again.

"You're quiet," Mom says to me the following night. We've just watched Zach open his presents, and he loved the stethoscope and the frame. He's trying out the stethoscope on Kate right now.

Which was awkward, so I moved into the kitchen.

"Sorry," I say. I'm leaning against Mom's kitchen counter, stuffed with salad but apparently about to eat cake, because she's putting the candles in it.

That's okay. There's always room for cake.

"Anything you want to talk about?" she asks.

I watch her stick a candle through a frosting balloon. "Mom, when you and Dad started dating, did you already know him?"

She squinches her lips together as she thinks. "Yes." She nods. "I'd known him for about six months."

"Were you friends?"

She nods again. "He was my brother's roommate's best friend."

I follow that connection in my brain before I nod. "Okay. So you hung out with them a lot?"

"Not a lot. He was always over at my brother's apartment, and Gene and I went to the same school." She gets a soft smile. "He was so cute, Maya. He had thick, shaggy brown hair and was always carrying a guitar."

I giggle, trying to picture my balding, nonmusical-that-I-knew-of father as a child of the seventies.

"Dad did?"

"Yep. He even played me a song the first time he asked me out." She starts giggling, too.

I can't help the grinning. "What did he sing?"

"He wrote a song. I don't remember exactly what it said, but the gist of it was that he thought I was beautiful and asked if I could be his girl." Mom blushes in a really cute flashback-to-her-twenties kind of way.

"Aw!"

Dad comes in the kitchen right then. "Uh-oh. What's going on in here?"

"Dad! You're so romantic!"

He gives me a look. "What?"

"You played a song for Mom when you asked her out?"

He grins suddenly at Mom. "I did, didn't I?"

She nods, still rosy-cheeked. "It was very sweet."

"Yeah?" He goes around the counter and lightly kisses her cheek. I smile. "So, you'll still be my girl?"

She giggles. "Only if you take out the trash."

He sighs. "Workhorse. I swear, Maya, this is the only reason she married me." He winks at Mom, pulls out the garbage can, and leaves.

"Why the questions, sweetie?" Mom asks after he's gone.

I try to shrug my way out of it, but Mom knows me better than that.

"Yes?" she persists.

"Well, I, uh, got asked out," I stutter.

Mom grins. "Oh yeah? Who asked you?"

I clear my throat. "Um. Jack."

She blinks, and her eyes widen. "Wow."

"I know."

"Did you know he liked you?"

"No," I say, still in disbelief.

"Wow," she says again.

"I know."

She sticks in a few more candles before talking. "Well, do you like him?"

I put in a candle, too. "I don't dislike him," I hedge.

"Maya."

"He's my best friend, Mom."

"Ah," she says knowingly. "Thus the questions about your dad and I."

I start fiddling with one of the extra candles. "I don't know what to do. He's probably the nicest guy I've ever known, but if I wreck this relationship like I did with Travis—"

"Honey," Mom interrupts, "you didn't wreck the relationship with Travis. It takes two. And look at it this way. If God had wanted you and Travis to end up together, you'd still be together. Right?"

I nod. "I know."

"So, don't miss out on Jack just because of Travis." She finishes with the candles and smiles at me. "Okay?"

"All right."

She starts searching for a lighter, and I look down at the candle. I've carved a little squiggly design with my thumbnail.

Jack would be making so much fun of me right now.

"You who can't sit still," he'd tease.

Which is probably when I'd hit him with the candle and break my pretty design.

Mom's mumbling questions to herself as she digs through the cabinets, looking for the lighter.

I turn the candle over and over in my hands.

Knowing Jack, after I broke the candle on him, he'd probably send me another batch of daisies and another strange poem.

"Maya?"

Or he'd leave candles hidden all over the place for me, and I'd keep finding them for the next two weeks.

"Maya?"

I'd pretend to get mad at him, and he'd get that grin on his face that I see only when he is annoying me.

"Maya!"

I jump and crack the candle in half. "What? What? Why are you yelling at me?" I gasp, looking at Mom.

She apparently found the lighter because the cake is halfway lit.

"I said your name three times." She gives me a look. "I was going to ask you to call everyone in here, but . . ." She puts the lighter down and grabs my cell phone off the kitchen table. "Just call him, okay?"

She finishes lighting the cake and walks out into the living room. I stare at my cell phone for a long minute and then hold the speed dial down.

"Hi, Nutkin."

I smile.

ABOUT THE AUTHOR

ERYNN MANGUM plans her life around caffeine, but when she's not tipping the coffee mug, she's spending time with her husband, Jon O'Brien, or hanging out with family and friends. She's the author of *Miss Match*, *Rematch*, and *Match Point*. Learn more at www.erynnmangum.com.

Coming in July 2010: *Latte Daze,* the second book in the Maya Davis series

Latte Daze
Erynn Mangum
978-1-60006-712-9

When Maya Davis's ex-boyfriend proposes to her room-mate and best friend, Jen, their apartment becomes Wedding Central. As if that weren't enough, Jen's obnoxious mom moves in to help plan the wedding, Maya's genius brother and sister-in-law announce their pregnancy, and then to top it off there's the whole matter of Jack—is it love? Who wouldn't need a coffee break!

To order copies, call NavPress at 1-800-366-7788 or log on to www.navpress.com.

NAVPRESS

Discipleship Inside Out™

Check out the Lauren Holbrook series from Erynn Mangum!

Miss Match
Erynn Mangum
978-1-60006-095-3

Lauren Holbrook has found her life's calling: matchmaking for the romantically challenged. Lauren sets out to introduce Nick, her carefree singles' pastor, to Ruby, her neurotic coworker who plans every second of every day. What could possibly go wrong? Just about everything.

Rematch
Erynn Mangum
978-1-60006-096-0

Lauren's dad might be getting remarried—and Lauren is still looking for the love of her life! Join Lauren on her adventure of caffeine, chocolate, girl talk, and spiritual insights as she continues to search for the right match.

Match Point
Erynn Mangum
978-1-60006-309-1

Matchmaker Lauren Holbrook is happy after putting together four successful couples—that is, until the tables are turned and she's on the receiving end of the matchmaking! Lauren and her boyfriend, Ryan, devise a plan to make it look as if they've broken up so people will get off their backs about marriage. No problem, right? That's of course until Lauren realizes she's in love.